Elsie's Children

Elsie's Children

A Sequel to Elsie's Motherhood

Martha Finley

The bearing and training of a child
is woman's wisdom.

—Tennyson

An Imprint of
Holly Hall Publications

Elsie's Children
Book 6 of The Elsie Books

by Martha Finley

Any revisions or special features in this edition:

ISBN 1-888306-39-4

Published by:
Holly Hall Publications
255 S. Bridge Street
P.O. Box 254
Elkton, MD 21922-0254

Send requests for information to the above address.

Cover illustration by Kathleen Taylor Kist

Printed in the United States of America.

Preface

WITH THIS VOLUME, bringing the story of Elsie and her children down to the present time, the series closes.

It was not by request of the author's personal friends, that either this or any one of the previous volumes was written, but in acquiescence to the demands of the public — the friends and admirers of Elsie herself. We know that as child, as young girl, as wife and mother, she has had many friends who have been loath to part with her. May they find neither Elsie nor her children less lovable in this, than in the earlier volumes, and may their society prove sweet, comforting and helpful to many readers and friends both old and new.

M. F.

Chapter First

Of all the joys that brighten suffering earth,
What joy is welcom'd like a new-born child.

— Mrs. Norton

There is a merry scene in the nursery at Viamede, where the little Travillas are waiting for their morning half-hour with "dear mamma." Mammy comes in smiling and mysterious, her white apron thrown over something held carefully in her arms and bids the children guess what it is.

"A new dolly for me?" says Vi; "I'm going to have a birthday tomorrow."

"A kite," ventured Harold. "No, a balloon."

"A tite! A tite!" cried little Herbert, clapping his hands.

"Pshaw! It's nothing but a bundle of clothes mammy's been doing up for one of you girls," said Eddie. "I see a bit of lace or work, or something, hanging down below her apron."

"Is it a new dress for Vi, mammy?" asked Elsie, putting her arm about her sister and giving her a loving kiss.

"Yah, yah; you ain't no whar nigh it yet, chillens," laughed mammy, dropping into a chair, and warding off an attempt on the part of little Herbert to seize her prize and examine it for himself.

"Oh, it's alive," cried Harold, half breathlessly, "I saw it move!" Then as a slight sound followed the movement, "A baby! A baby!" they all exclaim. "O, mammy, whose is it? Where did you get it? Oh, sit down and show it to us!"

"Why, chillen, I reckon it 'longs to us," returned mammy, complying with the request, while they gathered closely about her with eager and delighted faces.

"Ours, mammy? Then I'm glad it isn't black or yellow like the babies down at the quarter," said Harold, eyeing it with curiosity and interest.

"So am I too," remarked Violet, "but it's got such a red face and hardly any hair on the top of its head."

"Well, don't you remember that's the way Herbie looked when he first came?" said Eddie.

"And he grew very white in a few weeks," remarked Elsie. "But is it mamma's baby, mammy?"

"Yes, honey, dat it am; sho's yer born 'nother pet for ole mammy, de bressed little darlin'," she answered, pressing the little creature to her breast.

The information was received with a chorus of exclamations of delight and admiration.

"Tate a bite of cacker, boy," said Herbert, offering a cracker which he was eating with evident enjoyment.

Mammy explained, amid the good-natured laughter of the older children, that the newcomer had no teeth and couldn't eat anything but milk.

"Oh, poor 'ittle fing!" he said, softly touching its velvet cheek. "Won't 'oo tum and pay wis Herbie?"

"No, it can't play," said Violet, "it can't walk and it can't talk."

"Where's mamma, mammy?" asked Eddie, glancing at the clock. "It's past her time. I wonder too she didn't come to show us the new baby herself."

"She's sick, chile," returned mammy, a grave and anxious look coming into her old eyes.

"Mamma sick?" exclaimed little Elsie, "Oh, may I go to her?"

"Mammy shook her head. "Not jes now, honey darlin', byme by, when she's bettah."

"Mamma sick?" echoed Violet, "Oh, I'm so, so sorry!"

"Don't fret, chillen, de Lord make her well again soon," said mammy, with cheerful hopefulness. She could not bear to see how sad each little face had grown, how the young lips quivered, and the bright eyes filled with tears; for dearly, dearly, they all loved their sweet, gentle mother.

"Herbie wants mamma," sobbed the baby boy, clinging to his eldest sister.

"Don't cry, pet," Elsie said touchingly, hugging him close and kissing away his tears. "We'll all ask God to make her well, and I'm sure He will."

"Why! Why! What's the matter here?" cried a cheery voice, as the door opened and Mr. Travilla stepped into their midst. "What's the matter with papa's darlings?" he repeated, gathering them all into his arms, and caressing each in turn.

"Is mamma, dear mamma, very sick?" they asked. Vi immediately added in joyous tones, "No, no, she isn't, or papa wouldn't look so happy."

"I am very happy," he said with emotion, glancing toward the bundle in mammy's lap. "We are both very happy over the new treasure God has given us; and I trust she will soon be well."

"Can we go and speak to her?" they asked.

"After a while," he said, "she is trying to sleep now. What do you think of the little sister?"

"Sister," cried Elsie, "oh, that is nice! I thought it was a boy. What's its name, papa?"

"It has none yet."

"I sorry for it," remarked Herbert, gazing with curious interest at the tiny creature, "I sorry for it 'cause can't walk, can't talk, can't eat good fings, dot no teef to eat wis. Do, boy, try to eat cacker, cacker dood, Herbie likes," and breaking off a fragment, he would have forced it into the wee mouth if papa and mammy had not interfered for its protection.

"No, no, my son, you would choke it," said Mr. Travilla, gently drawing him away.

"It isn't a boy; it's a girl, Herbie," corrected Harold.

"Oh!" cried Vi, who was gently feeling the top of the tiny head. She looked aghast at her father, "O, papa, its head's rotten!"

"No, daughter, don't be alarmed," he said smiling slightly, "there's nothing wrong there; all young babies' heads are soft like that on the top."

"Oh, are they?" she said with a sigh of relief. "I was afraid it would spoil soon and we couldn't keep her."

"No, she seems to be all right," he said with a grave and tender smile. "God has been very good to us."

"Yes, papa. Oh such a pretty darling as it is!" said Elsie.

"Yes, indeed," chimed in the others. Vi added, "And I'm so glad she's a girl 'cause now we have two sisters, Elsie, same as the boys."

"Oh, but we have three now!" said Eddie, laughing good naturedly at Vi's crestfallen look.

"Oh, yes," she acknowledged, then brightening, "but we have three brothers, and you have two; so it's even all around after all, isn't it, papa?"

The children were full of delight over their treasure, and eager to show it to grandpa, grandma, Aunt Rosie, Aunt Wealthy, and Aunt May; regretting much that the rest of their friends had left Viamede before the advent of the little stranger.

She proved a frail, gentle creature, with violet eyes and pale golden hair, so fair and delicate that Lily was the name that most readily suggested itself and the one finally settled upon as really hers.

Lily became a great pet with them all, but Violet claimed a special property in her because as she would say, "the darling came to us almost on my birthday and she's just the sweetest, prettiest birthday present mamma ever gave me."

The weather was growing warm at Viamede and Aunt Wealthy and the little Duncans found the heat oppressive; so when Lily was three weeks old and dear mamma was able to be up again, looking bright and well, that party bade goodbye and set out on their return to Lansdale.

The Dinsmores and Travillas lingered until the middle of May, when they too set their faces northward, not parting company till very near to Ion and the Oaks.

Chapter Second

Envy is but the smoke of low estate,
Ascending still against the fortunate.

—Brooke

It was dark and raining a little when the carriage turned into the avenue at Ion; but the front of the house was ablaze with lights. The hall door stood wide open, and a double line of servants in holiday attire, each sooty face dressed in smiles, stood waiting to welcome the weary travelers home.

There were many hearty shakings and kissings of hands; many frequent exclamations: "God bless you Massa and Missus!" "Tank de Lord you's got home again honey. We's been pinin for you darlins and for de sight of de new baby," and with the last words the voices were lowered at a sign from Aunt Chloe, in whose arms the little Lily lay sleeping sweetly.

There was some fretting among the weary little ones, but mamma and nurses were kind and gentle, and a good supper and bed soon cured all their troubles for that night.

Little Elsie was roused from her slumbers by a gentle shake, and sitting up in bed, found the sun shining and Vi standing by her side with eager, excited face.

"Come, come to the window!" she cried. "It does seem as if I must be dreaming; it wasn't there before, I'm sure."

"What?" asked Elsie, springing out upon the floor and hurrying after Vi to the window from which she had witnessed the burning of the schoolhouse.

"There!" exclaimed Elsie, clasping her hands in a sort of ecstasy of delight, "Oh, aren't papa and mamma good?

How did they ever come to think of it? And how could they get it done while they were away?"

"Grandpa, Uncle Horace and Cal," suggested Vi. "Oh, aren't you glad? Aren't you glad Elsie?"

"I should think so! And the boat is ever so pretty. Let's hurry and get dressed and go down and see it closer."

Rowing and sailing upon the bayou and lake had been the children's greatest pleasure at Viamede, their greatest regret in leaving it. Knowing this, their ever-indulgent parents had prepared a pleasant surprise for them, causing a small tract of barren land on the Ion estate to be turned into an artificial lake. It was this, shining in the golden beams of the morning sun, and a beautiful boat moored to the hither shore that had called forth from the lips of the little girls those exclamations of almost incredulous wonder and delight.

"Yes, I'll ring for Dinah," cried Vi, skipping across the room and putting out her hand to lay hold of the bell pull.

"Wait, Vi, our prayers first, you know," said Elsie.

"Oh, yes! I do want to thank God for being so good to us — the pretty lake and boat and all."

"Dear kind parents, safe journey home, too, and oh more things than we can count," added Elsie, as they knelt down side by side.

This duty performed with no irreverent haste, the maid was summoned and a careful dressing made in time to take a walk before mamma would be ready to see them.

They found their father on the lower veranda talking with the overseer, while Solon stood waiting with Beppo's bridle in his hand, the horse pawing the ground with impatience.

Eddie was there, too, caressing Bruno who seemed as glad to be at home again as any of the rest. Uttering a joyous bark, he left his young master and bounded to meet the little girls.

Mr. Travilla turned at the sound and with a kind fatherly smile, held out his hands.

"Oh, papa," they cried, running to him, "how good of you to have made it for us!"

"Good morning, my darlings," he said, giving and receiving caresses, "but what are you talking about?"

"Why the lake, papa, the lake and the boat."

"Lake?" exclaimed Eddie, "why, where?"

"Oh, you couldn't see it from your windows," said Elsie. "Papa, papa, may we go now and look at it?"

"Yes," he said, taking a hand of each. "Larkin, I'll see you again after breakfast. Come, Eddie, my son, you, too, and Bruno."

A brisk five minutes walk brought them to the shore of the lake, a tiny one, scarce a quarter of a mile in circumference, not very deep and the water so clear that the pebbly bottom could be distinctly seen. And there were gold and silvery fish, too, gliding hither and thither, while a pretty, gaily painted row boat lying at the water's edge, rocked gently in the morning breeze.

Eddie hailed the scene with a shout of delight; the little girls danced about gleefully, Vi clapping her hands and asking eagerly if they might get into the boat.

Papa looked at his watch, "Yes, there will be time for a row, one trip around the lake. Step in, all of you, and I will take the oars."

Vi was quite ready and Eddie gallantly handed her in, then turned and offered his hand to Elsie. She demurred. "But mamma! Shouldn't we have mamma with us the first time?" she looked up inquiringly into her father's face.

"Yes, yes, of course!" cried the others, making haste to step ashore again. "We want dear mamma with us the very first time."

Papa smiled approval. "Then we will go back," he said, "and after breakfast, if mamma is willing, we will all come and take a row together. The boat is large enough to carry us all at once."

Mamma's consent was readily obtained, for to please her children was her great delight. So, shortly after breakfast they all repaired to the lake and rowed round and across it several times, a merry, happy party.

At Roselands the family was gathered about the breakfast table and the principal topic of conversation was the return of the party from Viamede. Calhoun had been to the Oaks the previous evening and learned of their safe arrival.

"We must all go this morning and call upon them," said Mr. Dinsmore.

"We'll divide our forces," said Cal, laughing. "Suppose grandpa, mother and Aunt Enna, go first to the Oaks, and we younger ones to Ion?"

"Very well," replied the old gentleman, "I shall spend an hour with my son, then ride over to see Elsie and her little flock. How many of you young folks want to go to Ion in the first division?"

"I" "And I!" "And I!" cried one and then another.

"But you can't go all at once," returned their grandfather, looking around on them with an amused smile; "the carriage is roomy, but, really, you are too many for it. Besides, wouldn't there be some danger of overwhelming your cousins?"

"Well, I'm going, let who will stay at home," observed Molly Percival with cool decision. "The boys can ride, I mean Cal and Art, and Dick and Wal; they all have ponies and the two carriages will hold the rest of us if we crowd a little."

"I'm not going to be bothered with Bob or Betty," said her mother. "They may go with you or wait till another time."

"Then they'll wait," remarked Isadore Conly, "for I shall wear my best silk suit, and I have no notion of being tumbled."

"Last year's suit is quite good enough for the occasion," said her mother. "They're only cousins."

"But rich ones, that can afford to dress, and I'll not go a step if I have to look shabby."

"Nor I," chimed in her sister. "So, mamma, you may as well resign yourself to the situation. It's no good finding fault or objecting," she added with a laugh.

"Have your own way, then," returned her mother indifferently, "but remember there will be no more dresses this season."

"Dear me, why aren't we rich as the Travillas?" pouted Isadore. "I do think things are very unequally divided in this world."

"Never mind. The wheel of fortune often takes a turn," said her mother. "You may have money left you some day (some of your father's relations are still rich); and you may make a grand match."

"How long will it take you girls to don your finery?" asked Cal, pulling out his watch. "We'd better start as soon as we can; the sun will be getting hot."

"I'm done," said Molly, jumping up, "and I'll be ready by the time the carriage can be brought to the door. Come Isa and Virgy, you've eaten enough. Cousin Elsie will be sure to treat us to something good." And she ran gaily from the room.

Molly, just turned thirteen, and already as tall as her mother, was a bright, lively girl, full of fun and frolic. She was not a beauty, but had clear complexion and fine dark eyes; and good humor and intelligence lent a charm to her face that made it more that ordinarily attractive.

Dick had always been fond of her and was beginning to take a brotherly pride in her good looks and intellectual gifts.

Enna's feelings toward her were divided between motherly pride and affection on the one hand, and on the other the dread of being made to appear old by the side of so tall a daughter — dread that made her jealous of Dick, also.

The Conly girls, too, were growing fast, giving promise of fair, graceful womanhood. Isadore was particularly of great beauty, which her mother fondly hoped would be the means of securing her a wealthy husband, for Mrs. Conly's affections were wholly set upon the things of this life. By her and her sister Enna, wealth and beauty were esteemed the highest good, and their children were trained in accordance with that view. The moral atmosphere of this house was very different from that of Ion. At Ion the lives and conversation of the parents were such as to leave no doubt in the minds of their children that to them the things of time and sense were as nothing in comparison with those of eternity.

Enna followed her daughter into the dressing room they used in common.

"Wear the very best you have, Molly," she said, "I don't want you looked down upon as a poor relation, or to have it said that the Conlys dress better than my children."

"I'm sure they don't," said Molly, ringing for the maid, "though they'd like to if they could, and are always jealous when grandpa makes me a present."

"Of course they are, and they manage to get more than their fair share, too," acquiesced the mother in a tone of irritation. "But you see to it that they don't get ahead of you at Ion. Remember, Elsie is as rich as a Jew, and likes the credit of being generous; so, keep on the right side of her if you want handsome presents."

"I'm sure she is generous and doesn't give only for the credit of it," said Molly.

"Don't give me any impudence," returned her mother sharply. "Rachel," to the maid, who just then came in answer to the bell, "dress Miss Molly first, and be quick about it."

Enna superintended the business in person, and in a way that sorely tried the temper and nerves of both Molly and the maid. The child's sash must be tied and retied, her hat bent this way and that, her collar and brooch changed again and again, till she was ready to cry with impatience. When, at last, she started for the door, she was called back, and Rachel ordered to change her slippers with walking boots.

"I don't want to wear them!" cried Molly, fairly stamping with impatience. "The heels are so high and narrow, I can't bear them."

"They're just the style and make your foot look beautiful," said her mother. "Sit down and let Rachel put them on you."

"Grandpa says they're dangerous, and so does Dr. Barton, too," grumbled Molly.

"Put them on her, Rachel," commanded Enna. "Molly, behave yourself, or you'll stay at home."

The child submitted rather sullenly, muttering that she would be late.

Rachel was fastening the second boot, when Isadore and Virginia were heard running down the stairs, calling out that the carriage was at the door.

"There! I knew you'd make me late!" cried Molly. "Oh, Rachel, do hurry!"

"Yes, Miss Molly, best I kin; dar dat's de las' button."

Up sprang Molly, and away in hot haste. She gained the landing, caught her heel in the carpet on the first step of the next flight, and a wild shriek rang through the house, accompanied by the sound of a heavy body tumbling and rolling down the stairs.

Echoing the scream, Enna rushed out into the upper hall.

Calhoun, at the foot of the stairs, was picking Molly up.

"Is she hurt? Is she killed?" asked the mother. "Molly, Molly, how did you come to be so awkward?"

"I wasn't! It was those heels. I knew they'd throw me down some day!" cried the child in tones of mingled anger, fright and pain.

"H'm! You're not killed, haven't even had the temper knocked out of you," remarked Enna, going back to her dressing.

"Poor child, you must be hurt," said Calhoun, laying her gently on a sofa; "but no bones broken, I hope?"

"I — I don't know," sobbed Molly, "it's my back. Oh, dear! Oh, dear!"

"Oh, Molly, are you much hurt? Shall I go for the doctor?" asked Dick, coming to her side pale with fright. "Mac's right here at the door, ready saddled and bridled, and — ."

"Go for the doctor?" interrupted Molly. "No, indeed! It's very good of you, Dick, but I don't want him; I am going to Ion with the rest of you. I'm ready now."

"You don't look much like it; you're pale as a ghost," he said.

Calhoun added, "You'd better lie still for a while Molly. Dick or I will take you over this evening, if you find yourself able to go then."

"Thank you, but I'm going now," she answered with decision, getting up and taking Dick's arm.

He helped her to the carriage, where Isadore, Virginia, and some of the younger ones sat waiting, and placed her in it.

She wiped away her tears and tried to smile, while answering the questions and condolences of the others, and the party moved on.

By the time Ion was reached, most of them has nearly forgotten Molly's accident, till Elsie remarked that she was looking pale, and asked if she were quite well.

That brought out the story of her fall.

Elsie heard it with grave concern but asked few questions, as Molly seemed annoyed that the subject had been introduced. It was a habit of her mother's to scold her for awkwardness, and the child was sensitive on that point.

When the young people had left and the older members of the Roselands family called, Elsie seized a favorable opportunity to speak of Molly's pale looks. She urged the importance of calling in a physician so that if there were any reason to apprehend serious results from the fall, measures might be promptly taken to avert the danger.

"She can't have been seriously hurt," returned Enna coldly, "or she wouldn't have been ready to get into carriage the next minute and ride over here."

"By the way," said her father, "I haven't heard what caused her fall."

"She's an awkward child, always tumbling about," returned Enna, reddening.

"Especially since she wears those fashionable boots with the high narrow heels," he remarked.

"Had she them on when she fell?"

Enna reluctantly admitted that such was the fact.

"I'll send them into town today, with orders that full half the heel shall be taken off," he said with angry decision.

CHAPTER THIRD

'Tis a goodly scene—
Yon river, like a silvery snake, lays out
His coil i' the sunshine lovingly.

— HUNT

THE FAMILY AT ION presently fell into the old routine of study, work and play, Elsie resuming the duties of governess; but as the heated term drew on, she and the little ones, especially the babe, began to droop.

"You must go north for the summer," said Dr. Barton. "Start as soon as possible and don't return till October."

"Would you recommend the seashore?" asked Mr. Travilla.

"H'm! That might answer very well, but mountain air would, I think, be better."

"Oh then, mamma!" cried Vi, who was present and had been an eager but hitherto silent listener, "won't you accept Aunt Lucy's invitation?"

"Perhaps, daughter," Elsie said smiling indulgently into the bright little face, "but we will take time to consider what will be best."

"Where is that?" asked the doctor. "Lucy Ross, I suppose, but I've forgotten where they live."

On the banks of the Hudson, a few miles south of Newburgh, the Crags they call their place, and a beautiful one it is. 'Twas only yesterday I received a letter from Lucy, urging us to come and spend the summer with her."

"I should say go by all means," said the doctor, taking leave.

There were reasons for hesitation on the part of the careful parents of which the physician knew nothing. The young Rosses, all unused to control, were a willful set not likely to exert a beneficial influence over the children — that was the hesitation.

However, the final decision was in favor of the visit; and a few days later they set out upon their journey, Mr. Horace Dinsmore taking charge of them, as business made it inconvenient for Mr. Travilla to leave just at that time.

From New York they passed up the Hudson in a steamboat. The carriage from the Crags was found in waiting at the landing, and a short drive brought them to the house, which stood high up above the river, in the midst of magnificent mountain scenery.

The Ion children, taught from early infancy to notice the beauties of nature, were in ecstasies of delight. They were exclaiming anew at every turn in the road, calling each other's, mamma's, or grandpa's attention to the sparkling river, the changing shadows of the mountainsides, here a jutting crag, there a waterfall or secluded glen. Having rested the previous night, sleeping soundly at a hotel, they were not wearied with travel but seemed fresher now than when they left their home.

Lucy and her little flock, gathered on the front porch to receive their guests, gave them a warm welcome. The two ladies had lost none of the affection for each other, which had been one of the happinesses of their childhood and early youth. Each loved the children of the other for the mother's sake if not their own. They numbered the same, but Sophie, Lucy's youngest, was now in her fifth year, and baby Lily was greeted with many expressions and demonstrations of delight.

Lucy excused her husband's absence — he was away on business, she said, but would be at home before night.

"Where's Phil?" asked Eddie, turning to Gertrude.

"Oh, he's at boarding school, don't you know?" she answered. "He'll be home for vacation; but that doesn't begin for two weeks yet."

Mr. Dinsmore tarried for a few days, then returned to the neighborhood of Philadelphia, where he had left his wife and Rosie, who were visiting their northern relatives.

Miss Fisk was still governess at the Crags, and when the children had had a week of play together, it was thought best by the mammas that two hours each morning should be devoted to lessons.

Knowing Miss Fisk to be not only well educated and refined, but also a conscientious and good woman, Elsie was willing to entrust her children to her care; the more so, because Lily in her feeble state, required much of her own time and attention.

In the midst of a beautiful grove of oaks and maples, on the side of a hill, scarce more than a stone's throw from the mansion, and within full view of its windows, stood a small brick building owned by Mr. Ross. It was used as a summer schoolroom for the children.

It was a cool shady spot, enlivened by the songs of the wild birds who built their nests in the trees and the musical tinkle of a little waterfall that came tumbling down from the heights above not half a dozen yards from the door.

Mr. Ross had furnished the room with comfortable and convenient chairs and desks, and Lucy had made it pretty and tasteful with white muslin curtains and neatly papered walls of a neutral tint, enlivened by a few gaily-colored pictures. Woodwork and floor were stained a rich dark brown, bright soft rugs were scattered here and there. Altogether, the place was as inviting as a lady's parlor.

The Ion children were well content to spend here two or three hours of that part of the day when the sun was too hot for them to be exposed to its rays with safety and comfort. The others found lessons made much more agreeable by the companionship of their new guests. And Miss Fisk was glad to take them under her charge, because by their intelligence they added greatly to the interest of her work, while their respectful obedient behavior exerted an excellent influence upon her own pupils.

Before leaving home, Elsie, after careful and prayerful consideration, thought it best to have a plain talk with her older children about the temptations that were likely to assail them during their visit to the Crags.

They had had some past experience with the ways of Lucy's children, and she knew they had not forgotten it. Reminding them of the Bible declaration that "evil communications corrupt good manner," she bade them, while refraining as far as possible from judging their little friends, at the same time to carefully avoid following their example in anything they knew to be wrong.

"Mamma," said Vi, "perhaps sometimes we mightn't know if it was wrong!"

"I think you will, daughter, if you take a moment to think; and if you are doubtful, you may be pretty sure it is wrong."

"Mamma, we mustn't tell tales to you?"

"No, dear, but perhaps you can consult me without that; and do not forget that you can always lift up your heart to God for help to know and do right."

"Yes, mamma," returned the little girl thoughtfully, "and I do believe Elsie will 'most always be there and know what's right."

"I'm not sure," said her sister, with a grave shake of her head. "I wish we could always have mamma by to tell us."

"But mamma cannot be with you always, darlings," Elsie said, regarding them with yearning tenderness. "And so, as your papa and I have often told you, you must learn to think and decide for yourselves — about some things now, and about other things as you grow older and wiser. Some things the Bible tells us plainly, and in regard to those we have nothing to do but obey."

Chapter Fourth

A child left to himself bringeth his mother to shame.

— Proverbs XXIX. 15

LUCY, TOO, HAD A TALK with her children, in which she begged them quite pathetically, not to disgrace her before the expected guests, Mr. Dinsmore especially, who was so very strict in his ideas of how children ought to be brought up, and how they should behave.

They promised readily enough to "behave splendidly" and for a few days did so astonishingly well that, as she laughingly said, "she began to grow frightened lest they were becoming too good to live."

But she need not have been alarmed; the reaction was not long in coming and was sufficient to relieve all apprehension that they were in immediate danger from a surplus of goodness.

It began on the morning after Mr. Dinsmore's departure. Gertrude was late to breakfast, and when reproved by her mother, answered in a manner so disrespectful as to quite astonish the young Travillas. They expected to see her banished at once from the table and the room; but her mother only looked grave and said in a tone of displeasure, "Gertrude, I cannot have you speak to me in that way. Don't do it again."

"I don't care. You needn't scold so about every little trifle then," muttered the delinquent in an undertone, pulling the dish of meat toward her, helping herself and spilling the gravy on the clean tablecloth.

Mrs. Ross did not seem to hear. She was spreading a piece of bread with the sweetest and freshest butter for Sophie.

"I don't want it; I want waffles!" screamed the child, snatching up the bread the instant it was laid on her plate, and dashing it on the carpet.

"You are not well this morning, dear, and mamma thinks waffles might make her darling worse," said Lucy in a soothing tone. "Come now, be a good baby and eat the bread. Shall mamma spread another piece?"

"No, no, naughty mamma! I'll jus' frow it on the floor if you do," cried the child, bursting into angry sobs.

"Shall mamma have some toast made for her?" she said coaxingly.

"No, no! Waffles! And butter on waffles, and 'lasses on butter, and sugar on 'lasses!"

The mother laughed. It seemed to irritate the child still further; and she screamed louder than ever, slid down from her chair and stamped her foot with rage.

Mrs. Ross was deeply mortified at the exhibition. "Pick her up and carry her to the nursery," she said to a servant.

Sophie kicked and struggled, but the girl — a strong and determined one — carried her away by main force.

"I'm dreadfully ashamed of her Elsie," Lucy said, turning to her friend; "but she's a nervous little creature and we must try to excuse her."

"A few hearty slaps would reverse the nervous currents and do her an immense amount of good, Mrs. Ross," remarked the governess in her slow, precise way.

"Slaps, Miss Fisk," returned Lucy reddening, "I don't approve of corporal punishment, as I have told you more than once. I was never whipped, and I don't intend that any of my children shall be."

"Most assuredly not, madam, but I was recommending it, not as a punishment for disobedience or ill temper, but simply as a remedial agent. I have never experienced anything of the kind myself, Mrs. Ross, but have heard it remarked that nervousness occasions greater suffering than is generally understood by the term pain; therefore, I suggest it as I should the amputation of a diseased member when necessary in order to preserve life."

"Permit me to remark," returned Lucy, "that unasked advice is seldom acceptable, and now a truce to discussion, if you please. My dear Elsie," turning to Mrs. Travilla, "I beg you to excuse our ill-manners. It strikes me that none of us is behaving quite as we ought this morning. Hal and Archie, what's wrong between you now?" The two boys, seated side by side, were scowling at each other and muttering angrily half under their breath.

"Why, ma, he went and took the very piece of meat I just said I was going to have," whimpered Archie, digging his fists into his eyes.

"Well, I don't care," retorted Harry, I'd as good a right as you, and I was ready first."

"Give him a part of it, can't you?" said his mother.

"'Tain't more'n I want myself."

"I won't have it after it's been on his plate," exclaimed both together.

"Boys, I'm ashamed of you!" said Lucy, "I wish your father were here to keep you straight. You don't dare behave so before him. I'm sure your little friends would never act so. Don't you see how your naughtiness astonishes them? Vi, would you talk to your mamma as my children do to me?"

The large blue eyes opened wide upon the questioner in half incredulous, reproachful surprise, then turned upon the beautiful gentle face of Mrs. Travilla with an expression of ardent affection mingled with admiration and respect. "Oh, Aunt Lucy! Could you believe I'd do that to my mamma?"

The very thought of so wounding that tender mother heart was evidently so full of pain to the little one that Elsie could not refrain from responding to the appeal. "Mamma knows you would not, darling."

"Oh, no, mamma, 'cause I love you!" cried the child, her young face growing bright with smiles.

"Atmospheric influences have often a great deal to do with these things; do you not find it so?" Elsie said, turning to her friend.

"Yes, I have noticed that!" Lucy said, catching gladly

at the suggestion. "And the air is certainly unusually oppressive this morning. I feel nervous myself. I think we'll have a gust before night."

The last words were spoken in an undertone, but the quick ear of Gertrude caught them. "Then I shan't go to school," she announced decidedly.

"Nonsense," said her mother, "'twon't be here till afternoon, probably not till night, if at all."

"Now, ma, you're just saying that. Aunt Elsie do you really think it won't come soon?"

Glancing through the open window at the mountains and the sky, Elsie answered that she saw no present indications of a storm. There was nothing to suggest it but the heat and closeness of the air.

"Are you afraid of thunder, Aunt Elsie?" asked Harry.

"Lightning, you silly boy," corrected Gertrude, "nobody's afraid of thunder."

"Yes, you are," he retorted. "You just ought to see, Ed, how scared she gets," and Harry laughed scornfully.

Gertrude was ready with an indignant retort, but her mother stopped her. "If you are really brave, Gertrude, you can have an excellent opportunity to show it when the storm comes." Then to Harry, "Let your sister alone, or I'll send you to your room."

The gust, a very severe one, came in the afternoon. Before it was fairly upon them, Lucy, herself pale with terror, had collected her children in a darkened room and seated them all on a feather bed. They remained there during the storm, half stifled by the heat, the little ones clinging to their mother, hiding their heads in her lap and crying with fear.

Elsie and her children formed a different group. The mother was the central figure here also, her darlings gathered closely about her, in her dressing room — at a safe distance from the open windows. They watched with awed delight the bursting of the storm clouds over the mountain tops, the play of the lightning, the sweep of the rain down from the heights into the valleys and river below. They listened to the crash and roar of the thunder as it reverberated among the hills, one echo taking it up after another, and repeating it to the next, till it sounded like the explosions of many batteries of heavy artillery, now near at hand, now farther and farther away.

"Mamma, isn't it grand?" exclaimed Eddie in one of the brief pauses in the wild uproar of the elements.

"Yes," she said, "the thunder of His power, who can understand?"

"Is it God, mamma? Does God make it?" asked little Herbert.

"Yes, dear. 'When He uttereth his voice, there is a multitude of waters in the heavens, and He causeth the vapors to ascend from the ends of the earth; He maketh lightning with rain, and bringeth forth the wind out of his treasuries.' "

"We needn't be 'fraid mamma?"

"No, darling, no, for God is our Father; He loves us and will take care of us."

The storm was very violent while it lasted, but soon passed away. The sun shone out, and a beautiful rainbow spanned the eastern sky above the mountaintops.

Elsie's children clapped their hands in ecstasy, and ran to call their little friends to enjoy the sight with them. Mrs. Ross followed, looking so pale and exhausted, that Elsie inquired with concern if she were ill.

"Oh, it was the storm!" she said. "Wasn't it fearful? I was sure the house would be struck and some of us killed. Weren't you frightened?"

"No," Elsie said, with a kindly reassuring smile, "I presume my nerves are stronger than yours; and I am not timid in regard to thunder and lightning. Besides, I know so well that He who guides and controls it is my Father and my Friend. Come, look at His bow of promise."

The children were in a group about the window, gazing and admiring.

"Let's ask mamma for the story of it," Vi was saying.

"The story of it?" repeated Archie Ross.

"Yes, don't you know about Noah and the flood?"

"I never heard it."

"Oh, Archie, it's in the Bible; grandma told it to us once," exclaimed his sister Gertrude.

"I didn't hear it, anyhow," persisted the boy. "Do, Vi, coax Aunt Elsie to tell it."

The petition was readily granted. Mrs. Travilla was an inimitable storyteller, and Lucy, whose knowledge of Scripture history was but superficial, listened to the narrative with almost as much interest and pleasure as did the children.

"I would give anything for your talent for storytelling, Elsie," she said at its conclusion.

"Oh, another! Another! Please tell us another!" cried a chorus of young voices.

Mrs. Travilla drew out her watch, and holding it up with a smile said, "Not just now, my dears; see it is almost tea-time, and" she added playfully, "some of us have need to change our dresses and smooth our tangled tresses."

"That is true," said Lucy, rising hastily, "and I expect my husband home. I must send the carriage off at once to the depot, for the train is nearly due."

Thereupon a cry was raised among the Rosses as they flew after their mother. "I want to go for papa!" "And I!" "It's my turn, I say, and I will go!" "No, you shan't, for it's mine."

Chapter Fifth

She led me first to God;
Her words and prayers were my young spirit's dew.

— Pierpont

"Hello! This looks like welcome; everyone of you has been crying!" Mr. Ross said, catching up Sophie in his arms, and glancing upon his group of children, after an affectionate greeting to his wife and a cordially kind one to their guest.

"What's the trouble? So sorry papa was coming home, eh?"

"No, no, that wasn't it, papa," they cried, crowding around him, each eager to claim the first caress. "It wasn't that, but we wanted to go for you, and mamma wouldn't let us."

"Yes," said Lucy, "they all wanted to go, and as that couldn't be, and no one would give up to the others, I kept them all at home."

"Quite right," he said gravely, "I'm afraid you hardly deserve the pretty gifts I have brought."

"Oh, yes, yes, papa, we'll be good next time! Indeed we will! Mamma, coax him!"

"Yes, do let them have them, Phil," urged his wife. "What would be the use of keeping the things back after spending your money for them?"

"To teach them a good lesson. I'm afraid both you and I are foolishly indulgent, Lucy."

"Oh, they'll be good next time."

"This once, then, but only this once; unless they keep their word," he said, producing his gifts — a book or toy for each of his own children, and a package of sweetmeats which he divided among all present.

He had brought a new dog home with him, but no one but Eddie had noticed it yet. He was stroking and patting it, saying, "Poor fellow, what kind of dog are you?"

"A French poodle," said Mr. Ross, coming up to them. "He's a good watch dog, and excellent for scaring up the wild ducks for the sportsmen. Do you and papa keep up the shooting lessons, master Eddie?"

"Yes, sir, papa has always said he meant to make me as good a shot as himself, and mamma says it was never his way to give up till a thing's thoroughly done," returned the boy, proudly.

"And you don't equal him as a shot yet, eh?"

"No, sir! No, indeed! Why even cousin Cal Conly — a big man — can't shoot as well as papa."

"What an ugly dog!" exclaimed the other children, gathering round.

"What did you buy it for, papa?" asked Gertrude.

"Not for beauty, certainly," laughed Mr. Ross, stroking and patting the shaggy head of the dog, who was covered with curly hair of a dirty white, mottled with dull brown, "but for worth which is far better. Isn't it, Ranger?"

A wag of his bushy tail was Ranger's only reply.

"Will he bite?" asked little Herbert, shrinking back as the newcomer turned toward him.

"Tramps and burglars, but not good children," replied Mr. Ross. "You needn't be afraid of him, my little man."

Through the evening there was a great deal of romping between the children and the new dog, but little Elsie seemed unusually quiet, scarcely stirring from her mother's side. She was suffering with a toothache, but kept her trouble to herself; principally, because she had a great dread of the dentist's instruments.

But in the night, the pain grew so severe that she could not keep from crying and groaning. She did not want to wake anyone, so buried her face in the pillow to smother the sound of her sobs; but presently a gentle hand touched her caressingly, and mamma's sweet voice asked, "What ails my little daughter?"

"Oh, mamma, I did not mean to wake you!" cried the little girl, sitting up with her hand pressed to her cheek, "but the pain was so bad I couldn't help making a noise."

"My poor dear little girl! Did you think your mother would want to sleep when her child was in pain?" Elsie said, clasping her in her arms. "No, indeed! So do not try to bear any pain alone another time."

Mamma's loving sympathy was very sweet; the pain was soon relieved, too, by some medicine she put into the tooth; and presently all was forgotten in sound refreshing sleep.

Elsie came into her mamma's dressing room the next morning, along with the others, looking bright and well as was her wont, yet with the boding fear that something would be said to her about having the troublesome tooth extracted.

However, to her relief the subject was not broached at all; they had their usual reading and prayer, recitation of texts and talk with mamma about the lessons contained in them, and then the breakfast bell summoned them to their morning meal.

The tooth was quiet for a few days, then ached again for several hours harder than ever.

"Couldn't my little girl pluck up courage enough to have it out?" asked the mother tenderly.

"Oh, mamma, don't say I must! Please, don't! I'm so frightened at the very thought!'

"Ah, if I could only bear it for you, my darling! But you know I cannot."

"No, dear mamma, and I couldn't be so selfish as to let you, if I could. But must I have it out?"

"I have not said so; I should far rather my dear daughter would say must to herself."

"Ought I, mamma?"

"Ought you not? The tooth has become only a source of pain and trouble to you. If left, it will cause the others to decay, and decayed teeth injure the health. Health is one of God's best gifts and it is our duty to use every means in our power to preserve it."

"Yes, mamma, but oh, I'm so afraid!" cried the child, trembling and weeping.

"My darling, resolve to do your duty with God's help, and He will fulfill His promise to you. 'As thy days so shall thy strength be.' "

Little Elsie had long ago given her heart to Jesus. Love to Him was the ruling motive of her life, and to please and honor Him she was ready to do or endure anything. "I will try, mamma," she said, "and you too will ask God to help me?"

Mamma gave the promise, sealing it with a tender kiss.

Mr. Ross was going down to New York the next morning, and it was arranged that his wife, Mrs. Travilla and little Elsie should accompany him.

Mrs. Ross had some shopping to do, but would first take the two Elsies to her dentist, so that the little girl's trial might be over as soon as possible and would be able to enjoy some sight seeing afterward. Baby Lily was better and could be safely entrusted for the day to Aunt Chloe's faithful care.

The plan was concealed from the Ross children because, as their mother said, "It was the only way to have any peace." So they were allowed to sleep until the travelers had taken an early breakfast and gone.

The little Travillas however were up and saw the departure, bidding a cheerful goodbye to "mamma and sister Elsie," sending wistful, longing looks after the carriage as it rolled away, but making no complaint that they were left behind.

"Poor dear Elsie!" Vi said with tears in her eyes. "It's just dreadful that she must have that tooth extricated."

"Extracted," corrected Eddie. "Vi, you seem to forget what mamma says — that you should never use a big word unless you are sure you have it right, or when a little one would do as well."

"What little one?"

"Pulled."

"Couldn't it be pulled and not come out?"

"Well then, you might say pulled out."

"I like the other word best," persisted Vi. "But you needn't be particular about words when Elsie's going to be so dreadfully hurt."

Herbert burst out crying at that.

"Why, Herbie, what ails you?" asked Vi, putting her arms round his neck and giving him a kiss.

"I don't want the man to hurt my Elsie," sobbed the little fellow. "Maybe dey'll kill her."

"Oh, no, they won't! Mamma will never let them do that. They'll only take away the naughty tooth that hurts her so."

"Come, let's go and walk round the garden," said Eddie, taking Herbert's hand. "Mamma said we might."

The breakfast bell called them in to find the Rosses making a perfect bedlam in their anger and disappointment at being left behind by their parents. Sophie was screaming and stamping with rage, the boys and Kate were whimpering and scolding, and Gertrude walking about with flashing eyes was saying, "I'll never forgive mamma for this! No, I never will, for she'd promised to take me along next time she went to the city."

Violet, Eddie, and Harold, hearing these words, looked at each other in horrified silence. "How could she speak so of her own mother?"

Miss Fisk came in, in her quiet, deliberate way and stood looking for a moment from one to another of her pupils in a sort of amazed, reproving silence that presently had the effect of quieting them down a little. Then she spoke.

"Young ladies and young gentlemen, I am astonished — especially at your expressions and behavior, Miss Gertrude Ross! How you can permit yourself to indulge in such invectives against parents so extremely indulgent as Mr. and Mrs. Ross, I cannot conceive."

Sophie, whose screams had sunk to sobs, now permitted the servant to lift her to her high chair; Kate and the boys slunk shamefacedly into their seats at the table; and Gertrude, muttering something about "people not keeping their promises," followed their example.

"Come, sit down my dears," Miss Fisk said, turning to

Violet and her brothers. "The tempest seems to have nearly subsided and I hope will not resume its violence."

Herbie was clinging to Vi in a frightened way, sobbing "I want mamma!" and Harold's eyes were full of tears. It took coaxing and soothing to restore equanimity. Then the breakfast proceeded, everybody seeming to grow brighter and more good-humored with the satisfying of the appetite for food.

Vi was a merry little creature, a veritable bit of sunshine wherever she went. And under the influence of her bright looks and ways, sweet rippling laughter and amusing speeches, the whole party at length grew quite merry — especially after Miss Fisk announced that there would be no lessons that day but instead a picnic in the woods.

Chapter Sixth

By sports like these are all their cares beguil'd,
The sports of children satisfy the child.

— Goldsmith

"Good! Good!" cried the children. "Oh, delightful! But where are we going?"

"To the grove adjacent to the schoolhouse," replied the governess. "We could not find a lovelier spot, and its proximity to the mansion renders it most eligible."

"'Proximity, eligible, adjacent,' what do you mean by those words, Miss Fisk?" asked Gertrude, a little contemptuously.

"I desire that you consult one of our standard lexicographers. You will then be far more likely to retain the definitions in your memory," returned the governess, ignoring the tone of her pupil.

Gertrude shrugged her shoulders, with impatience, muttering audibly, "I wish you'd talk like other people, and not like a dictionary."

"You quarrel with my phraseology, because you do not understand it," observed Miss Fisk nonchalantly, "which is very irrational; since, were I never to employ, in conversing with you, words beyond your comprehension, you would lose the advantage of being induced to increase your stock of information by a search for their meaning."

"If that's what you do it for, you may as well give it up at once," returned Gertrude, "for I don't care enough about your meaning to take half that trouble."

"Miss Gertrude, permit me to remark that you are

lacking in respect to your instructor," returned Miss Fisk, reddening.

"Do you mean that it is convenient, because of being so near this house, Miss Fisk?" asked Eddie respectfully.

"Yes, convenient and safe, on which account both Mrs. Travilla and Mrs. Ross stipulated that our picnic for today should be held there."

"Well, let's go right away," said Gertrude, jumping up and pushing back her chair.

"Immediately, Miss Ross," corrected the governess. "Right away is exceedingly inelegant."

"How tiresome!" muttered Gertrude. Then, aloud to Violet, as the governess left the room, "I say, Vi, does your mamma reprove you for saying right away?"

"I don't remember that I ever said it. Mamma —"

"Said it?" interrupted Gertrude, with a twinkle of fun in her eyes. "Why don't you say 'used the expression?' my dear," mimicking Miss Fisk's tones. "You should never condescend to make use of a nickel word, when a fifty cent one would express your sentiments fully as correctly, or perchance even more so."

Vi could not help joining in the laugh with which Gertrude concluded, though feeling rather ashamed of herself, as she seemed to see the grave look of disapproval mamma would have given her if present.

"Oh, Gertrude," she said, "we oughtn't to — ."

"Yes, we ought," returned Gertrude as they ran out of the room together. "Mamma always laughs when I take off on old finicky Fisk. She wouldn't want me to talk like her for the world. Would your mamma wish you to?"

"No, but she never says — ."

"Right away? No, of course not. She says 'immediately' or 'at once' or something that sounds nice. Well, so will I when I'm grown up."

Miss Fisk was on the porch taking an observation of the weather, the children crowding about her, clamoring to be allowed to set out immediately for the grove. The day was fine and there seemed every indication that it would continue so.

"Yes," said the governess, "you may request your maids to see that you are suitably arrayed for the occasion, and as promptly as possible. We will repair to the appointed place — taking our departure in precisely thirty minutes."

The children were ready and impatiently waiting when Miss Fisk came down from her room, "suitably arrayed for the occasion."

They set out at once, the whole party in high good humor. The boys carried their balls, marbles, and fishing rods; the girls had their dolls and a set of toy dishes to play tea party with.

Miss Fisk had a bit of fancy work and a book, and two servants brought up the rear with camp chairs, an afghan and rugs to make a couch for the little ones when they should grow sleepy. Luncheon was in course of preparation by the cook, and was to be sent by the time the young picnickers were likely to feel an appetite for it.

The boys took the lead, bounding on some distance ahead, with Ranger in their midst. They were in no mood just then to be sitting still; so, depositing their fishing tackle in the schoolhouse, they went roving about in search of more active amusement than that of catching trout.

"That'll be good fun when we want to sit down and rest," said Eddie.

"Oh, I see a bird's nest, and I'm going to have it!" exclaimed Archie, beginning to climb a tree.

"Oh, don't," cried Harold, "mamma says it's very cruel and wicked to rob the poor little birds."

"Pooh! You're a baby!" answered Archie, half breathlessly, pulling himself up higher and yet higher. "There, I'll have it in a minute," reaching out his hand to lay hold of the branch that held the nest.

Ranger was barking loudly at the foot of the tree, Harry and Eddie were calling Archie to "Take care!" and he hardly knew how it was himself, but he missed the branch, lost his hold of the tree, and fell, lighting upon Ranger's back.

The boy gave a scream, the dog a yelp, and the rest of the party came running to ask what was the matter.

Archie picked himself up, looking quite crestfallen, and the fright of the others was turned to laughter as they discovered that he had received no damage beyond a slight scratch on his hand and a tear in his jacket.

Miss Fisk, making him promise not to repeat the experiment, went back to her seat under the trees and the book she had brought from the house for her own enjoyment.

The morning passed without any further incident worth recording, the children amusing themselves with various quiet plays — the girls keeping house, each under her own particular tree, and exchanging visits; the boys catching trout, which they sent to the house to be cooked for dinner. They wanted to make a fire and cook them themselves, but Miss Fisk wisely forbade it.

She would have had the meal served in the schoolhouse, but yielded to the clamor for an outdoor repast. Several desks were brought out into the shade of the trees, a dainty tablecloth spread over them and the party presently sat down to a delightful collation, to which they brought keen appetites.

Ranger had disappeared. They missed him as they were leaving the table.

"Where can he have gone?" Harry was saying, when Vi cried out, "Oh, yonder he is! And he has a dear little bird in his mouth! Oh, you wicked, cruel dog!" And running to him, she tried to take it from him.

He dropped it and snapped at her, Eddie jerking her back just in time to save her from his teeth, while Archie, who was very fond of Vi, struck the dog a blow with a stick, crying furiously, "You just do that again, sir, and I'll kill you."

Ranger then flew at him, but the boy avoided the attack by jumping nimbly behind a tree.

The other children were screaming with fright, and a catastrophe appeared imminent, but one of the maids came running with some tempting morsels for Ranger, which appeased his wrath, and the danger was averted.

Ranger's attention being absorbed with the satisfying of his appetite, the children now looked about for the bird. It was not quite dead, but soon breathed its last in Vi's lap with her tears dropping fast upon it.

"Oh, don't Vi!" said Archie. "I can't bear to see you feel so sorry. And the bird isn't being hurt now, you know; 'twon't ever be hurt any more, will it, Ed?"

"No," said Harry, "we might as well let the dog have it."

"No, no!" said Eddie. "It would just encourage him to catch another."

"So it would," said Gertrude. "Let's make a grand funeral and bury it at the foot of a tree. If we only knew now which one it used to live in."

The motion was about to be carried by acclamation, but Vi entered a decided protest. "No, no, I want to keep it."

"But you can't, Vi," remonstrated Eddie, "dead things have to be buried, you know."

"Not the skin and feathers, Eddie; they do stuff them sometimes and I'll ask mamma to let me have this one done."

"Oh, what's the use?" expostulated Gertrude. "It's only a common robin."

"But I love it — the poor dear little thing — and mamma will let me, I know she will," returned Vi, wiping away her tears as though comforted by the very thought.

The other children wandered off to their play leaving her sitting where she was, on a fallen tree, fondling the bird. But Archie soon came back and seated himself by her side.

"Such a pity, isn't it?" he said. "I hate that Ranger, don't you, Vi?"

"No-o, I hope not, Archie," she answered doubtfully. "Folks kill birds to eat them and maybe 'tain't any worse for dogs," she added, with a fresh burst of tears. "Poor little birdie! Maybe there are some young ones in the nest that have no mamma now to feed or care for them."

"That old Ranger! And he snapped at you, too. Here he comes again. I'll kill him!" cried the boy with vehemence. "Oh, no, I know what I'll do! Here, Ranger! Here, Ranger!" and starting up, he rushed away in a direction to take him farther from the schoolhouse and the rest of his party.

He had spied in the distance a farmer's boy, a lad of fourteen, with whom he had some slight acquaintance. "Hello, Jared Bates!" he shouted.

"Well, what's wantin'?" and Jared stood still, drawing the lash of his carter's whip slowly between his fingers. "Hurry up now, for I've got to go back to my team. Whose dog's that?" as Ranger came running up and saluted him with a sharp, "bow, wow, wow!"

"Ours," said Archie, "and I'm mad at him 'cause he killed a bird and tried to bite Vi Travilla, when she went to take it from him."

"Like enough," returned Jared, grinning, "but what about it?"

"I thought maybe you'd like to have him."

"So I would; what'll you sell him for?"

"Ten cents."

"I hain't got but two."

"Haven't you, Jared? Truly, now?"

"No, nary red, 'cept them," and diving into his pantaloons' pocket, Jared produced a handful of odds and ends — a broken knife, a plug of tobacco, some rusty nails, a bit of twine — from which he picked out two nickels. There, them's um, and they's all I got in the world," he said gravely, passing them over to Archie.

"Well, it's very cheap," observed the latter, pocketing the cash, "but you can have him. Goodbye!" And away he ran back to the spot where he had left Vi.

"You're a green un!" laughed Jared, looking after him; then, whistling to the dog to follow, he went on his way.

Chapter Seventh

But this I say, he which soweth sparingly shall reap also sparingly; and he which soweth bountifully shall reap also bountifully.

— 2 Corinthians 9:6

All the children, Gertrude excepted, were gathered on the front porch, Vi with the dead bird in her hands, when the carriage drove up with the returning travelers.

There was a chorus of welcome, and most of the young faces were bright and happy. Elsie's troop had nothing but smiles, caresses and loving words for her, and tender, anxious inquires about "sister Elsie."

"Is the tooth out? Did the dentist hurt much?"

"It was hard to bear," she said, "but the doctor was very kind, and tried not to hurt her. And, oh, mamma had made her such a lovely present for being brave and willing to have her tooth out." She took out a beautiful little gold watch and chain from her bosom, and held them up to their admiring gaze.

"Oh, I'm so glad, so glad! Dear mamma, how good of you!" cried Vi, without a touch of envy, embracing first her sister, and then her mother.

Eddie and the two younger ones seemed equally pleased, and "sister Elsie" allowed each in turn to closely inspect her treasure.

In the meantime, Mr. and Mrs. Ross had been busy bestowing caresses and small gifts upon their children, who received them with noisy glee mingled with some reproaches because they had been left at home.

"Come, come, no complaints," said their father. "I

think you have fared well — a holiday, a picnic, and these pretty presents. Where's Gertrude?"

"Sure enough, where is she?" asked Lucy, looking round from one to another.

"She's mad because you did not take her along," remarked Harry. "She says you didn't keep your promise."

"Dear me, I'd forgotten all about it!" exclaimed Mrs. Ross. "I should have taken her though, but there wasn't time to get her up and dressed."

"Gertrude! Gertrude!' called Mr. Ross, in tones of authority. "Gertrude, come here and show yourself."

At that the child came out slowly from the hall — whence she had been watching the scene through the crack behind the door — looking red and angry.

"What's the matter with you?" asked her father, with some displeasure in his tone.

"Nothing, I'm not crying."

"Nor pouting either, I suppose? What's it all about?"

"Mamma promised to take me along the next time she went to the city."

"Perhaps she will the next time."

"But this was the next time, because she promised it when she went before and took Kate."

"Well, such promises are always conditional. She took no one this time but me, and there was a good reason why."

Gertrude smiled slightly, then laughed outright, as she glanced up into his face, saying, "I thought it was you, papa, who took mamma."

"Oh, now you begin to look something like the little girl I'm used to hearing called Gertrude Ross, the one I like to buy presents for. The other one that was here just a moment ago gets nothing bought with my money."

"See here," said her mother, and with a cry of delight Gertrude sprang forward and caught from her hand a watch and chain very nearly the counterparts of those little Elsie was displaying to her sister and brother.

"Oh, joy, joy!" she cried, dancing up and down.

"Thank you, papa! I'd rather have this than a dozen visits to New York. See, Kate, isn't it a beauty?"

"Yes," returned her sister sullenly, "but I don't see why you should have a watch and I only this ring. You're hardly more than a year older that I am and not a bit better girl."

"Come, come, don't pout, Kitty," said her father, stroking her hair. "Your time will come. Harry's and Archie's, too; even little Sophie's," he added, catching the household pet up in his arms to give her a hug and a kiss.

It was not until after tea that Mr. Ross missed his dog. "Where's Ranger?" he asked of one of the servants.

"That, sir, I don't know," she answered. "Sure he went to the picnic wid the rest of the childer, an' it's mesilf as hasn't seen him since."

"Harry," stepping out on the porch where the children, except the very little ones — who had already been sent up to bed — were sitting listlessly about, too weary with the day's sports to care for any more active amusement, "where's Ranger?"

"Ranger?" cried Harry with a start, "Why sure enough, I haven't seen him since we came home! And I don't think he came with us either."

"No, he didn't," answered several young voices.

"I wonder where he can be," pursued Harry. "Shall I go and look for him, papa?"

Mr. Ross was about to say yes when his eye fell upon the face of his youngest son, who, he noticed, looked very red and somewhat troubled.

"What do you know about it, Archie?" he asked. "Can you tell us what has become of Ranger?"

"He behaved very bad indeed, papa," stammered the boy. "He killed a dear little bird and tried to bite Vi, and me too — and I sold him."

The truth was out and Archie heaved a sigh of relief.

"Sold him?" repeated his father in a tone of mingled surprise and displeasure.

"Yes, sir, to Jared Bates for two cents. Here they are.

I suppose they belong to you," said the little fellow, tugging at his pocket.

"For two cents!" exclaimed Mr. Ross laughing in spite of himself. "You'll never grow rich, my boy, making such bargains as that. But see here," he added, growing grave again, "whose dog was it?"

"I — I thought it was ours, papa."

"Ours? Yours to play with, but only mine to sell or give away. You'll have to go to Jared tomorrow, return his two cents, and tell him the dog is mine, and you sold what did not belong to you."

"Oh, where's my bird?" cried Violet, reminded of it by this little episode. "I laid it down to look at Elsie's watch and it's gone! Mamma, mamma, I'm so sorry!"

"I am too, dear, for your sake," the mother said, putting an arm about her and kissing the wet cheek, for the tears had begun to flow again. "Was it the bird Ranger killed?"

"Yes, mamma, I was going to ask you to get it stuffed for me."

"Some cat has got it, no doubt," said Mr. Ross. "But don't cry. It couldn't hurt it, you know, after it was dead."

"If it only had a heaven to go to," sobbed Vi.

"Perhaps it has," said the gentleman kindly. "I really don't think," turning to Mrs. Travilla, "that the Bible says anything to the contrary. It seems to me to simply leave the matter in doubt."

"I know," she answered thoughtfully, "that is the generally accepted belief that there is no hereafter for the lower animals; yet it has occurred to me, too, that the Bible does not positively assert it. And some of the poor creatures have such a suffering life in this world that it makes my heart ache to think there is no other for them."

"Papa," asked Archie, "don't you think Ranger deserved to be sold for killing that bird and trying to bite Vi?"

"That's a question you should have propounded before selling him, that, and another — 'May I sell him?' "

"I wish you'd let Phelium go and buy him back,"

remarked the boy, looking uncomfortable at the thought of having to do the errand himself.

"No, sir," returned the father decidedly. "The mischief you have done, you must undo yourself. Ah, Harry, go and ask if any letters came today."

"I asked," said Gertrude. "There was just one, from Phil," and she drew it from her pocket and handed it to her father.

"What does he say?" Mrs. Ross inquired when he had glanced over it.

"Not much, except that he's to be here tomorrow and wants the carriage sent to the depot for him," he answered, handing it to her.

"Good!" said Gertrude, with much satisfaction. "We always have more fun when Phil's at home."

"Except when he picks a quarrel with you or some of us," remarked Harry.

"For shame, Hal!" said his mother. "The quarrels, if there are any, are as likely to be begun by you, as anyone else."

Lucy was proud and fond of her firstborn, and always ready to shield him from blame. He was in his mother's eyes as the king, who could do no wrong; but to the others he was a spoiled child — a willful, headstrong, domineering boy.

Yet, he was not without his good qualities — brave, frank, affectionate, and generous to a fault. Many hearts besides those of his doting parents were drawn to him in sincere affection, Elsie's among the rest. Yet she dreaded exposing her little sons to Phil's influence. She was especially concerned for Edward, as nearer Phil's age; and because, though much improved by good training, his natural disposition was very similar. But she had not seen Philip for two years, and hoped he might have changed for the better.

It seemed so at first. He was a bright, handsome youth, and came home in fine spirits, and with a manner full of affection for parents, brothers and sisters. She did not wonder at Lucy's fond pride in her eldest son.

"Phil," said his mother, following him into his room that night, "you have made a good impression, and I'm very anxious you shouldn't spoil it; so do try to keep on your good behavior while the Travillas stay."

"I intend to, Mrs. Ross," he returned, with a laugh. "Elsie, little Elsie's been my little lady love since the first time my eyes lighted on her, and I know that if I want to secure the prize, I've got to keep on the right side of her father and mother."

"Lucy laughed. "You are beginning early, Phil," she said. "I advise you to not say a word of your hopes in their hearing for ten years to come."

"Trust me for managing the thing, ma," he returned, nodding his head wisely. "But do you s'pose now, they'd be so outrageously unreasonable as to expect a fellow to be quite perfect?" he queried, striking a match and lighting a cigar.

"Phil! Phil! Throw that away!" she said, trying to snatch it from him.

He sprang nimbly aside. "No, you don't, ma! Why shouldn't I smoke like my father? Ministers smoke too, and lots of good people."

"But you're too young to begin yet, and I know your Aunt Elsie would be horrified. She'd think you a very fast boy and hurry away with her children, lest they should be contaminated by your bad example."

"Well," he answered, puffing away, "I'll not let her or them know I ever indulge. I'll only smoke up here and at night, and the smell will be off my breath by morning."

"I wish you'd give it up entirely. Where did you ever learn it?"

"Comes natural! I guess I inherited the taste. But nearly all the fellows at school do it — on the sly."

"Ah, Phil, I'm afraid you're a sad fellow!" Lucy said, shaking her head reprovingly; but he could see the smile shining in her fond, admiring eyes, and lurking about the corners of her mouth.

"Oh, come now, ma, I'm not so bad — not the worst fellow in the world. I wouldn't do a mean thing."

"No, of course not," she said, kissing him goodnight, and leaving him with a parting "Don't forget to say your prayers, Phil."

Mr. and Mrs. Ross were not Christian parents. Careful and solicitous about the temporal welfare of their children, they gave little thought to their spiritual needs. Lucy taught them, in their infancy, to say their prayers before lying down to rest at night. As they grew older she sent them to Sunday school, took them to church on pleasant Sabbath mornings, when it was convenient, and she felt inclined to go herself, and provided each one with a copy of the Bible.

This was about the extent of the religious training they received, and it was strongly counteracted by the worldly atmosphere of their home, the worldly example set them by their parents, and the worldly maxims and precepts constantly instilled into their young minds.

From these they learned to look upon the riches, honors and pleasures of earth as the things to be most earnestly coveted, most worthy of untiring efforts to secure.

Life at the Crags was a strange puzzle to the Ion children — no blessing asked at the table, no gathering of the family morning or evening for prayer or praise or the reading of God's word.

"Mamma, what does it mean?" they asked. "Why doesn't Uncle Ross do as papa does?"

Elsie scarce knew how to answer them. "Don't let us talk about it, dears," she said, "but whatever others may do, let us serve God ourselves and seek His favor above everything else; for 'in His favor is life' and His loving kindness is better than life."

CHAPTER EIGHTH

To each his sufferings: all are men
Condemn'd alike to groan;
The tender for another's pain,
The unfeeling for his own.

— GRAY

THE WEATHER WAS DELIGHTFUL. Because of Phil's return, the children were excused altogether from lessons and nearly every day was taken up with picnics, riding, driving, and boating excursions up and down the river.

They were never allowed to go alone on the water or behind any horse but "Old Nan," an old slow-moving creature that Phil said "could not be persuaded or forced out of a quiet even trot that was little better than a walk, for five consecutive minutes."

The mothers were generally of the party — Lily continuing so much better that Elsie could leave her, without anxiety, in the faithful care of her old mammy — and always one or two trusty servants were taken along.

One day Philip got permission to take old Nan and the phaeton and drive out with the two older girls, Gertrude and Elsie.

They were gone several hours and on their return, while still some miles from home were overtaken by a heavy shower, from which they took refuge in a small log house standing a few yards back from the road.

It was a rude structure built in a wild spot among the rocks and trees, and evidently the abode of pinching poverty; but everything was clean and neat. The occupants were an elderly woman reclining in a high backer wooden rocking chair with her feet propped up on a rude bench, and a young girl who sat sewing by a window overlooking the road. She wore an air of refinement and spoke English more correctly and with a purer accent than sometimes is heard in the abodes of wealth and fashion.

Gertrude ran lightly in with a laugh and jest, Elsie following close at her heels.

The girl rose and setting out two unpainted wooden chairs, invited them to be seated, remarking as she resumed her work, that the shower had come up very suddenly, but she hoped they were not wet.

"Not enough to hurt us," said Gertrude.

"Hardly at all, thank you," said Elsie. "I hope our mammas will not be alarmed about us, Gerty."

"I don't think they need to be so long as there's no thunder and lightning," answered Gertrude. "Ah, see how it is pouring over yonder on the mountain Elsie?"

The pale face of the woman in the rocking chair, evidently an invalid, had grown still paler and her features worked with emotion.

"Child! Child!" she cried, fixing her wild eyes on Elsie, "who — are you?"

"They're the young ladies from the Crags, mother," said the girl soothingly.

"I know that Sally," she answered peevishly, "but one's a visitor, and the other one called her Elsie. She's just the age and very image of — child, what is your family name?"

"Travilla, madam," the little girl replied, with a look of surprise.

"Oh, you're her daughter. Yes, of course. I might have known it. And so she married him, her father's friend and so many years older."

The words were spoken as if to herself and she finished with a deep drawn sigh.

This woman had loved Travilla — all unsuspected by him, for he was not a conceited man — and there had been a time when she would have almost given her hopes for heaven for a return of her affection.

"Is it my mother you mean? Did you know her when she was a little girl?" asked Elsie, rising and drawing near the woman's chair.

"Yes, if she was Elsie Dinsmore and lived at Roselands — how many years ago? Let me see. It was a good many, long before I was married to John Gibson."

"That was mamma's name and that was where she lived, with her grandpa, while her papa was away in Europe so many years," returned the little Elsie. Then she asked with eager interest, "But how did you happen to know her? Did you live near Roselands?"

"I lived there; but I was a person of no consequence — only a poor governess," returned the woman in a bitter tone, an expression of angry discontent settling down upon her features.

"Are you Miss Day?" asked Elsie, retreating a step or two with a look as if she had seen a serpent.

Her mother had seldom mentioned Miss Day to her, but from her Aunts Adelaide and Lora she had heard of her many acts of cruelty and injustice to the little motherless girls committed to her care.

"I was Miss Day. I'm Mrs. Gibson now. I was a little hard on your mother sometimes, as I see you've been told; but I'd a great deal to bear, for they were a very proud, haughty family — those Dinsmores. I was not treated as one of them, but as a sort of upper servant, though a lady by birth, breeding and education," the woman remarked, her tone growing more and more bitter as she proceeded.

"But was it right? Was it just and generous to vent your anger upon a poor little innocent girl who had no mother and father there to defend her?" asked the child, her soft eyes filling with tears.

"Well, maybe not; but it's the way people generally do. Your mother was a good little thing, provokingly good sometimes; pretty too, and heiress, they said, to an immense fortune. Is she rich still? Or did she lose it all in the war?"

"She did not lose it all, I know," said Elsie, "but how

rich she is I do not know. Mamma and papa seldom talk of any but the true riches."

"Just like her, for all the world!" muttered the woman. Then aloud and sneeringly, "Pray what do you mean by true riches?"

"Those which can never be taken from us, treasures laid up in heaven where neither moth nor rust doth corrupt and thieves break not through to steal."

The sweet child voice ceased and silence reigned in the room for a moment, while the splashing of the rain upon the roof could be distinctly heard.

Mrs. Gibson was the first to speak again. "Well, I'd like to have that kind, but I'd like wonderfully well to try the other for a while first."

Elsie looked at the thin, sallow face with its hollow cheeks and sunken eyes, and wished mamma were here to talk of Jesus to this poor woman, who surely had but little time to prepare for another world.

"Is your mother at the Crags?" asked Mrs. Gibson, turning to her again.

Elsie answered in the affirmative, adding that they had been there for some time and would probably remain a week or two longer.

"Do you think she would be willing to come here to see me?" was the next question, almost eagerly put.

"Mamma is very kind and I am sure she will come if you wish to see her," answered the child.

"Then, tell her I do. Tell her I, her old governess, am sick and poor and in great trouble."

Tears rolled down her cheeks and for a moment her eyes rested upon her daughter's face with an expression of keen anguish. "She's going blind," she whispered in Elsie's ear, drawing the child toward her, and nodding in the direction of Sally, stitching away at the window.

"Blind! Oh, how dreadful!" exclaimed the little girl in low moved tones, the tears springing to her eyes. "I wish she could go to Dr. Thomsom."

"Dr. Thomson! Who is he?"

"An oculist. He lives in Philadelphia. A friend of mamma's had something growing over her eyes so that she was nearly blind, and he cut it off and she can see now as well as anybody."

"I don't think that is the trouble with Sally's; though, of course, I can't tell. But she's always had poor sight, and now that she has to support the family with her needle, her eyes are nearly wore out."

Sally had been for several minutes making vain attempts to thread a needle.

Elsie sprang to her side with a kindly, eager "Let me do it, won't you?"

It was done in a moment, and the girl thanked her with lips and eyes.

"It often takes me a full five or ten minutes," she said, "and sometimes I have to get mother to do it for me."

"What a pity! It must be a great hindrance to your work."

"Yes, indeed, and my eyes ache so that I can seldom sew or read more than an hour or two at a time. Ah, I'm afraid I'm going to lose my sight altogether."

The tone was inexpressibly mournful, and Elsie's eyes filled again.

"Don't fret about it," she said, "I think — I hope you can be cured."

The rain had nearly ceased, and Philip, saying the worst was over, and they were in danger of being late at dinner, hurried the girls into the phaeton.

"What was that woman whispering to you?" asked Gertrude, as soon as they were a distance away.

Elsie looked uncomfortable. "It was something I was to tell mamma," she replied.

"But what is it?"

"I'm afraid she wanted to keep it a secret from you, Gerty, or she would have spoken out loud."

"I think you're being mean and unaccommodating," retorted Gertrude, beginning to pout.

"No, she isn't," said Philip pompously, "she's honorable, and one of the few females who can keep a secret. But I overheard it, Elsie, and feel pretty sure that the reason she whispered it was to keep the poor girl from hearing. It's very natural she shouldn't want her to know she's afraid her sight's leaving her."

"Oh, yes, I suppose that was it!" returned Elsie. "But you were very wise to think of it, Phil."

"Don't flatter him," said Gertrude, "He thinks a great deal too much of himself already."

Dinner was just ready when they reached home, and their mammas were on the porch looking for them.

"So there you are at last! What detained you so long?" said Mrs. Ross.

"Went farther than we intended, and then the rain, you know," said Philip.

"And, oh, we had an adventure!" cried the girls, and hastened to tell it.

Mrs. Travilla had not forgotten her old governess, and though no pleasant recollection of her lingered in her memory, neither was there any dislike or revengeful feeling there. She heard of her sorrows with commiseration and rejoiced in the ability to alleviate them.

"That Mrs. Gibson!" exclaimed Lucy, "I've seen her many a time at the door or window, in driving past, and have often thought there was something familiar in her face, but never dreamed who she was. That hateful Miss Day as I used to call her. Elsie, I wouldn't do a thing for her, if I were you. Why she treated you with absolute cruelty."

"She was sometimes unjust and unkind." said Mrs. Travilla, smiling at her friend's vehemence, "but probably my sensitiveness, timidity and stupidity were often very trying."

"No such thing! If you will excuse me for contradicting you, everybody that knew you then would testify that you were the sweetest, dearest, most patient, industrious little thing that ever was made."

Elsie laughed and shook her head. "Ah, Lucy, you always flattered me; never were jealous even when I was held up to you as a pattern, an evidence that yours was a remarkably sweet disposition. Now, tell me, please, if you know anything about these Gibsons."

"Not much. They came to that hut years ago, evidently very poor, and quite as evidently — so reports say — having seen better days. The husband and father drank deeply, and the wife earned a scanty support for the family by sewing and knitting. That is about all I know of them, except that several of their children died of scarlet fever within a few days of each other, soon after they came to the neighborhood. And that a year ago last winter, the man, coming home drunk, fell into a snow drift, and next day was found frozen to death. I was told at that time they had two children — a son who was following in his father's footsteps, and this daughter."

"Poor woman!" sighed Elsie. "She is sorely tried and afflicted. I must go to her at once."

"Do, mamma, and get a doctor for her," said little Elsie. "She looked so sick and miserable."

Mrs. Ross offered her carriage, and the shower having cooled the air, Elsie went, shortly after the conclusion of the meal.

CHAPTER NINTH

I'll not chide thee;
Let shame cover when it will, I do not call it.

— SHAKESPEARE

"I NEVER SAW SUCH A likeness in my life!" said Mrs. Gibson, looking after the phaeton as it drove away. "She's the very image of her mother. I could just have believed it was the very little Elsie Dinsmore I used to teach more than twenty years ago."

"She's lovely!" exclaimed Sally with enthusiasm. "Mother, did you see what a pretty watch she had?"“

"Yes," gloomily, "some folks seem to have nothing but prosperity, and others nothing but poverty and losses and crosses. They're as rich as Midas and we have hardly enough to keep us from starving."

"Better times may come," said Sally, trying to speak hopefully. "Tom may reform and go to work. I do think, mother, if you'd try to —."

"Hush! I'm a great deal better to him than he deserves."

It was some moments before Sally spoke again, then it was only to ask, "Will you have your dinner now, mother?"

"No, there's nothing in the house but bread and potatoes, and I couldn't swallow either. Dear me, what a table they used to set at Roselands! There was enough to tempt the appetite of an epicure."

"I must rest my eyes a little. I can't see any longer," said the girl, laying down her work and going to the door.

"It's just dreadful," sighed the mother, "but don't get discouraged. These people will help us and it is possible some skillful oculist may understand your case and be able to help you."

The girl's eyes were fixed upon the distant mountaintops where, through a rift in the clouds, the sun shone suddenly out for a moment. "'I lift up mine eyes unto the hills whence cometh my help,'" she murmured softly to herself. Then from a full heart went up a strong cry, "Oh, God, my Father, save me, I beseech thee, from this bitter trial that I so dread! Nevertheless, not as I will, but as thou wilt. Oh, help me to be content with whatsoever Thou shalt send!"

"Sally, you're standing there for a long time." It was the mother's querulous voice again.

The girl turned toward her, answering in a patient tone. "Yes, mother, it rests my eyes to look at the sky and the mountains or any distant object."

"You'd better get yourself something to eat. It must be six or eight hours at least since breakfast."

An hour later Sally, again busied with her sewing by the window, lifted her head at the sound of wheels and exclaimed in a low tone, "There is the same carriage again! It has stopped and a lady is getting out of it."

But turning her head, she perceived that her mother, who was now lying on the bed, had fallen asleep. Dropping her work, she stepped quickly to the door in time to prevent a rap.

She recognized the lady at once from her likeness to her namesake daughter, and holding out her hand with a joyful and admiring smile said, "Mrs. Travilla, is it not? Thank you for coming; I am so glad, and mother will be so delighted to see you; but she is sleeping just now."

She had spoken softly, and Elsie answered in the same subdued tone, as she took the offered hand, then stepped in and sat down in a chair the girl hastened to set for her. "That is well; we must not wake her."

A long talk followed in which Elsie by her ready tact and sweet sympathy, free from the slightest approach to patronage, drew from the girl the story of their sorrows, privations and fears for the future.

Her mother had been gradually failing for some time, though she really did not know what was the nature of the disease. For awhile they had contrived by their united efforts to make the two ends meet; but now that all depended upon her, with her poor sight, it was no longer possible.

How are your eyes affected?" asked Elsie.

"The sight is dim. I can scarcely see to set my stitches. I have great difficulty in threading a needle; I always had. I could never read fine print, never read through a long sentence without shutting my eyes for an instant or looking off the book. It has always been an effort to see, and now I am forced to use my eyes so constantly that they grow worse and pain me very much. At times a mist comes over them so that I cannot see at all until I rest them a little. Indeed, I often seem to be going blind and I'm afraid I shall," she added, with a tremble in her tones, a tear rolling down her cheek. But she hastily wiped it away.

"My poor child, I hope not," Elsie said, laying a hand softly on hers. "There have been wonderful cures of diseased eyes. You must go to an oculist."

"The expense would be far beyond our means."

"You must let me assume that. No, don't shake your head. I have abundant means. The Lord has given me far more of this world's goods than I ought to use for myself or my family and I know it is because He would have me be His steward."

The girl wept for joy and thankfulness.

"Oh, how kind you are!" she cried. "I believe the Lord sent you and that my sight will be spared, for I have prayed so that it might — that He would send me help somehow. But mother, how can she do without me?"

"I will see that she has medical advicc, nursing, everything she needs."

Sally tried to speak her thanks but tears and sobs came instead.

The sound woke Mrs. Gibson. "Elsie Dinsmore!" she cried in feeble but excited tones, with difficulty raising herself to a sitting posture. "I should have known you anywhere."

"I cannot say the same; you are much changed," Elsie said, going to the bedside and taking the thin feverish hand in hers.

"Yes, I've grown an old woman, while you are fresh and young; and no wonder, for your life has been all prosperity — mine, nothing but trouble and trial from beginning to end."

"Oh, mother, dear, we have had a great many mercies," said Sally, "and your life in not ended. I hope your good times are yet to come."

"Well, maybe so, if Mrs. Travilla can help us to the medical aid we need, and put us in the way of earning a good living afterward."

"I shall do my best for you in both respects," Elsie said kindly, accepting a chair Sally set for her near the bed.

Chapter Tenth

When we see the flower seeds wafted,
From the nurturing mother tree,
Tell we can, wherever planted,
What the harvesting will be;
Never from the blasting thistle,
Was there gathered golden grain,
Thus the seal the child receiveth,
From its mother will remain.

— Mrs. Hale

For once Mrs. Gibson had the grace to feel a passing emotion of gratitude to this kind benefactor, and shame that she herself had been so ready with faultfinding instead of thanks.

As for Sally, she was completely overcome and, dropping into a chair, hid her face and cried heartily.

"Come, don't be a fool," her mother said at last. "There's too much to be done to waste time in crying, and besides you'll hurt your eyes."

Sally rose hastily, removed the traces of her tears, and began setting the table for their morning meal.

"How soon are you going?" her mother asked at its conclusion.

"Just as soon as I can get the things cleared away and the dishes washed, if you think you can spare me."

"Of course I can. I feel well enough this morning to help myself to anything I'm likely to want."

There was still half an hour to spare before breakfast when, after a round of five or six miles on their ponies, Philip and Elsie reached the Crags.

"What shall you do with yours?" asked Philip, remarking upon that fact.

"Read," she answered, looking back at him with a smile as she tripped lightly up the stairs.

Dinah was in waiting to smooth her hair and help her change the pretty riding hat and habit for a dress better suited to the house; then Elsie, left alone, seated herself by a window with her Bible in her hand.

For a moment her eyes rested upon the blue distant mountains, softly outlined against the deeper blue sky, watching the cloud shadows floating over the nearer hills and valleys — here richly wooded, there covered with fields of waving grain. All the while her ears were drinking in with delight many a sweet rural sound — the songs of the birds, the distant lowing of cattle, and bleating of sheep — her heart swelling with ardent love and thankfulness to Him who had given her so much to enjoy.

Dinah had left the door open, that the fresh air might course freely through the room, and Gertrude coming some minutes later in search of her friend, stood watching Elsie for a little unperceived.

"Dear me!" she exclaimed at length, "How many times a day do you pore over that book?"

Elsie looked up with a smile as sweet as the morning. "I am allowed to read it as often as I please."

"Allowed? Not compelled? Not ordered?"

"No, only I must have a text ready for mamma every morning."

"Getting one ready for tomorrow?"

"No, just reading. I had time for only a verse or two before my ride."

"Well, that would be plenty for me. I can read it, too, as often as I like, but a chapter or two on Sunday generally does me for all the week. There's the bell; come, let's go down."

Vi met them at the door of the breakfast room. "Oh, Elsie, did you have a pleasant ride? Is Sally Gibson coming soon?"

"I don't know. Mamma said I need not wait for an answer."

There was time for no more, and Vi must put a restraint upon herself, repressing excitement and curiosity for the present, as mamma expected her children to be very quiet and unobtrusive at the table when away from home.

Vi was delighted when just as they were leaving the table, a servant announced that a young person, who called herself Miss Gibson, was asking for Miss Travilla. Vi never liked waiting, and was always eager to carry out immediately any plan that had been set on foot.

Mrs. Gibson was not troubled with any delicacy of feeling about asking for what she wanted, and had made out a list of things to be provided for herself and Sally, which the girl was shamed to show, so extravagant seemed its demands.

When urged by her benefactor, she mentioned a few of the most necessary articles, modestly adding that the generous gift Mrs. Travilla had already bestowed ought to be sufficient to supply all else that might be required.

Elsie, seating herself at her writing desk and taking out pen, ink and paper, looked smilingly into the faces of her two little girls.

"What do you think about it, dears?"

"Oh, they must have more things — a good many more; and we want to help pay for them with our money."

"You see, Miss Sally, they will be sadly disappointed if you refuse to accept their gifts," said Elsie. "Now I'm going to make out a list and you must help me, lest something should be forgotten. Mrs. Ross has kindly offered us the use of her carriage, and we will drive to the nearest town and see what we can find there. The rest we will order from New York."

The list was made out amid much innocent jesting and merry laughter of both mother and children — Sally a deeply interested and delighted spectator of their pleasing exchange. The mother was so sweet, gentle and affectionate, the children so respectful and loving to her, so kind and considerate of each other.

In fact, the girl was so occupied in watching them that she was not aware till Mrs. Travilla read it over aloud that this new list was longer and more extravagant than the one she had suppressed.

"Oh, it is too much, Mrs. Travilla!" she cried, the tears starting to her eyes.

"My dear child," returned Elsie, playfully, "I'm a willful woman and will have my own way. Come, the carriage is in waiting and we must go."

The shopping expedition was quite a frolic for the children and a great treat to poor, overworked Sally. "She looks so shabby. I'd be ashamed to go with her to the stores or anywhere, or to have her ride in the carriage with me," Gertrude had said to Vi as the little girls were having their hats put on; Vi answered indignantly, "She's clean and tidy; and she isn't vulgar or rude, and I do believe she's good. And mamma says dress and riches don't make the person."

And that seemed to be the feeling of all. Elsie, too, had purposely dressed herself and her children as plainly as possible so that Sally, though painfully conscious of the deficiencies in her attire, soon forgot all about them and gave herself up to the thorough enjoyment of the pleasures provided for her.

She felt that it would be very ungrateful did she not share the hearty rejoicing of the children over "her pretty things" as they eagerly selected and paid for them with their own pocket money. They seemed fully to realize the truth of the Master's declaration, "It is more blessed to give than to receive."

Vi would have had the making of the new dresses begun at once, wanting Sally to return with them to the Crags, and let Dinah fit her immediately, but was overruled by her mamma.

"No, dear, Sally must go home to her sick mother now; and Dinah shall go to them after dinner."

"But, mamma, I want to begin my part. You know you

said I could hem nicely, and might do some on the ruffles or something."

"Yes, daughter, and so you shall; but you must rest awhile first."

Violet had often to be held back in starting upon some new enterprise, and afterward encouraged or compelled to persevere. Elsie was more deliberate at first, more steadfast in carrying out what she had once undertaken. Each had what the other lacked. Both were winsome and lovable, and they were extremely fond of one another — scarcely less so of their brothers and the darling baby sister.

"When may I begin, mamma?" asked Vi somewhat impatiently.

"After breakfast tomorrow morning you may spend an hour with your needle."

"Only an hour, mamma? It would take all summer at that rate."

"Ah, what a doleful countenance, daughter mine!" Elsie said laughingly, as she bent down and kissed the rosy cheek. "You must remember that my two little girls are not to carry the heavy end of this, and the sewing will be done in good season without overworking them. I could not permit that. I must see to it that they have plenty of time for rest and for healthful play. I appoint you one hour a day, and shall allow you to spend one more, if you wish, but that must be all."

Violet had been trained to cheerful acquiescence in the decisions of her parents, and now put it into practice; yet, she wished very much that mamma would let her work all day for Sally, till the outfit was ready. She was sure she would not tire of it; but she soon learned anew the lessons she had learned a hundred times before — that mamma knew best.

The first day she would have been willing to sew a little longer after the second hour's task was done; the next, two hours were fully sufficient to satisfy her appetite for work. On the third, it was weariness before the end of the first hour; on the fourth, she would have been glad to beg off entirely. Her mother said firmly, "No, dear, one hour's work is not too much for you, and you know I allowed you to undertake it only on the condition that you would persevere to the end."

"Yes, mamma, but I am very tired, and I think I'll never undertake anything again," and with a sigh the little girl seated herself and began her task.

Mamma smiled sympathetically, softly smoothed the golden curls, and said in her gentle voice, " 'Let's not be weary in well-doing'! Do you remember the rest?"

"Yes, mamma, 'for in due season we shall reap, if we faint not.' And you told us to faint was to get tired and stop. But mamma, what shall I reap by keeping on with this?"

"A much needed lesson in perseverance, for one thing, I hope; and for another, the promise given in the forty-first Psalm, 'Blessed is he that considereth the poor; the Lord will deliver him in time of trouble. The Lord will preserve him, and keep him alive; and he shall be blessed upon the earth; and thou wilt not deliver him unto the will of his enemies. The Lord will strengthen him upon the bed of languishing: thou wilt make all his bed in his sickness.' "

"How would you like to hear a story while you sit sewing by my side?"

"Oh, ever so much, mamma! A story! A story!" And all the little flock clustered about mamma's chair, for they dearly loved her stories.

This was an old favorite, but the narrator added some new characters and new scenes, spinning it out, yet keeping up the interest, till it and the hour came to an end very nearly together.

Then the children, finding that was to be all for the present, scattered to their play.

Mrs. Ross had come in a few minutes before, and signing to her friend to proceed, had joined the group of listeners.

"Dear me, Elsie, how can you take so much trouble with your children?" she said. "You seem to be always training and teaching them in the sweetest, gentlest ways; and, of course, they're good and obedient. I'm sure I love mine dearly, but I could never have the patience to do all you do."

"My dear friend, how can I do less, when so much of their future welfare, for time and for eternity, depends upon my faithfulness?"

"Yes," said Lucy softly, "but the mystery to me is, how you can keep that in mind all the time, and how you can contrive always to do the right thing?"

"I wish I did, but it is not so; I make many mistakes."

"I don't see it. You do wonderfully well anyhow, and I want to know how you manage it."

"I devote most of my time and thoughts to it. I try to study the character of each child. And above all, I pray a great deal for wisdom and for God's blessing on my efforts — not always on my knees — for it is a blessed truth, that we may lift our hearts to Him at any time and in any place. Oh, Lucy," she exclaimed with tearful earnestness, "if I can but train my children for God and heaven, what a happy woman I shall be! The longing desire of my heart for them is that expressed in the stanza of Watts' Cradle Hymn:

'Mayst thou live to know and fear him,
Trust and love him all thy days,
Then go dwell forever near him,
See his face and sing his praise!'

Chapter Eleventh

Beware the bowl! Though rich and bright,
Its rubies flash upon the sight,
An adder coils its depths beneath,
Whose lure is woe, whose sting is death.

— Street

Mrs. Ross had found a nurse for Mrs. Gibson and a seamstress to help with the sewing. A good many of the garments were ordered from New York ready made, and in a few days the invalid was comfortably established in the seaside cottage recommended by Dr. Morton.

In another week, Sally found herself in possession of a wardrobe that more than satisfied her modest desires. She called at the Crags in her new travelling dress to say goodbye, looking very neat and ladylike — happy, too, in spite of anxiety in regard to her sight.

Not used to the world, timid and retiring, she had felt a good deal of nervous apprehension about making the journey alone. But business called Mr. Ross to Philadelphia and he offered to take charge of her and see her safe in the quiet boarding place already secured by Mrs. Edward Allison, to whom Elsie had written on her behalf.

Adelaide had never felt either love or respect for the ill-tempered governess of her younger brothers and sisters, but readily undertook to do a kindness for her child.

"Have you the doctor's address?" Mr. Ross asked, when taking leave of the girl in her new quarters.

"Yes, sir; Mrs. Travilla gave it to me on a card, and I have it safe. I have a letter of introduction, too, from Dr. Morton. He says he is not personally acquainted with Dr.

Thomson, but knows him well by reputation; and if anybody can help me, he can."

"That is encouraging, and I hope you will have no difficulty in finding the place. It is on the next street and only a few blocks from here."

Sally thought she could find it readily. Mrs. Travilla had given her very careful directions about the streets and numbers in Philadelphia; besides, she could inquire if she were at a loss.

When Mr. Ross returned home, he brought someone with him at the sight of whom the Ion children uttered a joyous cry; and who, stepping from the carriage, caught their mamma in his arms and held her to his heart, as if he meant never to let her go.

"Papa! Papa!" cried the children. "We did not know you were coming; mamma did not tell us. Mamma, did you know?"

Yes, mamma had known; they saw it in her smiling eyes. And now they knew why it was that she had watched and listened so eagerly for the coming of the carriage — even more so than Aunt Lucy, who was expecting Uncle Philip, and who was very fond of him, too. But then, he had left her only the other day, and mamma and papa had been parted for weeks.

Mr. Travilla had rented a furnished cottage at Cape May and had come to take them all there. The doctors thought that that would be best for Lily now.

The young folks were greatly pleased, and ready to start at once. They had enjoyed their visit to the Crags, but had missed papa sadly; and now they would have him with them all the time — grandpa and the whole family from the Oaks, too, for they were occupying an adjoining cottage. And the delicious salt sea breeze, oh, how pleasant it would be!

Mrs. Ross was sorry to part with her guests. She had hoped to keep her friend with her all summer; but she was a good deal comforted in her disappointment be the knowledge that her mother, Sophie and her children would soon take their places.

As for young Philip he was greatly vexed and upset. "It is really too bad!" he said, seeking little Elsie out, and taking a seat by her side.

She was on the porch at some little distance from the others, and busied in turning over the pages of a new book her papa had brought her.

"What is too bad, Phil?" she asked, closing it, and giving her full attention to him.

"That you must be hurried away so soon. I've hardly been home two weeks, and we hadn't seen each other for two years."

"Well, a fortnight is a good while. And you will soon have your cousins here — Herbert and Meta —."

"Herbert!" he interrupted impatiently, "who cares for him? And Meta — prying, meddling, telltale Meta is worse than nobody. But there! Don't look so shocked, as if I had said an awfully wicked thing. I really don't hate her at all, though she got me in trouble more than once with grandma and Aunt Sophie that winter we spent at Ashlands. Ah, a bright thought strikes me!"

"Indeed! May I have the benefit of it?" asked the little girl, smiling archly.

"That you may. It is that you might as well stay on another week, or as long as you will."

"Thank you, but you must remember the doctor says we should go at once, on baby's account."

"I know that, but I was speaking only of you personally. Baby doesn't need you, and papa could take you to your father and mother after a while."

"Let them all go and leave me behind? Oh, Phil, I couldn't think of such a thing!"

The Travillas had been occupying their seaside cottage for two weeks when a letter came from Sally Gibson. This was the first she had written them, though she had been notified at once of their change of address. She'd been told that they would be glad to hear how she was and what Dr. Thomson thought of her case, and a cordial invitation to come to them to rest and recuperate as soon as she was ready to leave her physician.

Elsie's face grew very bright as she read.

"What does she say?" asked her husband.

"There is first an apology for not answering sooner (her eyes were so full of belladonna that she could not see to put pen to paper, and she had no one to write for her). Then, a burst of joy and gratitude — to God, to the doctor and to me — 'success beyond anything she had dared to hope' but she will be with us tomorrow and tell us all about it."

"And she won't be blind, mamma?" queried Violet, joyously.

"No, dear; I think that she must mean that her eyes are cured, or her sight made good in some way."

"Oh, then, I'll just love that good doctor!" cried the child, clasping her hands in delight.

The next day brought Sally, but they scarcely recognized her, she had grown so plump and rosy; and there was a light in the eyes that looked curiously at them through glasses clear as crystal.

Mrs. Travilla took her by both hands and kissed her.

"Welcome, Sally, I am glad to see you, but should scarcely have known you had we met in a crowd. You are looking so well and happy."

"And so I am, my dear kind friend," the girl answered with emotion. "I can see! I can see to read fine print that is all a blur to me without these glasses. And all the pain is gone — the fear, the distress of body and mind. Oh, the Lord has been good to me! And the doctor is so kind and interested! I shall be grateful to him and to you as long as I live!"

"Oh, did he make you those glasses? What did he do to you?" asked the eager, curious children. "Tell us all about it, please."

But mamma said, "No, she is too tired now. She must go to her room and lie down and rest till tea-time."

Little Elsie showed her the way, saw that nothing was wanting that could contribute to her comfort, then left her to her repose.

It was needed after all the excitement and the hot dusty

ride in the cars; but she came down from it quite fresh, and as ready to pour out the whole story of the experiences of the last two weeks as the children could desire.

When tea was over, they clustered round her on the cool breezy veranda overlooking the restless murmuring sea, and by her invitation, questioned her to their heart's content.

"Is he a nice kind old man, like our doctor at Ion?" began little Harold.

"Quite as nice and kind I should think, but not very old."

"Did he hurt you very much?" asked Elsie, who had great sympathy for suffering, whether mental or physical.

"Oh, no, not at all! He said directly that the eyes were not diseased; the trouble was malformation and could be remedied by suitable glasses. And oh, how glad I was to hear it!"

"I thought mamma read from you letter that he put medicine in your eyes."

"Yes, belladonna, but that was only to make them sick so that he could examine them thoroughly and measure them for glasses."

Turning to Mrs. Travilla, she said, "He is very kind and pleasant to everyone so far as I could see. He makes no difference between rich and poor, but is deeply interested in each case in turn — always giving his undivided attention to the one he has in hand at the moment, putting his whole heart and mind into the work."

"Which is doubtless one great reason why he is so successful," remarked Mrs. Travilla, adding "Remember that, my children. Half-hearted work accomplishes little for this world or the next."

"Weren't you afraid the first time you went?" asked timid little Elsie.

"My heart beat pretty fast," said Sally smiling. "I am rather bashful you see, and worse than that, I was afraid the doctor would say like others, that it was the nerve and I would go blind, or that some dreadful operation would be necessary. But, after I had seen him and found out how kind and pleasant he was, and that I'd nothing painful or dangerous to go through, and might hope for good sight at last, I didn't mind going at all."

"It was a little tedious sitting there in the outer office among strangers with no one to speak to, and with nothing to do for hours at a time, but that was nothing compared to what I was to gain by it."

Then the children wanted to know what the doctor measured eyes with, and how he did it. Sally amused them very much by telling how she had to say her letters every day and look at the gaslight and tell what shape it was, and on and on.

"The doctor told me," she said, addressing Mrs. Travilla, "that I would not like the glasses at first, hardly anyone does; but I do, though not so well, I dare say, as I shall after a while when I get used to them."

Mrs. Gibson's health was improving so that she was in a fair way to recover and as she was well taken care of and did not need her daughter, Sally felt at liberty to stay with these kind friends and enjoy herself.

She resolved to put away care and anxiety for the future, and take full benefit of her present advantages. Yet there was one trouble that would intrude itself and rob her of half her enjoyment. Tom, her only and dearly beloved brother, was traveling the downward road, seeming wholly given up to the dominion of the love of strong drink and kindred vices.

It was long since she had seen or heard from him and she knew not where he was. He had been in the habit of leaving their poor home on the Hudson without deigning to give her or his mother any information as to whither he was bound or when he would return. Sometimes he came back in a few hours, and then again, sometimes he stayed away for days, weeks, or months.

One day Elsie saw Sally turn suddenly pale while glancing over the morning paper. There was keen distress in the eyes she lifted to hers as the paper fell from her nerveless hand.

"Poor child! What is it?" Elsie asked compassionately,

going to her and taking the cold hand in hers. "Is there anything that I can relieve or help you to bear?"

"Tom!" and Sally burst into hysterical weeping.

He had been arrested in Philadelphia for drunkenness and disorderly conduct, fined and sent to prison till the amount should be paid.

Elsie did her best to comfort the poor sister who was in an agony of shame and grief. "Oh," she sobbed, "he is such a dear fellow if only he could let drink alone! But it's been his ruin, his ruin! He must be so disgraced that all his self-respect is gone and he'll never hold up his head again or have the heart to try to do better."

"Don't despair, poor child!" said Elsie, "He has not fallen too far for the grace of God to reclaim him. 'Behold the Lord's hand is not shortened, that it cannot save; neither his ear heavy, that it cannot hear.' "

"And oh, I cry day and night to Him for my poor Tom, so weak, so beset with temptations!" exclaimed the girl. "And will He not hear me at last?"

"He will if you ask in faith, pleading the merits of His Son," returned her friend in moved tones.

"He must be saved!" Mr. Travilla said with energy, when Elsie repeated to him this conversation with Sally. "I shall take the next train for Philadelphia and try to find him."

Tom was found, his fine paid, his release procured, his rags exchanged for neat gentlemanly attire, and hope of better things for this world and the next set before him. With self-respect and manhood partially restored by all this and the kindly considerate, brotherly manner of his benefactor, he was persuaded to go with the latter to share with Sally for a few weeks, the hospitality of that pleasant seaside home.

He seemed scarcely able to lift his eyes from the ground as Mr. Travilla led him onto the veranda where the whole family was gathered eagerly awaiting his coming. But in a moment Sally's arms were around his neck, her kisses and tears warm on his cheek, as she sobbed out in excess joy, "Oh, Tom, dear Tom, I'm so glad to see you!"

Then Mrs. Travilla's soft white hand grasped his in cordial greeting, and her low sweet voice bade him welcome. The children echoed her words, apparently with no other thought of him than that he was Sally's brother and it was perfectly natural he should be there with her.

So he was soon at ease among them; but felt very humble, kept close by Sally and used his eyes and cars far more than his tongue.

His kind entertainers exerted themselves to keep him out of the way of temptation and help him to conquer the thirst for intoxicating drink, Mrs. Travilla giving Sally carte blanche to go into the kitchen and prepare him a cup of strong coffee whenever she would.

"Sally," he said to his sister one evening when they sat alone together on the veranda, "what a place this is to be in! It's like a little heaven below. There is so much peace and love; the moral atmosphere is so sweet and pure. I feel as though I had no business here, such a fallen wretch as I am!" he concluded with a groan, hiding his face in his hands.

"Don't, Tom, dear Tom!" she whispered, putting her arm about his neck and laying her head on his shoulder. "You've given up that dreadful habit. You're never going back to it?"

"I don't want to! God knows I don't!" he cried as in an agony of fear, "but that awful thirst — you don't know what it is! And I'm weak as water. Oh, if there was none of the accursed thing on the face of the earth, I might hope for salvation! Sally, I'm afraid of myself, of the demon that is in me!"

"Oh, Tom, fly to Jesus!" she said, clinging to him. "He says, 'In me is thine help.' 'Fear not; I will help thee,' and He never yet turned a deaf ear to any poor sinner that cried to him for help. Cast thyself wholly on Him and He will give you strength. For 'everyone that asketh, receiveth; and he that seeketh, findeth; and to him that knocketh, it shall be opened.' "

There was a moment of silence, in which Sally's heart was going up in earnest prayer for him. Then, Mr. Travilla joined them and addressing Tom said, "My wife and I have been talking about your future, indeed, Sally's also. We suppose you would like to keep together."

"That we should," they said.

"Well, how would you like to emigrate to Kansas and begin life anew, away from all the old associates? I need not add that if you decide to go, the means shall not be wanting."

"Thank you, sir. You have been the best friends to us both, and to our mother, you and Mrs. Travilla," said Tom, with emotion. "This is just what Sally and I have been wishing we could do. I understand something of farming and should like to take up a claim out there in some good location where land is given to those who will settle on it. And if you, sir, can conveniently advance the few hundred dollars we shall need to carry us there and give us a fair start, I shall gladly and thankfully accept it as a loan, hoping to be able to return it in a year or two."

This was the arrangement made and preparations to carry it out were immediately set on foot. In a few days the brother and sister bade goodbye to their kind entertainers. Their mother, now nearly recovered, joined them in Philadelphia, and the three together turned their faces westward.

In biding adieu to Elsie, Sally whispered with tears of joy the good news that Tom was trusting in a strength mightier than his own. And so, as years rolled on, these friends were not surprised to hear of his steadfast adherence to the practice of total abstinence from all intoxicating drinks, and his growing prosperity.

Chapter Twelfth

You may as well
Forbid the sea to obey the moon,
As, or by oath, remove, or counsel, shake
The fabric of her folly.

— Shakespeare

Scarcely had the Gibsons departed when their places were more than filled by the unexpected arrival of a large party from Roselands comprising of Mr. Dinsmore, with his daughter Mrs. Conley and her entire family, with the exception of Calhoun, who would follow shortly.

They were welcomed by their relatives with true southern hospitality and assured that the two cottages could readily be made to accommodate them all comfortably.

"What news of Molly?" was the first question after the greetings had been exchanged.

Mrs. Conly shook her head and sighed, "She hasn't been able to set her foot on the floor for weeks, and I don't believe she ever will. That's Dr. Pancoast's opinion, and he's good authority. 'Twas her condition that brought us north. We've left her and her mother at the Continental in Philadelphia."

"There's to be a consultation tomorrow of all the best surgeons in the city. Enna wanted me to stay with her till that was over, but I couldn't think of it with all these children fretting and worrying to get down here out of the heat. So I told her I'd leave Cal to take care of her and Molly."

"Dick's with them, too. He's old enough to be useful now, and Molly clings to him far more than to her mother."

"Isn't it dreadful," said Virginia, "to think that that fall down the stairs has made her a cripple for life, though nobody thought she was much hurt at first?"

"Poor child! How does she bear it?" asked her uncle.

"She doesn't know how to bear it at all," said Mrs. Conly. "She nearly cries her eyes out."

"No wonder," remarked the grandfather, "it's a terrible prospect she has before her, to say nothing of the present suffering. And her mother has no patience with her, pities herself instead of the child."

"No," said Mrs. Conly, "Enna was never known to have patience with anybody or anything."

"But Dick's good to her," remarked Isadore.

"Yes," said Arthur, "it's really beautiful to see his devotion to her and how she clings to him. And it's doing the lad good — making a man of him."

"Surely Enna must feel for her child!" Elsie said, thinking of her own darlings and how her heart would be torn with anguish at the sight of one of them in so distressing a condition.

"Yes, of course, she cried bitterly over her when first the truth dawned upon her that Molly was so dreadfully injured. But, of course, that couldn't last and she soon took to bewailing her own hard fate in having such a burden on her hands — a daughter who must always live single and could never be anything but a helpless invalid."

Elsie understood how it was, for had she not known Enna from a child? Her heart ached for Molly, and as she told her own little ones of their poor cousin's hopeless, helpless state, she mingled her tears with theirs.

"Mamma, won't you 'vite her to come here?" pleaded Harold.

"Yes, dear mamma, do," urged the others, "and let us all try to amuse and comfort her."

"If I do, my dears, you may be called upon at times to give up your pleasures for her. Do you think you will be willing to do so?"

At that the young faces grew very grave, and for a moment no one spoke. Quick, impulsive Violet was the first to answer.

"Yes, mamma, I'm willing. I do feel so sorry for her I'd do anything to help her bear her pain."

"Mamma," said Elsie, softly, "I'll ask Jesus to help me, and I'm sure He will."

"So am I, daughter; and I think Vi means to ask His help too?"

"Oh, yes, mamma, I do!"

"And I," "And I," And I," responded the others.

So the invitation was sent for Molly and her mother and brother to come and pay as long a visit as they would.

A letter came in a few days, accepting it and giving the sorrowful news that all the surgeons agreed in opinion that the poor girl's spine had been so injured that she would never again have any use of her lower limbs.

It was Mrs. Conly who brought the letter to her niece, it having come in one addressed to her. She expressed strong sympathy for Molly, but was much taken up with the contents of another letter received by the same mail.

"I've just had a most generous offer from Mr. Conly's sister, Mrs. Delaford," she said to her niece. "She has no children of her own, is a widow and very wealthy. She's very fond of my Isadore, who is her godchild and namesake. She offers now to clothe and educate her, with the view of making the child her heir, and also to pay for Virgy's tuition, if I will send them both to the convent where she herself was educated."

"Aunt Louise, you will not think of it, surely?" cried Elsie, looking much disturbed.

"And why not, pray?" asked Mrs. Conly, drawing herself up, and speaking in a tone of mingled hauteur, pique and annoyance.

"You would not wish them to become Roman Catholics?"

"No, of course not; but that need not follow."

"It is very apt to follow."

"Nonsense! I should exact a promise that their faith would not be interfered with."

"But would that avail, since 'no faith with heretics,' has been for centuries the motto of the 'infallible, unchangeable,' Church of Rome?"

"I think you are inclined to see danger where there is none," returned the aunt. "I would not for the world be as anxious and fussy about my children as you are about yours. Besides, I think it quite right to let their father's relatives do for them when they are both able and willing."

"But Aunt Louise — ."

"There! Don't let us talk any more about the matter today, if you please," interrupted Mrs. Conly, rising. "I must go now and prepare for my bath. I'll be in again this evening to see Enna and the others. They'll be down by the afternoon train. Good morning."

And she sailed away, leaving Elsie sad and anxious for the future of her young cousins.

"What is it, daughter?" Mr. Dinsmore asked, coming in a moment later. "I have seldom seen you look so disturbed."

Her face brightened, as was its wont under her father's greeting, but this time only momentarily.

"I am troubled, papa," she said, making room for him on the sofa by her side. "Here is the note from Enna. The doctors give Molly no hope that she will ever walk again. One cannot help feeling very sad for her, poor child! And besides, something Aunt Louise has been telling me makes me anxious for Isadore and Virginia."

He was scarcely less concerned than she, when he heard what that was. "I shall talk to Louise," he said. "It would be the height of folly to expose her girls to such influences. It is true I once had some thoughts of sending you to a convent school, under the false impression that the accomplishments were more thoroughly taught there than in the Protestant seminaries. But with the light I have since gained upon the subject, I know that it would have been a fearful mistake."

"Dear papa," she said, putting her hand into his and looking at him with loving eyes, "I am so thankful to you that you did not — so thankful that you taught me yourself. The remembrance of the hours we spent together as teacher and pupil has always been very sweet to me."

"To me, also," he answered with a smile.

The expected quests arrived at the appointed time, Enna looking worn, faded and fretful; Dick, sad and anxious; and poor Molly, weary, exhausted and despairing — as if life had lost all brightness to her.

Her proud spirit rebelled against her helplessness, against the curious, even against the pitying looks it attracted to her from strangers in the streets and public conveyances.

The transit from one vehicle to another was made in the strong arms of a stalwart Negro whom they had brought with them from Roselands. Dick followed closely to guard his sister from accident and shield her as much as possible from observation, while Enna and Cal brought up the rear.

A room on the ground floor had been appropriated to Molly's use, and thither she was carried at once and gently laid upon a couch. Instantly her cousin Elsie's arms were about her, her head pillowed upon the gentle breast, while tears of loving sympathy fell fast upon her poor pale face, mingled with tender caresses and whispered words of endearment.

It did the child good. The tears and sobs that came in response relieved her aching heart of half its load. But it vexed Enna.

"What folly, Elsie!" she said. "Don't you see how you're making the child cry? And I've been doing my best to get her to stop it; for, of course, it does no good, and only injures her eyes."

"Forgive me, dear child, if I have hurt you," Elsie said low and tenderly, as she laid Molly's head gently back against the pillows."

"You haven't! You've done me good!" cried the girl,

flashing an indignant glance at Enna. "Oh, mother, if you treated me so, it wouldn't be half so hard to bear!"

"I've learned not to expect anything but ingratitude from my children," said Enna, coldly returning Elsie's kind greeting.

But Dick grasped his cousin's hand warmly, giving her a look of grateful affection, and accepted with delight her offered kiss.

"Now, I will leave you to rest," she said to Molly, "and when you feel like seeing your cousins, they will be glad to come in and speak to you. They are anxious to do all they can for your entertainment while you are here."

"Yes, but I want to see grandpa and Uncle Horace now, please; they just kissed me in the car, and that was all."

They came in at once, full of tender sympathy for the crippled, suffering girl.

"They're so kind," sobbed Molly, as they left the room.

"Yes, you can appreciate everybody's kindness but your mother's," remarked Enna in a piqued tone. "And everybody can be sorry for you, but my feelings are lost sight of entirely."

"Oh, mother, don't!" sighed Molly. "I'm sure I've enough to bear without your reproaches. I'd appreciate you fast enough if you were such a mother as Cousin Elsie."

"Or as Aunt Louise, why don't you say?" said Mrs. Conly, coming in, going up to the couch, and kissing her. "How d'ye do, Enna?"

"Yes, even you are sorrier for me than mother is, I do believe!" returned Molly, bursting into tears. "And if it was Isa or Virgy you'd be ever so good to her, and not scold her as mother does me."

"Why, I'm just worn out and worried half to death about that girl," said Enna in answer to her sister's query. "She'll never walk a step again — all the doctors say that." At these words Molly was almost convulsed with sobs, but Enna went on relentlessly. "And when they asked her how it happened, she up and told them her high-heeled shoe threw her down, and that she didn't want to wear them, but I made her do it."

"And so you did, and I only told it because one of the doctors asked if I didn't know they were dangerous. When I said yes, he wanted to know how I came to be so foolish as to wear them."

"And then he lectured me," Enna went on, "as if it was my fault, when of course it was her own carelessness. For if it wasn't, why haven't some of the rest of us fallen down? Accidents happen when nobody's to blame."

"I came near falling the other day, myself," said Mrs. Conly, "and I'll never wear a high, narrow heel again, nor let one of my girls do so. Now I'm going out. You two ought to take a nap — Molly especially, poor child! I'm very sorry for you, but don't cry any more now. It will only hurt your eyes."

Mrs. Conly was to stay to tea and spend the evening. Stepping into the parlor, she found all the adult members of the family there.

"I want to have a talk with you, Louise," her brother said, seating her comfortably on a sofa and drawing up a chair beside her.

"And I think I know what about," she returned with heightened color, glancing toward Elsie, "but let me tell you beforehand, Horace, that you may as well spare yourself the trouble. I have already accepted Mrs. Delaford's offer."

"Louise! How could you be so hasty in so important a matter?"

"Permit me to answer that question with another," she retorted, drawing herself up haughtily. "What right have you to call me to account for so doing?"

"Only the right of an older brother to take a fraternal interest in your welfare and that of his nieces."

"What is it, mother?" asked Calhoun.

She told him in a few words, and he turned to his uncle with the query why he so seriously objected to her acceptance of what seemed so favorable an offer.

"Because I think it would be putting in great jeopardy the welfare of your sisters, temporal and spiritual."

"What nonsense, Horace!" exclaimed Mrs. Conly

angrily. "Of course I shall expressly stipulate that their faith is not to be interfered with."

"And just as much, of course, the promise will be given and systematically broken without the slightest compunction; because, in the creed of Rome, the end justifies the means and no end is esteemed higher than that of adding members to her communion."

"Well," said Louise, "I must say you judge them hardly. I'm sure there are at least some pious ones among them and, of course, they wouldn't lie."

"You forget that the more pious they are, the more obedient they will be to the teachings of their church. And when she tells them it is a pious act to be false to their word or oath, for her advancement, or to burn, kill and destroy, or break any other commandment of the decalogue, they will obey — believing that thus they do God service."

"Really, the folly of Protestant parents who commit their children to the care of those who teach and put in practice, too, these two maxims, so utterly destructive of all truth and honesty, all confidence between man and man — 'the end sanctifies the means,' and 'no faith with heretics,' — is to me perfectly astounding."

"So you consider me a fool," said Mrs. Conly, bridling. "Thanks for the compliment."

"It is you who make the application, Louise," he answered. "I had no thought of doing so, and still hope you will prove your wisdom by reconsidering and letting Mrs. Delaford know that you revoke your decision."

"Indeed, I shall not; I consider that I have no right to throw away Isadore's fortune."

"Have you then a greater right to imperil her soul's salvation?" he asked with solemn earnestness.

"Pshaw! What a serious thing you make of it," she exclaimed, yet with an uneasy and troubled look.

"Uncle!" cried Calhoun in surprise, "do you not think there have been and are some real Christians in the Roman Catholic Church?"

"No doubt of it, Cal; some who, in spite of her idolatrous teachings, worship God alone and put their trust solely in the atoning blood and imputed righteousness of Christ. Yet who can fail to see in the picture of Babylon the Great so graphically drawn in Revelation, a faithful picture of Rome? And the command is, 'Come out of her, my people, that ye be not partakers of her sins, and that ye receive not of her plagues.' "

Mr. Dinsmore paused, but no one seeming to have anything to say in reply, went on to give his sister a number of instances which had come to his knowledge, of the perversion of Protestant girls while being educated in convents.

"Well," she said at last, "I'm not going to draw back now, but I shall be on the watch and if they do begin to tamper with my girls' faith, I'll remove them at once. There now, I hope you are satisfied!"

"Not quite, Louise," he said. "They are accomplished proselytizers and may have the foundations completely and incurably undermined ere you suspect that they have begun."

Chapter Thirteenth

Affliction is the wholesome soil of virtue;
When patience, honor, sweet humility,
Calm fortitude, take root, and strongly flourish.

— Mallet and Thomson's Alfred

A bath, a nap, and a dainty supper had refreshed Molly somewhat before the children were admitted to her room; but they found her looking pale and thin, and oh, so sorrowful, so different from the bright, merry, happy "Cousin Molly" of six months ago.

Their little hearts swelled with sympathetic grief, and tears filled their eyes as one after another they took her hand and kissed her lovingly.

"Poor child, I so solly for oo!" said Herbert, and Molly laughed hysterically, then put her hands over her face and sobbed as though her heart would break. First, it was the oddity of being called "child" by such a mere baby; then, it was the thought that she had become an object of pity to such a one.

"Don' ky," he said, pulling away her hand to kiss her cheek. "Herbie didn't mean to make oo ky."

"Come, Herbie dear, let us go now; we mustn't tease poor sick cousin," whispered his sister Elsie, drawing him gently away.

"No, no! Let him stay. Let him love me," sobbed Molly. "He is a dear little fellow," she added, returning his caresses, and wiping away her tears.

"Herbie will love oo, poor old sing," he said, stroking her face, "and mamma and papa, and all de folks will be ever so dood to oo."

Molly's laugh was more natural this time, and under

its enlivening influence, the little ones grew quite merry, really amusing her with their prattle, till their mammy came to take them to bed.

Elsie was beginning to say goodnight too, thinking there was danger of wearying the invalid, but Molly said, "I don't wonder you want to leave me — mother says nobody could like to stay with such a —," she broke off suddenly. Again she hid her face in her hands and wept bitterly.

"Oh, no, no! I was only afraid of tiring you," Elsie said, leaning over her and stroking her hair with a soft, gentle touch. "I should like to stay and talk if you wish, to tell you all about our visit to the Crags, and mamma's old governess, and —."

"Oh, yes, do! Anything to help me forget, even for a few minutes. Oh, I wish I was dead! I wish I was dead! I can't bear to live and be a cripple!"

"Dear Molly, don't cry. Don't feel so dreadfully about it!" Elsie said, weeping with her. "Jesus will help you bear it. He loves you and is sorrier for you than anybody else is. He won't let you be sick or in pain in heaven."

"No, He doesn't love me! I'm not good enough. And if He did, He wouldn't have let me get such a dreadful fall."

Little Elsie was perplexed for the moment, and knew not what to answer.

"Couldn't He have kept me from falling?" demanded Molly, almost fiercely.

"Yes, He can do everything."

"Then, I hate Him for letting me fall!"

Elsie was inexpressibly shocked. "Oh, Molly!" in an awed, frightened tone, was all that she could say.

"I'm awfully wicked, I know I am; but I can't help it. Why did He let me fall? I couldn't bear to let a dog be so dreadfully hurt, if I could help it!"

"Molly, the Bible says 'God is love.' And in another place, 'God so loved the world, that He gave His only begotten Son, that whosoever believeth in Him should not perish, but have everlasting life.' 'God commendeth his love toward us, in that while we were yet sinners,

Christ died for us.' He must have loved you, Molly, when He died that dreadful death to save you."

"Not me."

"Yes, if you will believe. 'Whosoever believeth.' "

"It was just for everybody in a lump," said Molly, sighing wearily. "Not for you or me, or anybody in particular — at least not for anybody that's living now. Because we weren't made then, so how could He?"

"But mamma says He knew He was going to make us, just the same as He does now. And that He thought of each one and loved and died for each one just as much as if there was only one."

"Well, it's queer if He loved me so well as that, and yet would let me fall and be so awfully injured. What's this? You didn't have it before you came north," taking hold of the gold chain about Elsie's neck.

Out came the little watch and Elsie told about the aching tooth and the trip to New York to have it extracted.

"Seems to me," was Molly's comment, "you have all the good things — such as a nice mother and everything else. Such a good father, too; and mine was killed when I was a little bit of a thing, and mother's so cross."

"But Dick's good to me, dear old Dick," she added, looking up at him with glistening eyes as he came in and going up to her couch, asked how she was.

"You'd better go to sleep now," he said. "You've been talking quite a while, haven't you?"

At that Elsie slipped quietly away and went in search of her mother.

She found her alone on the veranda looking out meditatively upon the restless moonlit waters of the sea.

"Mamma," said the child softly, "I should like a stroll on the beach with you. Can we go alone? I want to talk with you about something."

"Come, then, daughter," and hand in hand they sought the beach, only a few yards distant.

It was a clear still night, the moon nearly full, and the cool salt breeze from the silver-tipped waves was exceedingly refreshing after the heat of the day, which had been one of the hottest of the season.

For a while they paced to and fro in silence; then, little Elsie gave her mother the substance of her conversation with Molly in which the latter expressed her disbelief in God's love for her because He had not prevented her fall. "Mamma," she said in conclusion, "how I wished you were there to make her understand."

"Poor child!" said the mother, in low, moved tones, "only He who permitted this sore trial can convince her that it was sent in love."

"But you will talk to her, mamma?"

"Yes, when a suitable opportunity offers; but prayer can do more for her than any words of ours addressed to her."

The presence of Molly and her mother proved a serious drawback to the enjoyment of the party during the remainder of their sojourn at the seashore. The burden fell heaviest upon Elsie and her children,as the principal entertainers. And the mother had often to counsel patience and forbearance, and to remind her darlings of their promise to be ready to do all they could for the comfort and happiness of the sufferer.

All made praiseworthy efforts to fulfill their engagement. And Elsie and Vi, particularly the former, as nearest to Molly in age, and therefore most desired by her as a companion, gave up many a pleasure excursion for her sake, staying at home to talk with and amuse her when all the rest were out driving or boating.

Chapter Fourteenth

Ah! Who can say, however fair his view,
Through what sad scenes his path may lie?

Mrs. Conly adhered to her resolve in regard to the education of her daughters. And about the middle of September left with them and her younger children for a visit to Mrs. Delaford, at whose house the wardrobes of the two girls were to be made ready for their first school year at the convent chosen by their aunt.

Arthur went with them as their escort. A week later the rest of the Roselands party returned home and early in October the Oaks and Ion rejoiced in the return of their families.

Baby Lily had been so benefited by the trip that Elsie felt warranted in resuming her loved employment as acting governess to her older children.

They fell into the old round of duties and pleasures, as loving and happy a family as one might wish to see. This was a striking and most pleasant contrast to the one at Roselands — that of Enna and her offspring, where the mother fretted and scolded, and the children, following her example, were continually at war with one another.

Only between Dick and Molly there was peace and love. The poor girl led a weary life pinned to her couch or chair, wholly dependent upon others for the means of locomotion and for anything that was not within reach of her hand.

She had not yet learned submission under her trial, and her mother was far from being any assistance in bearing it. Molly was greatly depressed in spirits, and her mother's scolding and fretting were often almost beyond endurance.

Her younger brother and sister thought it a trouble to wait on her and usually kept out of her way. But Dick, when present, was her faithful slave, always ready to lift and carry her, or to bring her anything she wanted. But much of Dick's time was necessarily occupied with his studies and in going to and from his school, which was two or three miles distant.

He was very thoughtful for her comfort and it was through his suggestion, that their grandfather directed that one of the pleasantest rooms in the house, overlooking the avenue, so that all the coming and going could be seen from its windows, should be appropriated to Molly's use.

There Dick would seat her each morning, before starting for school, in an invalid's easy chair presented to her by her Cousin Elsie, and there he would be pretty sure to find her on his return. Unless, as occasionally happened, their grandfather, Uncle Horace, Mr. Travilla, or some one of the relatives had taken her out for a drive.

One afternoon about the last of November, Molly, weary of sewing and reading, weary, inexpressibly weary, of her confinement and enforced quietude, was gazing longingly down the avenue. She was wishing that someone would come to take her out for an airing, when the door opened and her mother came in dressed for the open air, in hat, cloak and furs.

"I want you to button my glove, Molly," she said, holding out her wrist. "Rachel's so busy on my new silk, and you have nothing to do. What a fortunate child you are to be able to take your ease all the time."

"My ease!" cried Molly bitterly, "I'd be gladder than words can tell to change places with you for awhile."

"Humph! You don't know what you're wishing! The way I have to worry over my sewing for four beside myself is enough to try the patience of a saint. By the way, it's high time you began to make yourself useful in that line. With practice, you might soon learn to accomplish a great deal, having nothing to do but stick at it from morning to night."

Molly was in the act of buttoning the second glove. Tears sprang to her eyes at this evidence of her mother's heartlessness, and one bright drop fell on Enna's wrist.

"There, you have stained my glove!" she exclaimed angrily. "What a baby you are! Will you have done with this continued crying?"

"It seems very easy for you to bear my troubles, mother," returned poor Molly, raising her head proudly, and dashing away the tears. "I will try to learn to bear them too, and never again appeal to my mother for sympathy."

"You get enough of that from Dick. He cares ten times as much for you as he does for me — his own mother."

At that moment Betty came running in. "Mother, the carriage is at the door, and grandpa's ready. Molly, grandpa says he'll take you too, if you want to go.'

Molly's face brightened, but before she could speak, Enna answered for her. "No, she can't. There isn't time to get her ready."

Mrs. Johnson hurried from the room, Betty following close at her heels, and Molly was left alone in her grief and weariness.

She watched the carriage as it rolled down the avenue, then turning from the window, indulged in a hearty cry.

At length, exhausted by her emotion, she laid her head back and fell asleep in her chair.

How long she had slept she did not know. Some unusual noise downstairs woke her, and the next moment Betty rushed in screaming, "Oh, Molly, Molly, mother and grandfather's killed — both of 'em! Oh dear! Oh dear!"

For an instant Molly seemed stunned; she scarcely comprehended Betty's words. Then, as the child repeated, "They're killed! They're both killed. The horses ran away and threw 'em out," she too uttered a cry of anguish, and grasping the arms of her chair, made desperate efforts to rise. But all was in vain, and with a groan she sank back, and covering her face with her hands, shed the bitterest tears her impotence had ever yet cost her.

Betty ran away again, and she was all alone. Oh, how hard it was for her to be chained there in such an agony of doubt and distress! She forcibly restrained her groans and sobs, and listened intently.

The Conlys, except Cal, were still up North. The house seemed strangely quiet, only now and then a stealthy step or a murmur of voices and occasionally a half smothered cry from Bob or Betty.

A horseman came dashing furiously up the avenue. It was her uncle, Mr. Horace Dinsmore. He threw himself from the saddle and hurried into the house, and the next minute two more followed at the same headlong pace.

These were Cal and Dr. Barton, and they dismounted in hot haste and disappeared from her sight beneath the veranda. Certainly something very dreadful had happened. Oh, would nobody come to tell her?

The minutes dragged their slow length along, seeming like hours. She lay back in her chair in an agony of suspense, the perspiration standing in cold drops on her brow.

But the sound of wheels roused her and looking out she saw the Oaks and Ion carriages drive up, young Horace and Rosie alight from one, Mr. Travilla and Elsie from the other.

"Oh!" thought Molly, "Cousin Elsie will be sure to think of me directly and I shall not be left much longer in this horrible suspense."

Her confidence was not misplaced. Not many minutes had elapsed when her door was softly opened, a light step crossed the floor and a sweet fair face, full of tender compassion, bent over the grief-stricken girl.

Molly tried to speak; her tongue refused its office. But Elsie quickly answered the mute questioning of the wild, frightened, anguished eyes.

"There is life," she said, taking the cold hands in hers, "life in both, and 'while there is life there is hope.' Our dear old grandfather has a broken leg and arm and a few slight cuts and bruises, but is restored to consciousness now, and able to speak. Your poor mother has fared still worse, we fear, as the principal injury is to the head, but we will hope for the best in her case also."

Molly dropped her head on her cousin's shoulder while a burst of weeping brought partial relief to the overburdened heart.

Elsie clasped her arms about her and strove to soothe and comfort her with caresses and endearing words.

"If I could only nurse mother now," sobbed the girl, "how glad I'd be to do it. Oh, cousin, it most breaks my heart now to think how I've vexed and worried her since — since this dreadful trouble came to me. I'd give anything never to have said a cross or disrespectful word to her. And now I can do nothing for her! Nothing! Nothing!" and she wrung her hands in grief and despair.

"Yes, dear child, there is one thing you can do," Elsie answered, weeping with her.

"What, what is that?" asked Molly, half incredulously, half hopefully, "What can I do chained here?"

"Pray for her, Molly, plead for her with Him unto whom belong the issues from death; to Him who has power in heaven and in earth and who is able to save to the uttermost."

"No, no, even that I can't do," sobbed Molly. "I've never learned to pray, and he isn't my friend as He is yours and your children's!"

"Then first of all make Him your friend. Oh, He is so kind and merciful and loving! He says 'Come unto me, all ye that labor and are heavy laden, and I will give you rest.' 'Him that cometh to me, I will in no wise cast out.' "

"Oh, if I only knew how!" sighed Molly. "Nobody needs such a friend more than I. I'd give all the world to have Him for mine."

"But you can not buy His friendship — His salvation. It is 'without money and without price.' What is it to come to Him? Just to take Him at His word, give yourself to Him and believe His promise that He will not cast you out."

There was a tap at the door and Rosie came in, put her arms round Molly, kissed her and wept for her.

Then young Horace followed and after that his father. Both seemed to feel very much for Molly and to be anxious to do everything in their power to help and comfort her.

Mr. Dinsmore was evidently in deep grief and soon withdrew, Elsie going with him. They stood together for a few minutes in the hall.

"My dear father, how I feel for you!" Elsie said, laying her hand on his arm and looking up at him through gathering tears.

"Thank you my child; your sympathy is always sweet to me," he said. "And you have mine; for I know this trial touches you also though somewhat less nearly than myself."

"Is grandpa suffering much?" she asked.

"Very much; and at his age — . But I will not anticipate sorrow; we know that the event is in the hands of Him who doeth all things well. Ah, if he were only a Christian! And Enna! Poor Enna!"

Sobs and cries coming from the nursery broke upon the momentary silence that followed the exclamation.

"Poor little Bob and Betty. I must go to them," Elsie said, gliding away in the direction of the sounds, while Mr. Dinsmore returned to the room where his father lay groaning with the pain of his wounds. Mr. Travilla, Calhoun and the doctor were with him, but he was asking for his son.

"Horace," he said, "can't you stay with me?"

"Yes, father, night and day while you want me."

"That's right! It's a good thing to have a good son. Dr. Barton, where are you going?"

"To your daughter, sir, Mrs. Johnson."

"Enna! Is she much hurt?" asked the old man, starting up, but falling back instantly with almost a scream of pain.

"You must lie still, sir, indeed you must," said the doctor, coming back to the bed. "Your life depends upon your keeping quiet and exciting yourself as little as possible."

"Yes, yes, but Enna?"

"Has no bones broken."

"Thank God for that! Then she'll do. Go, doctor, but don't leave the house without seeing me again."

They were glad he was so quickly satisfied, but knew he would not be if his mind were quite clear.

Dick had come home in strong excitement, rumors of the accident having met him on the way. The horses had taken fright at the sudden shriek of a locomotive, and the breaking of a defective bit had deprived the old gentleman of the power to control them. They ran madly down a steep embankment, wrecking the carriage and throwing both passengers out upon a bed of stones.

Pale and trembling the lad went straight to his mother's room where he found her lying moaning on the bed, recognizing no one, unconscious of anything that was going on about her.

He discovered that he loved her far more than he would have believed. He thought she was dying, and his heart smote him as memory recalled many a passionate, undutiful word he had spoken to her. Often, it is true, under great provocation; but, oh, what would he not now have given to recall them.

He had much ado to control his emotion sufficiently to ask the doctor what he thought of her case. He was somewhat comforted by the reply.

"The injury to the head is very serious, yet by no means despair of her life."

"What can I do for her?" was the boy's next question in an imploring tone as though he would esteem it a boon to be permitted to do something for her relief.

"Nothing. We have plenty of help here, and you are too inexperienced for a nurse," Dr. Barton said, not unkindly. "But see to your sister Molly," he added. "Poor child! She will feel this sorely."

The admonition was quite superfluous. Dick was already hastening to her.

Another moment and she was weeping out her sorrow and anxiety on his shoulder.

"Oh, Dick," she sobbed, "I'm afraid I can never speak to her again, and — and my last words to her, just before she went, were a reproach. I said I'd never ask her for her sympathy again; and now I never can. Oh, isn't it dreadful, dreadful!" and she wept as if her very heart would break.

"Oh, don't, Molly!" he said hoarsely, pressing her closer to him and mingling his tears with hers. "Who could blame you, you poor suffering thing! And I'm sure you must have been provoked to it. She hadn't been saying anything kind to you?"

Molly shook her head with a fresh burst of grief. "No, oh, no! Oh, if we'd parted like Cousin Elsie and her children always do — with kind and loving words and caresses!"

"But we're not that sort, you know," returned Dick with an awkward attempt at consolation. "And I'm a great deal worse than you, a great deal, for I've talked up to mother many a time and didn't have the same excuse."

There was sickness at Pinegrove. Mrs. Howard was slowly recovering from an attack of typhoid fever. This was why she had not hastened to Roselands to the assistance of her injured father and sister.

And Mrs. Rose Dinsmore was at Ashlands, helping Sophie nurse her children through the scarlet fever. And so, Mrs. Conly being still absent up North, the burden of these new responsibilities must fall upon Mr. Horace Dinsmore and his children.

Mr. Dinsmore undertook the care of his father, Mr. Travilla and young Horace engaging to relieve him now and then. Elsie undertook that of Enna. Elsie's children, except the baby who must come to Roselands with mammy, could do without her for a time. It would be hard for both her and them, she knew, but the lesson in self-denial for the sake of others might prove more than compensation. And Enna must not, in her critical state, be left to the care of servants.

Rosie volunteered to see that Molly was not neglected, and to exert herself for the poor girl's entertainment; and Bob and Betty were sent to the Oaks to be look after by Mrs. Murray and their cousin Horace.

It would be no easy or agreeable task for the old lady, but she was sure not to object in view of the fact that quiet was essential to the recovery of the sufferers at Roselands.

Chapter Fifteenth

Great minds, like heaven, are pleased in doing good,
Though the ungrateful subjects of their favors
Are barren in return.

— Rowe

The short winter day was closing in. At Ion, five eager, expectant little faces were looking out upon the avenue where slowly and softly, tiny snowflakes were falling, the only moving thing within range of their vision.

"Oh, dear, what does keep papa and mamma so long!" cried Vi, impatiently. "It seems most like a year since they started."

"Oh, no, Vi, not half a day yet!"

"I don't mean it is, Eddie, but it does seem like it to me. Elsie, do you think anything's happened?"

"One of the horses may have lost a shoe," Elsie said, trying to be very cheerful. She put her arm round Violet as she spoke. "I remember that happened once a good while ago. But if mamma were here, don't you know what she would say, little sister?"

"Yes, 'don't fret; don't meet trouble half way, but trust in God, our Father, who loves us so dearly that He will never let any real harm come to us.' "

"I think our mamma is very wise," remarked Eddie, "so very much wiser than Aunt Lucy, who gets frightened at every little thing."

"Oh, Eddie dear, would mamma or papa like that?" said Elsie softly.

"Well, it's true," he said, reddening.

"But they've both told us that unkind remarks

should not be made even if true, unless it is quite necessary."

"Oh, why don't papa and mamma come?" "Oh, I wis dey would! I so tired watchin' for 'em!" burst out Harold and Herbert, nearly ready to cry.

"Look, look!" cried the others in chorus, "they are coming! The carriage is just turning in at the gate!"

But it was growing so dark now, and the tiny flakes were coming down so thick and fast, that none of them were quite sure the carriage was their own until it drew up before the door and two dear familiar forms alighted and came up the veranda steps.

They were greeted with as joyous a welcome as if they had been absent for weeks or months, and returned the sweet caresses as lovingly as they were bestowed, smiling tenderly upon each darling of their hearts.

But almost instantly little Elsie perceived something unusual in the sweet, fair face she loved so dearly, and was wont to study with such fond, tender scrutiny.

"Mamma, dear mamma, what is wrong?" she asked.

"A sad accident, daughter," Elsie answered, her voice faltering with emotion. "Poor grandpa and Aunt Enna have been badly hurt."

"Our dear grandpa, mamma?" they all asked, lips and voices tremulous with grief.

"No, darlings, not my own dear father," the mother answered, with a heart full of gratitude that it was not he, "but our poor old grandfather who lives at Roselands."

"My dear little wife, you are too much overcome to talk any more just now," Mr. Travilla said, wheeling an easy chair to the fire, seating her in it, and removing her hat and cloak, with all the tender gallantry of the days when he wooed and won his bride. "Let me tell it." He took a seat near her side, lifted "bit Herbie" to his knee, and with the others gathered close about him, briefly told how the accident had happened, and that he and their mother had met a messenger coming to acquaint them with the disaster, and summon them to Roselands. Then he gave the children some idea of the present situation of their injured relations.

When he had finished, and his young hearers had expressed their sorrow and sympathy for the sufferers, a moment of silence ensued, broken by little Elsie.

"Mamma, who will take care of them?"

"God," said Herbert. "Won't He, papa?"

"But I mean who will nurse them while they are sick," said Elsie.

"My father will take care of grandpa," Mrs. Travilla answered, "Uncle Horace and papa helping when needed."

"And Aunt Enna, mamma?"

"Well, daughter, who do you think should nurse her? Aunt Louise is away, Aunt Lora sick herself, grandma at Ashlands with Aunt Sophie and her sick children."

"Oh, mamma, it won't have to be you, will it?" the child asked almost imploringly.

"Oh, mamma, no! How could we do without you?" chimed in the others. Herbert added tearfully, "Mamma stay wis us; we tan't do wisout you."

They left their father to cluster about and cling to her, with caresses and entreaties.

"My darlings," she said, returning their endearments, "can you not feel willing to spare your mother for a little while to poor, suffering Aunt Enna?"

"Mamma, they have plenty of servants."

"Yes, Vi, but she is so very ill that we can not hope she will get well without more careful, tender nursing than any servant would give her."

"Mamma, it will be very hard to do without you."

"And very hard for me to stay away from my dear children; but what does the Bible say? Seek your own pleasures and profit, and let others take care of themselves?"

"Oh, mamma, no! 'Thou shalt love thy neighbor as thyself.' "

" 'Do good to them that hate you,' " quoted Eddie in an undertone.

"But we were not speaking of enemies, my son," his mother said in surprise.

"I think Aunt Enna is your enemy, mamma; I think she hates you," he said, with flashing eyes. "For I've many a time heard her say very hateful things to you. Mamma, don't look so sorry at me. How can I help being angry at people who say unkind things to you?"

" 'Forgive and you shall be forgiven," she said gently. " 'Do good and lend.' Can't you lend you mother for a few week, dears?"

"Weeks, mamma! Oh, so long!" they cried. "How can we? Who will take care of us, and hear our lessons and teach us to be good?"

"Dinah will wash and dress you, Elsie will help you little ones to learn your lessons, and I think papa," looking at him, "will hear you recite."

"Yes," he said, smiling on them, "we will do our best, so that dear mamma may not be anxious and troubled about us in addition to all the care and anxiety for the suffering ones at Roselands."

"Yes, papa," they answered, returning his smile half tearfully; then, they questioned their mother as to when she must go, and whether they should see her at all while Aunt Enna was sick.

"I can wait only long enough to take supper with you, and have our talk together afterwards," she said, "because I am needed at Roselands. Perhaps papa will bring you sometimes to see me for a little while if you will be very quiet. And it may be only for a few days that I shall be wanted there. We cannot tell about that yet."

She spoke cheerfully, but it cost her an effort because of the grieved, troubled looks on her dear little faces.

"But baby, mamma!" cried Vi, "baby can't do without you!"

"No, dear, she and mammy will have to go with me."

They were not the usual merry party at the tea table, and a good many tears were shed during the talk with mamma afterward.

They all consented to her going, but the parting with her and the thought of doing without her for "so long" were the greatest trials they had ever known.

She saw all the younger ones in bed, kissed each one good night, and reminding them that their heavenly Father was always with them, and that she would not be too far away to come at once to them if needed, she left them to their sleep.

Elsie followed her mother to her dressing room and watched for every opportunity to assist in her preparations for her absence. They were not many, and with some parting injunctions to this little daughter and the servants, she announced herself ready to go.

Elsie clung to her with tears at the last, as they stood together in the lower hall waiting for the others.

"Mamma, what shall I do without you? I've never been away from you for a whole day in all my life."

"No, dearest, but be my brave, helpful little girl. You must try to fill mother's place to the little ones. I shall not be far away, you know, and your dear father will be here nearly all the time. And don't forget, darling, that your best Friend is always with you."

"No, mamma," said the child, smiling through her tears. "It is so sweet to know that; and please don't trouble about us at home. I'll do my best for papa and the children."

"That is right, daughter. You are a very great comfort to me now and always," the mother said, with a last caress, as her husband joined her and gave her his arm to lead her to the carriage.

"Don't come out in the cold, daughter," he said, seeing the child was about to follow.

Mammy had just come down with the sleeping babe in her arms, warmly wrapped up to shield her from the cold.

Elsie sprang to her side, lifted the veil that covered the little face, and softly touched her lips to the delicate cheek. "Goodbye, baby darling. Oh, mammy, we'll miss her sadly and you, too."

"Don't fret, honey, 'spect we all be comin' back soon," Aunt Chloe whispered, readjusting the veil, and hurrying after her mistress.

Elsie flew to the window, and watched the carriage

roll away down the avenue, till lost to sight in the darkness, tears tumbling in her eyes, but a thrill of joy mingling with her grief. "It was so sweet to be a comfort and help to dear mamma."

She set herself to considering how she might be the same to her father and brothers and sister, what she could do now.

She remembered that her father was very fond of music and that mother often played and sang for him in the evenings. He had said he would probably return in an hour. Going to the piano, she spent the intervening time in the diligent practice of a new piece of music he had brought her a day or two before.

At the sound of the carriage wheels, she ran to meet him, her face bright with welcoming smiles.

"My little sunbeam," he said, taking her in his arms. "You have been nothing but a comfort and blessing to your mother and me, since the day you were born."

"Dear papa, how kind of you to tell me that!" she said, her cheek flushing and her eyes glistening with pleasure.

He kept her with him till after her usual hour for retiring, listening to, and praising her music and talking with her quite as if she were fit to be a companion for him.

Both the injured ones were very ill for some weeks, but by means of competent medical advice and careful nursing, their lives were saved. Yet, neither recovered entirely from the effects of the accident.

Mr. Dinsmore was feeble and ailing, and walked with a limp for the rest of his days. Enna, though her bodily health was quite restored, rose from her bed with an impaired intellect, her memory gone, her reasoning powers scarcely equal to those of an ordinary child of five or six.

She did not recognize her children, or indeed anyone. She had everything to relearn and went back to childish amusements — dolls, dollhouses, and other toys.

The sight was inexpressibly painful to Dick and Molly, far worse than following her to her grave.

She remained at her father's, a capable and kind

woman being provided to take constant care of her. Bob and Betty stayed on at the Oaks, their uncle and aunt bringing them up with all the care and kindness bestowed upon their own children. Dick and Molly made their home at Ion.

Molly was removed tither as soon as the danger to her mother's life was past, the change being considered only temporary at the time. Afterward it was decided to make it permanent, in accordance with the kind and generous invitation of Mr. and Mrs. Travilla to her and her brother, and their offer to become responsible for the education and present support of both.

Little Elsie was bravely and earnestly striving to fill her mother's place in the household. She was making herself companionable to her father. She was helping Eddie, Vi and Harold with their lessons; comforting Herbie when his baby heart ached so sorely with its longing for mamma, and in all his little griefs and troubles; and settling the slight differences that would sometimes arise between the children or the servants. She found Molly an additional burden, for she too must be cheered and consoled and was often fretful, unreasonable, and exacting.

Still the little girl struggled on, now feebly and almost ready to despair, now with renewed hope and courage gathered from an interview with her earthly or her heavenly Father.

Mr. Travilla was very proud of the womanly way in which she acquitted herself at this time. He regarded her diligence, utter unselfishness, patience, and thoughtfulness for others and did not withhold the reward of well earned praise. This, with his advice and sympathy, did much to enable her to persevere to the end.

But oh what relief and joy when at last the dear mother was restored to them and the unaccustomed burden lifted from the young shoulders!

It would have been impossible to say who rejoiced most heartily in the reunion — father, mother or children. But every heart leaped lightly, every face was bright with smiles.

Mrs. Travilla knew she was adding greatly to her cares and to the annoyances and petty trials of everyday life in taking Dick and especially Molly into her family, but she realized it more and more as the months and years rolled on. Both had been so spoiled by Enna's unwise and capricious treatment, that it was a difficult thing to control them. And poor Molly's sad affliction caused her frequent fits of depression that rendered her a burden to herself and to others. Also, she inherited to some extent, her mother's infirmities of temper and her envy, jealousy and unreasonableness made her presence in the family a trial to her young cousins.

The mother had to teach patience, meekness and forbearance by precept and example, ever holding up as the grand motive, love to Jesus, and a desire to please and honor Him. Such constant sowing of the good seed, such patient, careful weeding out of the tares, such watchfulness and prayerfulness as Elsie bestowed upon the children God had given her, could not fail of their reward from Him who has said, "Whatsoever a man soweth, that shall he also reap." And as the years rolled on, she had the unspeakable joy of seeing her darlings, one after another gathered into the fold of the Good Shepherd. One by one consecrating themselves in the dew of their youth to the service of Him who had loved them and washed them from their sins in His own blood.

She was scarcely less earnest and persistent in her efforts to promote the welfare, temporal and spiritual, of Molly and Dick. She far more than supplied the place of the mother, now almost worse than lost to them.

They had always liked and respected her; they soon learned to love her deeply, and grew happier and more lovable under the refining, elevating influence of her conduct and conversation.

She and her husband gave to both the best advantages of education that money could procure, aroused in them the desire, and stimulated them to earnest efforts to become useful members of society.

Elsie soon discovered that one grand element of Molly's depression was the thought that she was cut off from all the activities of life and doomed, by her sad affliction, to be a useless burden upon others.

"My poor dear child!" she said clasping the weeping girl in her arms, "that would be a sad fate indeed, but it is not yours. There are many walks of usefulness still open to you — literature, several of the arts and sciences, music, painting, authorship, to say nothing of needle work both plain and fancy. The first thing will be a good education in the ordinary sense of the term. And that you can take as easily as one who has the use of all her limbs. Books and masters shall be at your command, and when you have decided to what employment you will especially devote yourself, every facility shall be given you for perfecting yourself in it."

"Oh, Cousin Elsie," cried the girl, her eyes shining, "do you think I could ever write books or paint pictures? I mean, such as would be really worth the doing, such as would make Dick proud of me and perhaps give me money to help him with, because you know the poor fellow must make his own way in the world."

"I scarcely know how to answer that question," Elsie said, smiling at her sudden enthusiasm, "but I do know that patience and perseverance will do wonders, and if you practice them faithfully, it will not surprise me to see you some day turn out a great author or artist."

"But don't fret because Dick has not a fortune to begin with. Our very noblest and most successful men have been those who had to win their way by dint of hard and determined struggling with early disadvantages. 'Young trees root the faster with shaking!' "she added with a smile.

"Oh, then Dick will succeed, I know, dear, noble fellow!" cried Molly flushing with sisterly pride.

From that time she took heart and though there were occasional returns of despondency and gloom, she strove to banish them and was upon the whole brave, cheerful, and energetic in carrying out the plans her cousin had suggested.

Chapter Sixteenth

It is as if the night should shade noonday,
Or that the sun was here, but forced away;
And we were left, under that hemisphere,
Where we must feel it dark for half a year.

— Ben Johnson

Since the events recorded in our last chapter, six years have rolled their swift, though noiseless round, ere we look in upon these friends again. Six years bring such changes as they must — growth and development to the very young, a richer maturity, a riper experience to those who had already attained an adult life, and to the aged, increasing infirmities, reminding them that their race is nearly run. It may be so with others; it must be so with them.

There have been gains and losses, sickness and other afflictions, but death has not yet entered any of their homes.

At Ion, the emerald, velvety lawn, the grand old trees, the sparkling lakelet, the flower gardens and conservatories gay with rich autumn hues, were looking their loveliest in the light of a fair September morning.

The sun was scarcely an hour high and, except in the region of the kitchen and stables, quiet reigned within and without the mansion. Doors and windows stood wide open and servants were busied here and there cleaning and setting in order for the day, but without noise and bustle. In the avenue before the front entrance stood Solon with the pretty gray ponies, Prince and Princess, ready saddled and bridled. While on the veranda sat a tall, dark-eyed, handsome youth, a riding whip in one hand, the other gently stroking and patting the head of

Bruno, as it rested on his knee — the dog receiving the caress with demonstrations of delight.

A light, springing step passed down the broad stairway, crossed the hall, and a slender fairy-like form appeared in the doorway. It was Violet, now thirteen, and already a woman in height, though the innocent child-like trust in the sweet fair face and azure eyes told another tale.

"Good morning, Eddie," she said. "I am sorry to have kept you waiting."

"Oh, good morning," he cried, jumping up and turning toward her. "No need for apology, Vi, I've not been here five minutes."

He handed her gallantly to the saddle, then mounted himself.

"Try to cheer up, little sister; one should not be sad on such a lovely morning as this," he said as they trotted down the avenue side by side.

"Oh, Eddie," she answered, with tears in her voice, "I do try, but I can't yet. It isn't like home without them."

"No, no indeed, Vi; how could it be? Mr. and Mrs. Daly are very kind, yet not in the least like our father and mother. But it would be impossible for anyone to take their places in our hearts or home."

"The only way to feel at all reconciled is to keep looking forward to the delight of seeing them return with our darling Lily well and strong," Vi said, struggling bravely with her tears.

Eddie answered, "I cannot help hoping that that may be in spite of all the discouraging things the doctors have said."

Lily, always frail and delicate, had drooped more and more during the past year. And only yesterday the parents had left with her for the north, intending to try the effect of different watering places, in the faint hope that the child might yet be restored to health, or her life at least prolonged for a few years.

They had taken with them their eldest daughter, an infant son, and several servants.

Aunt Chloe and Uncle John were not of the party, increasing infirmities compelling them to stay behind.

The separation from her idolized mistress caused the former many tears, but she was much comforted by Elsie's assurance that to have her at home to watch over the children there would be a great comfort and relief from anxiety on their account.

It had seemed to Mr. and Mrs. Travilla, a very kind Providence that had sent them an excellent tutor and housekeeper in the persons of Mr. and Mrs. Daly, their former guests at Viamede.

Since the winter spent together there, an occasional correspondence had been kept up between the two families. Learning from it that Mr. Daly was again in need of a change of climate just as they were casting about for some suitable persons to take charge of their house and children during their contemplated absence from home, Elsie suggested to her husband that the situations should be offered to him and his wife.

Mr. Travilla approved, the offer was made at once, and promptly and thankfully accepted.

Frank Day, now a fine lad of eleven, was invited to come with his parents, and to share his father's instructions.

They had now been in the house for more than a week, and seemed eminently suited to the duties they had undertaken. Yet, home was sadly changed to the children, deprived for the first time in their lives of the parents whom they so dearly loved, and who so thoroughly understood and sympathized with them.

Eddie was growing very manly, was well advanced in his studies, easy and polished in manner. Vi and the younger ones looked up to him with pride and respect, as the big brother who knew a great deal, and in papa's absence would be their leader and protector.

He, on his part, was fond and proud of them all, but more especially of Elsie and Vi, who grew daily in beauty and grace.

"You can't think how sorely I have missed Elsie this

morning," Vi said, breaking a slight pause in the talk, "and yet I am glad she went, too. She will be such a comfort to mamma and Lily, and she promised me to write every day — which, of course, mamma could not find time to do."

"Yes, and her absence will give you an opportunity for practice in that line and in being motherly to Rosie," Eddie said with a smile.

"To Herbie, too," she answered. "We are to meet in mamma's dressing room every morning just as usual, only it will be a strange half hour without mamma. But we will say our texts to each other, talk them over and read together."

"Yes, I promised mamma that I would be with you. Which way now?" he asked as they came to the crossroads.

"To the Oaks. I want to see grandpa. A caress, or even a word or smile from him would do me good this morning."

"He may not be up."

"But I think he will. You know he likes to keep early hours."

Mr. Dinsmore was up and pacing the veranda thoughtfully to and fro, as the young riders came in sight.

He welcomed them with a smile, and lifting Vi from her pony, held her close to his heart as something very dear and precious.

"My darling," he said, "your face is sad this morning, and no wonder. Yet, cheer up, we will hope to see our dear travelers at home again in a few weeks, our poor fading flower restored to bloom and health."

He made them sit down and regale themselves with some fine fresh oranges, which he summoned a servant to bring. Their grandma, aunt and uncle joined them presently and they were urged to stay to breakfast, but decline. "The little ones must not be left alone this first morning without papa and mamma."

On their return, Rosie, a merry, healthy, romping child of five, with a rich, creamy complexion, dark hair and eyes, forming a strong contrast to Vi's blonde beauty, came bounding to meet them.

"Oh, Vi, I've been wanting you! You'll have to be mamma to us now, you know, till our real own mamma comes back. And, Eddie, you'll have to be the papa. Won't he, Vi? Come let's all go to mamma's dress-room; my verse is ready."

"What is your text, Rosie?" Violet asked when they reached the room, sitting down and drawing the child to her side.

"Take me in your lap like mamma does and I'll say it."

"Now then," Vi said, complying with the request.

"'When my father and my mother forsake me then the Lord will take me up.'"

"Who taught you that, pet?" asked Vi, with a slight tremble in her low sweet tones.

"Cousin Molly. I was crying for mamma and papa and she called me in there and told me I mustn't cry, 'cause Jesus loves me and will never, never go away from me."

"That's like my text," said Herbert. "Mamma gave it to me for today. 'I will never leave thee, nor forsake thee.'"

"And mine," said Harold, "'Lo, I am with you always, even unto the end of the world.'"

"'This God is our God for ever and ever; He will be our guide even unto death,'" repeated Vi feelingly.

"That's a nice one," said Rosie.

"Yes," said Edie, "and this is a nice one for us to remember just now in connection with the dear ones on their journey, and for ourselves when we go away. Yes, now, and at all times. 'Behold I am with thee, and will keep thee in all places whither thou goest, and will bring thee again into this land.'"

"Isn't the Bible the sweetest book!" exclaimed Vi. "The Book of books — it has been a comforting word for everybody and in every time of need."

The breakfast bell ran.

"Oh, dear!" cried Rosie, clinging to Violet, her chest heaving with sobs, "how can we go to the table and eat without papa and mamma?"

"Don't cry, little pet, don't cry. You know they want us to be cheerful and make it pleasant for Mr. and Mrs. Daly," the others said, and with a great effort the child swallowed her sobs. Then, wiping away her tears, she allowed Vi to lead her down to the breakfast room.

Mrs. Daly met them with a smiling face and kind motherly greeting. Mr. Daly had a pleasant word for each and talked so entertainingly all through the meal that they had scarcely time for sad or lonely thoughts.

Family worship followed immediately after breakfast, as was the custom of the house. Mr. Daly's prayers were short, comforting them all, and simple enough for even little Rose to understand.

There was still time for a walk before school, but first Vi went to Molly to ask how she was and to carry her a letter from Dick which had come by the morning mail.

Dick was in Philadelphia studying medicine. He and Molly corresponded regularly and she knew no greater treat than a letter from him. Vi was glad she could carry it to her this morning. It was so great a pleasure to be the bearer of anything so welcome.

There were no more pleasant or better-furnished rooms in the house than those appropriated to the use of the poor, dependent crippled cousin. Molly herself tastefully and becomingly dressed, blooming, bright, and cheerful, sat in an invalid chair by the open window. She was reading, and so absorbed in her book that she did not hear the light step of her young relative.

Vi paused in the doorway a moment, thinking what a pretty picture Molly made — with her intellectual countenance, clear complexion, rosy cheeks, bright eyes and glossy braids — framed by the vine-wreathed window.

Molly looked up and laying aside her book, "Ah, Vi, this is kind!" she said. "Come in, do; I'm ever so glad to see you."

"And what of this?" asked Vi, holding up the letter.

"Oh, delightful! Dear old fellow to write so soon. I was not expecting it till tomorrow."

"I knew you'd be glad," Vi said, putting it into her

hand, "and now I'll just kiss you good morning and run away, that you may enjoy it fully before lesson time."

Rosie's voice was summoning Vi. The children were on the veranda ready for their morning walk, waiting only for "Sister Vi."

"Let's walk to the Oaks," said Rosie, slipping her hand into Vi's. "It's a nice shady walk, and I like to throw pebbles into the water. But I'll feed the fishes first. See what a bag full of crumbs mammy has given me."

Violet was very patient and indulgent toward the little sister, yet obliged to cut short her sport with the pebbles and the fishes, because the hour for lessons drew near.

Chapter Seventeenth

The lilies faintly to the roses yield,
As on the lovely cheek they struggling vie,
And thoughts are in thy speaking eyes revealed,
Pure as the fount the prophet's rod unseal'd.

— Hoffman

"Dr. Arthur lef 'dis for you, Miss Wi'let," said one of the maids, meeting her young mistress on the veranda and handing her a note.

"Cousin Arthur? Was he here?"

"Yes, miss. He axed for you, but hadn't no time to stop, not even to see po' Miss Molly. Spect somebody's mighty sick."

Arthur Conley had entered the medical profession, and for the last two years had been practicing in partnership with Dr. Barton.

Vi glanced over the note and hastened to Eddie, whom she found in the schoolroom — its only occupant at the moment.

"Here's a note from Isa, asking us to bring Rosie and come to Roselands for the rest of the day, after lessons are done. She thinks I must feel lonely. It is very kind, but what shall I do about it? Rosie would enjoy going, but would it be kind to you or the boys or Molly?"

"I might take the boys over to the Oaks, but I don't know — oh, I think Molly would probably prefer solitude, as I happen to know that she has some writing to do. Well, what now?" seeing a hesitating, perplexed look on Vi's face.

"I cannot ask permission of papa or mamma."

"No, of course not. We must go to Mr. Daly for that now."

"I don't like it," she answered, coloring. "It does seem as if nobody has the right to control us except our father and mother and our grandparents."

"Only that they have given him the right for the present."

Mr. Daly came in at that instant and Vi, placing the note in his hand, said, "Will you please to look at this, sir, and tell me if I may accept the invitation?"

"I see no objection," he said, returning it with a kindly smile, "provided your lessons are well recited."

Mr. Daly was an excellent teacher, thoroughly prepared for his work by education, native talent for imparting the knowledge he possessed, love for the employment, and for the young ones entrusted to his care.

The liking was mutual, and study hours were soon voted only less enjoyable than when mamma was their loved instructor.

Molly occupied her place in the schoolroom as regularly as the others. It adjoined her apartments and her wheeled chair required a very slight exertion of strength on the part of friend or servant to propel it from room to room.

Molly had already made herself a very thorough French and German scholar, and was hoping to turn her ability to translate to good account in the way of earning her own support. There was no pauper instinct in the girl's noble nature, and able and willing as her cousin was to support her, she greatly preferred to earn her own living, though at the cost of much wearisome labor of hand and brain.

She was not of those who seem to forget that the command "Six days shalt thou labor and do all thy work," is equally binding with that other, "In it (the seventh day) thou shalt not do any work." This lesson — that industry is commanded, idleness forbidden — was one which Elsie had ever been careful to instill into the minds of her children from their earliest infancy. Nor was it enough, she taught them, that they should be doing something. They must be usefully employed, remembering that they were but stewards who must one day give an account to their Lord of all they had done with the talents entrusted to them.

"Is Dick well? Was it a nice letter?" Violet asked, leaning over her cousin's chair when lessons were done.

"Oh, very nice! He's well and doing famously. I must answer it this afternoon."

"Then you will not care for company?"

"Not particularly. Why?"

Vi told of her invitation.

"Go, by all means," said Molly. "You know Virgy has a friend with her, a Miss Reed. I want you to see her and tell me what she's like."

"I fear you'll have to see her yourself to find that out. I'm no portrait painter," Violet said with a smile as she ran lightly away to order the carriage and see to her own grooming and Rosie's.

They were simple enough — white dresses with blue sashes and ribbons for Vi, the same but pink for Rosie.

Miss Reed, dressed in a stiff silk and loaded with showy jewelry, sat in the drawing room at Roselands in a bay window overlooking the avenue. She was gazing eagerly toward its entrance, as though expecting someone.

"Yes, I've heard of the Travillas," she said in answer to a remark from Virginia Conly who stood by her side almost as showily attired as Miss Reed. "I've been told she was a great heiress."

"She was; and he was rich, too; though I believe he lost a good deal during the war."

"They live splendidly, I suppose?"

"They've everything money can buy, but are nearly breaking their hearts just now over one of their little girls who seems to have some incurable disease."

"Is that so? Well, they ought to have some trouble as well as other folks. I'm sorry though, for I'd set my heart on being invited there and seeing how they live."

"Oh, they're all gone away except Vi and Rosie and the boys. But maybe Vi will ask us there to dinner or tea. Ah, here they come!"

"What splendid match horses! What an elegant

carriage!" exclaimed Miss Reed, as a beautiful barouche, drawn by a pair of fine bays came bowling up the avenue.

"Yes, they've come. It's the Ion carriage."

"But that's a young lady Pomp's handing out of it!" exclaimed Miss Reed the next moment. "And I thought you said it was only two children you expected."

"Yes, Vi's only thirteen," answered Virginia running to the door to meet her. "Vi, my dear, how good of you to come. How sweet you look!" kissing her. "Rosie, too," bestowing a caress upon her also. "Pink's so becoming to you, little pet, and blue equally so to Vi. This is my friend Miss Reed, Vi. I've been telling her about you."

Violet gave her hand, then drew back blushing and slightly disconcerted by the almost rude stare of the black eyes that seemed to be taking an inventory of her personal appearance and attire.

"Where is Isa?" she asked.

"Here, and very glad to see you, Vi," answered a silvery voice. A tall, queenly looking girl of twenty in rustling black silk and with roses in her hair and at her throat took Violet's hand in hers and kissed her on both cheeks; then, letting her go, saluted the little one in like manner.

"Why don't you do that to me? Guess I like kisses as well as other folks. Ha! Ha!" cried a shrill voice. A little withered up, faded woman with a large wax doll in her arms came skipping into the room.

Her hair, plentifully sprinkled with gray, hung loosely about her neck, and she had bedecked herself with ribbons and faded artificial flowers of every hue.

"Well, Griselda," she continued, addressing the doll, which she bounced in her arms, regarding it with a look of fond admiration, "we don't care, do we, dear? We love and embrace one another and that's enough.

"Oh, go back to your own room," said Virginia in a tone of annoyance. "We don't want you here."

"I'll go when I get ready, and not a minute sooner," was the rejoinder in a peevish tone. "Oh, here's visitors! What a pretty little girl! What's your name, little girl? Won't you come and play with me? I'll lend you

Grimalkin, my other wax doll. She's a beauty — almost as pretty as Griselda. Now, don't get mad at that, Grissy, dear," kissing the doll again and again.

Rose was frightened and clung to her sister, trying to hide behind her.

"It's Aunt Enna. She won't hurt you," whispered Vi. "She never hurts anyone unless she is teased or worried into a passion."

"Won't she make me go with her? Oh, don't let her, Vi."

"No, dear, you shall stay with me. And here is the nurse come to take her away," Violet answered, as the poor lunatic was led from the room by her attendant.

"Dear me!" exclaimed Miss Reed, who had not seen or heard Enna before. Turning to Virginia, she asked, "does she belong in the house? Aren't you afraid of her?"

"Not at all; she's perfectly harmless. She is my mother's sister and lost her reason some years ago by an accidental injury to the head."

"I wonder you don't send her to an asylum."

"Perhaps it might be well," returned Virginia indifferently, "but it's not my affair."

"Grandpa would never hear of such a thing!" said Isadore indignantly.

"Mamma would not either, I am sure," said Violet. "Poor Aunt Enna! Should she be sent away from all who love her just because she is unfortunate?"

"Everyone to their taste," remarked the visitor, shrugging her shoulders.

Vi inquired for her Aunt Louise and the younger members of the family, and was told that they and the grandfather were spending the day at Pinegrove.

"I was glad they decided to go today," said Isadore, seating Vi and herself comfortably on a sofa; then, taking Rose on her lap and caressing her, "because I wanted you here, and to have you to myself. You see these two young ladies," glancing smilingly at her sister and guest, "are so fully taken up with each other, that for the most of the time I am quite alone, and must look for entertainment elsewhere than in their company."

"Yes," said Virginia, with more candor than politeness, "Josie and I are all sufficient for each other, are we not mon amie?"

"Very true, machere, yet I enjoy Isa's company, and am extremely delighted to have made the acquaintance of your charming cousin," remarked Miss Reed, with an insinuating bow directed to Violet.

"You do not know me yet," said Vi, modestly. "Though so tall, I am only a little girl and do not know enough to make an interesting companion for a young lady."

"Quite a mistake, Vi," said Isadore rising. "But there is the dinner bell. Come let us try the soothing and exhilarating effect of food and drink upon our flagging spirits. We will not wait for Art. There's no knowing when he can leave his patients, and Cal's away on business."

On leaving the table, Isadore carried off her young cousins to her apartments. Rose was persuaded to lie down and take a nap, while the older girls conversed together in an adjoining room.

"Isn't it delightful to be at home again, after all those years in the convent?" queried Vi.

"I enjoy home, certainly," replied Isa, "yet I deeply regretted leaving the sisters; for you cannot think how good and kind they were to me. Shall I tell you about it? About my life there?"

"Oh, do! I should so like to hear it."

Isadore smiled at the eager tone, the bright interested look, and at once began a long and minute description of the events of her school days at the nunnery, ending with a eulogy upon convent life in general and the nuns who had been her educators in particular. "They lived such holy, devoted lives, were so kind, so good, so self-denying."

Violet listened attentively, making no remark, but Isadore read disapproval more than once in her speaking countenance.

"I wish your mamma would send you and Elsie there to finish," remarked Isa, breaking the pause that followed the conclusion of her narrative. "Should you not like to go?"

"No, oh no, no!"

"Why not?"

"Isa, I could never, never do some of those things you say they require — bow to images or pictures, or kneel before them, or join in prayers or hymns to the Virgin."

"I don't know how you could be so wicked as to refuse. She is the queen of Heaven, and mother of God."

"Isa!" and Violet looked inexpressibly shocked.

"You can't deny it. Wasn't Jesus God?"

"Yes, He is God. 'In the beginning was the Word, and the Word was with God, and the Word was God.' 'and the Word was with God, and the Word was God.' 'and the Word was made flesh, and dwelt among us.' "

"Ah! And was not the Virgin Mary His mother?"

Vi looked perplexed for a moment, then brightening, "Ah, I know now," she said. "Jesus was God and man both."

"Well?"

"And — mamma told me — Mary was the mother of his human nature only, and it is blasphemous to call her the mother of God. And to do her homage is idolatry."

"So I thought before I went to the convent," said Isadore, "but the sisters convinced me of my error. Vi, I should like to show you something. Can you keep a secret?"

"I have never had a secret from mamma. I do not wish to have any."

"But you can't tell her everything now while she's away, and this concerns no one but myself. I know I can trust your honor," and taking Vi's hand, she opened a door and drew her into a large closet, lighted by a small circular window quite high up on the wall. The place was fitted up as an oratory, with a picture of the Virgin and child, and a crucifix, standing on a little table with a prayer book and rosary beside it.

Vi had never seen such things, but she had heard of them and knew what they signified. Glancing from the picture to the crucifix, she started back in horror, and without a word hastily retreated to the dressing-room, where she dropped into a chair, pale, trembling, and distressed.

"Isadore, Isadore!" she cried, clasping her hands, and lifting her troubled eyes to her cousin's face, "Have you — have you become a Roman Catholic?"

"I am a member of the one true church," returned her cousin coldly. "How bigoted you are, Violet. I could not have believed it of so sweet and gentle a young thing as you. I trust you will not consider it your duty to betray me to mamma?"

"Betray you? Can you think I would? So Aunt Louise does not know? Oh, Isa, can you think it right to hide it from her — your own mother?"

"Yes, because I was directed to do so by my father confessor; and because my motive is a good one; and 'the end sanctifies the means.' "

"Isa, mamma has taught me, and the Bible says it too, that it is never right to do evil that good may come."

"Perhaps you and your mamma do not always understand the real meaning of what the Bible says. It must be that many people misunderstand it, else why are there so many denominations of Protestants, teaching opposite doctrines, and all professing to get them from the Bible?"

Violet in her extreme youth and want of information and ability to argue was not prepared with an answer.

"Does Virgy know?" she asked.

"About my change of views and my oratory? Yes."

"And does she —."

"Virgy is altogether worldly, and cares nothing for religion of any kind."

Vi's face was full of distress. "Isa," she said, "may I ask you a question?"

"What is it?"

"When you pray, do you kneel before that — that —."

"Crucifix? Sometimes, at others before the Virgin and child."

Vi shuddered. "Oh, Isa, have you forgotten the second commandment? 'Thou shalt make unto thee any graven image or likeness of anything that is in heaven above, or that is in the earth; thou shalt not bow down thyself to them nor serve them,' "

"I have not forgotten, but am content to do as the church directs," returned Isadore, coldly.

"Isa, didn't they promise Aunt Louise that they would not interfere with your religion?"

"Yes."

"And they broke their promise. How can you think they are good?"

"They did it to save my soul. Was not that a good and praiseworthy motive?"

"Yes; but if they thought it their duty to try to make you believe as they do, they should not have promised not to do so."

"But in that case I should never have been placed in the convent, and they would have had no opportunity to labor for my conversion."

Earnestly, constantly had Elsie endeavored to obey the command, "Therefore shall ye lay up these my words in your heart and in your soul, and bind them for a sign upon your hand, that they may be as guards between your eyes. And ye shall teach them to your children, speaking of them when thou sittest in thy house, and when thou walkest by the way, when thou liest down, and when thou risest up."

Thus Violet's memory was stored with texts, and those words from Isaiah suggested themselves as a fit comment upon Isadore's last remark. "Woe unto them that call evil good and good evil; that put darkness for light and light for darkness; that put bitter for sweet and sweet for bitter."

Chapter Eighteenth

But all's not true that supposition saith,
Nor have the mightiest arguments most faith.

— Drayton

Examples I could cite you more;
But be contented with these four;
For when one's proofs are aptly chosen,
Four are as valid as four dozen.

— Prior

Isa's conversion, Isa's secret, weighed heavily upon the heart and conscience of poor Violet; the child had never been burdened with a secret before.

She thought Aunt Louise ought to know, yet was not at all clear that it was her duty to tell her. She wished it might be discovered in some way without her telling, for "it was a dreadful thing for Isa to be left to go on believing and doing as she did. Oh, if only she could be talked to by someone old enough and wise enough to convince her of her errors!"

Isadore with the zeal of a young convert, had set herself the task of bringing Vi over to her new faith. The opportunity afforded by the absence of the vigilant parents was too good to be lost, and should be improved to the utmost.

She made daily errands to Ion, some trifling gift to Molly often being the excuse. She was sweet and gracious to all, but devoted herself especially to Violet, insisting on sharing her room when she stayed overnight, coaxing her out for long walks and drives, rowing with her on the lake, learning to handle the oars herself in order that they might go alone.

And all the time she was on the watch for every favorable opening to say something to undermine the child's faith, or bias her mind in favor of the tenets of the Church of Rome.

Violet grew more and more troubled and perplexed, and now not on Isa's account alone. She could not give up the faith of her fathers, the faith of the Bible. (To that inspired word she clung as to the Rock which must save her from being engulfed in the wild waters of doubt and difficulty that was surging around her.) But neither could she answer all of Isadore's questions and arguments. And there was no one to whom she might turn in her bewilderment, lest she should betray her cousin's secret.

She prayed for guidance and help, searching the Scriptures and "comparing spiritual things with spiritual," and thus was kept from the snares laid for her inexperienced feet. She stumbled and walked with uncertain step for a time, but did not fall.

Those about her, particularly Eddie and her old mammy, noticed the unwonted care and anxiety in her innocent face, but attributed it wholly to the unfavorable news in regard to Lily's condition, which reached them from time to time.

The dear invalid was reported as making little or no progress toward recovery, and the hearts of brothers and sisters were deeply saddened by the tidings.

Miss Reed was still at Roselands and had been brought several times by Virginia for a call at Ion. At length, Violet having written for and obtained permission of her parents, and consulted Mrs. Daly's convenience in reference to the matter, invited the three girls for a visit of several days, stipulating, however, that it was not to interfere with lessons.

To this the girls readily assented. "They would make themselves quite at home and find their own amusement. It was what they should like above all things."

The plan worked well, except that under this constant

association with Isadore, Vi grew daily more careworn and depressed. Even Mr. Daly noticed it, and spoke to her of Lily's state as hopefully as truth would permit.

"Do not be too troubled, my dear child," he said, taking her hand in a kind fatherly manner. "She is in the hands of One who loves her even better than her parents, brothers and sisters do, and will let no real evil come nigh her. He may restore her to health, but if not — if He takes her from us, it will be to make her infinitely happier with Himself; for we know that she has given her young heart to Him."

Violet bowed a silent assent, then hurried from the room — her heart too full for speech. She was troubled, sorely troubled for her darling, suffering little sister, and with this added anxiety, her burden was hard indeed to bear.

Mr. Daly was reading in the library that afternoon, when Violet came running in as if in haste, a flush of excitement on her fair face.

"Ah, excuse me, sir! I fear I have disturbed you," she said, as he looked up from his book. "But, oh, I'm glad to find you here for I think you can help me! I came to look for a Bible and concordance.

"They are both here on this table," he said. "I am glad you are wanting them, for we cannot study them too much. But in what can I help you, Vi? Is it some theological discussion between your cousins and yourself?"

"Yes, sir. We were talking about a book — a storybook that Miss Reed admires — and I said mamma would not allow us to read it because it teaches that Jesus Christ was only a good man. Miss Reed said that was her belief, and yet she professes to believe the Bible. I wish to show her that it teaches that he was very God as well as man."

"That will not be difficult," he said, "for no words could state it more directly and clearly than these, 'Christ, who is over all, God blessed forever.' " And opening the Bible at the ninth chapter of Romans, he pointed to the latter clause of the fifth verse.

"Oh, let me show her that!" cried Vi.

"Suppose you invite them in here," he suggested, and she hastened to do so.

Miss Reed read the text as it was pointed out to her. "I don't remember noticing that before," was all she said.

Silently Mr. Daly turned over the leaves and pointed out the twentieth verse of the first Epistle of John, where it is said of Jesus Christ, "This is the true God and eternal life," and then to Isaiah 9:6. "For unto us a child is born, unto us a son is given; and the government shall be upon his shoulder; and his name shall be called Wonderful, Counselor, the Mighty God, the Everlasting Father, the prince of Peace," and several other passages equally strong and explicit in their declaration of the divinity of Christ. "Well," said Miss Reed, "if He was God, why didn't he say so?"

"He did, again and again," was the reply. "Here in John 8:58 we read, "Jesus said unto them, 'Verily, verily, I say unto you, before Abraham was, I am.' "

"I don't see it!" she said sneeringly.

"You do not? Just compare it with this other passage in Exodus 3:14, 15. 'And God said unto Moses, I AM THAT I AM: and he said, thus shalt thou say unto the children of Israel, the Lord God of your fathers, the God of Abraham, the God of Issac, and the God of Jacob, hath sent me unto you; this is my name forever, and this is my memorial unto all generations.' The Jews who were present understood those words of Jesus as an assertion of His divinity and took up stones to cast at Him."

Isadore seemed interested in the discussion, but Virginia showed evident impatience. "What's the use of bothering ourselves about it?" she exclaimed at length. "What difference does it make whether we believe in His divinity or deny it?"

"A vast difference, my dear young lady," said Mr. Daly. "If Christ be not divine, it is idolatry to worship Him. If He is divine, and we fail to acknowledge it and to trust in Him for salvation, we must be eternally lost for 'neither is their salvation in any other; for there is none other name under heaven given among men, whereby we must be saved.' 'But whosoever believeth in Him shall receive remission of sins.' "

Virginia fidgeted uneasily and Miss Reed inquired with affected politeness if that were all.

"No," he said, "far from it. Yet, if the Bible be — as I think we all acknowledge — the inspired word of God, one plain declaration of a truth is as authoritative as a dozen."

"Suppose I don't believe it is all inspired?" queried Miss Reed.

"Still, since Jesus asserts His own divinity, we must either accept Him as God or believe Him to been an imposter and therefore not even a good man. He must be to us everything or nothing. There is no neutral ground. He says, 'He that is not with me is against me.' "

"And there is only one true church," remarked Isadore, forgetting herself, "the holy Roman Church, and none without her limits can be saved."

Mr. Daly looked at her in astonishment. Violet was at first greatly startled, then inexpressibly relieved. Since Isa's secret being one no longer, a heavy weight was removed from her heart and conscience.

Virginia was the first to speak. "There!" she said, "You've let it out yourself. I always knew you would sooner or later."

"Well," returned Isadore, drawing herself up haughtily, determined to put a brave face upon the matter, now that there was no retreat. "I'm not ashamed of my faith, nor afraid to attempt its defense against any who may see fit to attack it," she added with a defiant look at Mr. Daly.

He smiled a little sadly. "I am very sorry for you, Miss Conly," he said, "and do not feel at all belligerent toward you; but let me entreat you to rest your hopes of salvation only upon the atoning blood and imputed righteousness of Jesus Christ."

"I must do works also," she said.

"Yes, as an evidence, but not as the ground of your

faith. We must do good works not that we may be saved but because we are saved. 'If a man love me, he will keep my words.' Well, my little Vi, what is it?" for she was looking at him with eager, questioning eyes.

"Oh, Mr. Daly, I want you to answer some things Isa has said to me. Isa, I have never mentioned it to anyone before. I have kept your secret faithfully till now that you have told it yourself."

"I don't blame you, Vi," she answered, coloring. "I presume I shall be blamed for my efforts to bring you over to the true faith, but my conscience acquits me of any bad motive. I wanted to save your soul. Mr. Daly, I do not imagine you can answer all that I have to bring against the claims of Protestantism. Pray where was that church before the Reformation?"

"Wherever the Bible was made the rule of faith and practice," he said, "there was Protestantism though existing under another name. All through the dark ages, when Popery was dominant almost all over the civilized world, the light of the pure gospel — the very same that the Reformation spread abroad over other parts of Europe — burned brightly among the secluded valleys of Piedmont. And twelve hundred years of bloody persecution on the part of the apostate Rome could not quench it."

"I know that Popery lays great stress on her claims to antiquity. But Paganism is older still, and evangelical religion — which, as I have already said, is Protestantism under another name — is as old as the Christian Era, as old as the human nature of its founder, the Lord Jesus Christ."

"You are making assertions," said Isadore bridling, "but where are your proofs?"

"They are not wanting," he said. "Suppose we undertake the study of ecclesiastical history together and see how Popery was the growth of centuries, as one error after another crept into the Christian church."

"I don't believe she was ever the persecutor you would make her out to have been," said Isadore.

"Popish historians bear witness to it as well as Protestant," he answered.

"Well, it's persecution to bring up those old stories against her now."

"Is it? When she will not disavow them, but maintains that she has always done right? And more than that, tells us she will do the same again if she ever has the power."

"I'm sure all Roman Catholics are not so cruel as to wish to torture or kill their Protestant neighbors," cried Isadore indignantly.

"And I quite agree with you there," he said. "I have not the least doubt that many of them are very kindhearted; but I was speaking, not of individuals, but of the Roman Church as such. She is essentially a persecuting power."

"Well, being the only true church, she has the right to compel conformity to her creed."

"Ah, you have already imbibed something of her spirit. But we contend that she is not the true church. 'To the law and to the testimony; if they speak not according to this word, it is because there is no light in them.' Brought to the touchstone of God's revealed word, she is proved to be reprobate silver — her creed spurious Christianity. In second Thessalonians, second chapter, we have a very clear description of her as that 'Wicked whom the Lord shall consume with the spirit of His mouth, and shall destroy with the brightness of His coming.' Also, in the seventeenth chapter of Revelation, where she is spoken of as Babylon the great, the mother of the harlots and abominations of the earth.' "

"How do you know she is meant there?" asked Isadore, growing red and angry.

"Because she, and she alone, answers to the description. It is computed that fifty millions of Protestants have been slain in her persecutions. May it not then be truly said of her that she is drunken with the blood of the saints?"

"I think what you have been saying shows that the priests are right in teaching that the Bible is a dangerous book in the hands of the ignorant, and should therefore be withheld from the laity," retorted Isadore hotly.

"But," returned Mr. Daly, "Jesus said, 'search the Scriptures; for in them ye think ye have eternal life; and they are they which testify of me.' "

CHAPTER NINETEENTH

Let us go back again, mother,
Oh, take me home to die.

"AND SO, ISA, my uncle's predictions that your popish teachers would violate their promise not to meddle with your faith have proved only too true," said Calhoun Conly, stepping forward as Mr. Daly finished his last quotation from the Scriptures.

In the heat of their discussion, neither the minister nor Isadore had noticed his entrance, but he had been standing there, an interested listener, long enough to learn the sad fact of his sister's conversion.

"They richly deserve the blame, and you cannot prevent it from being given them," he answered firmly and with flashing eyes. "I have come by my mother's request to take you and Virginia home, inviting Miss Reed to accompany us."

"I am ready," said Isadore, rising, the others doing likewise.

"But you will stay to tea?" Violet said. "Cal, you are not in too great haste for that?"

"I'm afraid I am, little cousin," he answered with a smile of acknowledgment of her hospitality. "I must meet a gentleman on business, half an hour from now."

Vi expressed her regrets, and ran after the girls, who had already left the room to prepare for their drive.

They seemed in haste to get away.

"We've had enough of Mr. Daly's prosing about religion," said Virginia.

"I'm sick of it," chimed in Miss Reed. "What difference does it make what you believe, if you're only sincere and live right?"

"With the heart man believeth unto righteousness," said Violet, "and 'the just shall live by faith.' "

"You're an apt pupil," sneered Virginia.

"It's mamma's doing that my memory is stored with texts," returned the child, reddening.

Isadore was silent and gloomy and took leave of her young cousin so coldly as to quite sadden her sensitive spirit.

Violet had enjoyed being made much of by Isa, who was a beautiful and brilliant young lady, and this sudden change in her manner was far from pleasant. Still the pain it gave her was greatly overbalanced by the relief of having her perplexities removed, her doubts set free.

Standing on the veranda, she watched the carriage as it rolled away down the avenue. Then she hailed with delight a horseman who came galloping up, alighted and, giving the bridle to Solon, turned to her with open arms and a smile that proclaimed him the bearer of good tidings before he uttered a word.

"Grandpa," she cried, springing to his embrace, "oh, is Lily better?'

"Yes," he said, caressing her; then, turning to greet Rosie and the boys who came running at the sound of his voice, he declared, "I have had a letter from your mother in which she says the dear invalid seems decidedly better."

"Oh, joy! joy!" cried the children, Rosie hugging and kissing her grandfather, the boys capering about in a transport of gladness.

"And will they come home soon, grandpa?" asked Eddie.

"Nothing is said about that but I presume they will linger up north till the weather begins to grow too cool for Lily," Mr. Dinsmore answered, shaking hands with Mr. Daly, who, hearing his voice on the veranda, stepped out to inquire for news of the absent ones.

While they talked together Vi ran away in search of Aunt Chloe.

She found her on the back veranda enjoying a chat with Aunt Dicey and Uncle Joe.

"Oh, mammy, good news, good news!" Vi cried, half-breathless with haste and happiness. "Grandpa had a letter from mamma and our darling Lily is better, much better."

"Bress de Lord!" exclaimed her listeners in chorus.

"Bress His holy name! I hope de chile am gwine to discover her health agin," added Uncle Joe. "I'se been a prayin' pow'ful strong for her."

"'Spect der is been more'n you at dat business, Uncle Joe," remarked Aunt Dicey. "'Spect I knows one ole niggah dat didn't fail to disremember de little darlin' at de throne ob grace."

"De bressed lamb!" murmured Aunt Chloe, dropping a tear on Violet's golden curls as she clasped her to her breast. "She's de Lord's own, and He'll take de bes' care of her in dis world and in de nex'; be sho' ob dat honey. Ise mighty glad for her and my dear missus and for you, too, Miss Wi'let. You's been frettin' yo' heart out 'bout Miss Lily."

"I've been very anxious about her, mammy, and something else has been troubling me too, but it's all right now," Violet answered with a glad look. Then, releasing herself, she ran back to her grandfather.

She had seen less than usual of him for several weeks past, and wanted an opportunity to pour out all her heart to him.

He had gone up to Molly's sitting room and she followed him there.

With Rosie on his knee, Harold and Herbert standing on either side, and Eddie sitting near, he was chatting gaily with his crippled niece, who was as bright and cheery as any of the group, all of whom were full of joy over the glad tidings he had brought.

"Grandpa," said Vi, joining them, "it seems a good while since you were here for more than a short call. Won't you stay now for the rest of the day?"

"Yes, and I propose that we drive down to the lake — Molly and all — and have a row. I think it would do you all good. The weather is delightful."

The motion was carried by acclamation. Molly's maid

was summoned. Eddie went down to order the carriage and the rest scattered to prepare for the expedition.

It was a lovely October day, the air balmy, the woods gorgeous in their richly colored autumn robes — gold, scarlet and crimson, russet and green mingled in gay profusion. The slanting beams of the descending sun fell across the lakelet like a broad band of shimmering gold, and here and there lent an added glory to the trees. The boat glided swiftly over the rippling waters, now in sunshine, now in shadow, and the children hushed their merry chatter, silenced by the beauty and stillness of the scene.

Tea was waiting when they returned and on leaving the table the younger ones bade goodnight and went away with Vi to be put to bed.

She had a story or some pleasant talk for them every night, doing her best to fill mamma's place.

Vi was glad to find her grandpa alone in the library when she came down again.

"Come, sit on my knee as your dear mamma used to do at your age," he said, "and tell me what you have been doing these past weeks while I have seen so little of you.'

"It is so nice," she said as she took the offered seat, and he passed his arm about her, "so nice to have a grandpa to love me, especially when I've no father or mother at home to do it."

"So we are mutually satisfied," he said. "Now what have you to tell me? Any questions to ask? Any doubts or perplexities to be cleared away?"

"Grandpa, has anybody been telling you anything?" she asked.

"No, nothing about you."

"Then I'll just tell you all." And she gave him a history of Isadore's efforts to convert her and their effect upon her. She also told of the conversation of that afternoon in which Mr. Daly had answered the questions of Isadore that had most perplexed and troubled her.

Mr. Dinsmore was grieved and distressed by Isa's

defection from the evangelical faith and indignant at her attempt to lead Vi astray also.

"Are you fully satisfied now on all the points?" he asked.

"There are one or two things I should like to ask you about, grandpa," she said. "Isa thinks a convent life so beautiful and holy, so shut out from the world with all its cares and wickedness, she says. It's so quiet and peaceful, so full of devotion and the self-denial the Lord Jesus taught when He said, 'If any man will come after me, let him deny himself and take up his cross and follow me.' Do you think leaving one's dear home and father and mother, and brothers and sisters to be shut up for life with strangers in a convent was the cross He meant, grandpa?"

"No, I am perfectly sure it was not. The Bible teaches us to do our duty in the place where God puts us. It recognizes the family relationships, teaches the reciprocal duties of kinsmen — parents and children, husbands and wives — but has not a word to say to monks and nuns.

"It bids us take up the cross God lays upon us, and not one of our own invention; nor did any one of the holy men and women it tells of live the life of a recluse. Nor can peace and freedom from temptation and sin be found in a convent any more than elsewhere, because we carry our evil natures with us wherever we go.

"No, peace and happiness are to be found only in being 'followers of God as dear children,' doing our duty in that station in life where he has placed us. Our motive should be to love Him, leading us to desire above all things to live to His honor and glory."

Violet sat with downcast eyes, her face full of earnest thought. She was silent for a moment after Mr. Dinsmore had ceased speaking; then, lifting her head and turning to him with a relieved look, "Thank you, grandpa," she said. "I am fully satisfied on that point. Now, there is just one more. Isa says that divisions among Protestants show that the Bible is not a book for common people to read for themselves. They cannot understand it right. If they did, they would all believe alike."

Mr. Dinsmore smiled. "Who is to explain it?"

"Oh, Isa says that is for the priests to do; and they and the people must accept the decisions of the church."

"Well, my child, it would take too much time to tell you just how impossible it is to find out what are the authoritative decisions of the Roman Church on more than one important point. One council would contradict another; one pope would affirm what his predecessors had denied, and vice versa. Why, even councils contradict popes and popes, councils.

"As to the duty of studying the Bible for ourselves — we have the Master's own command: 'Search the Scriptures,' — which settles the question at once for all His obedient disciples. And no one who sets himself to the work humbly and teachably, looking to the Holy Spirit for enlightenment will fail to find the path to heaven. 'The way-faring men, though fools shall not err therein.' Jesus said 'the Comforter which is the Holy Ghost, whom the father will send in my name, He shall teach you all things.'

"And, my child, none of us is responsible for the interpretation that his neighbor puts upon God's word, His letter addressed to us all. Each of us must give account of himself to God."

Violet's doubts and perplexities had vanished like morning mist before the rising sun. Her natural gaiety of spirits returned, and she became again, as was her wont, the sunshine of the house, full of life and hope, with a cheery word and sunny smile for everyone — from Mr. Daly down to Rosie, and from Aunt Chloe to the youngest child in the quarter.

She had not been so happy since the departure of her parents.

Eddie, Molly and the younger ones reflected in some measure her bright hopefulness and the renewed ardor with which she pursued her studies. For some days all went on prosperously at Ion.

Then came a change.

One evening Vi, having seen Rosie to bed and bade Harold and Herbert goodnight also, returned to the schoolroom where Eddie and their cousin were busied with their preparations for the morrow's recitations.

She had settled herself before her desk and was taking out her books when the sound of horses' hooves coming swiftly up the avenue caused her to spring up and run to the window.

"It is grandpa," she said. "He seldom comes so late. Oh, Eddie!" and she dropped into a chair, her heart beating wildly.

"Don't be alarmed," Eddie said, rising and coming toward her, his own voice trembling with apprehension. "It may be good news again."

"Oh, do you think so? Can it be?" she asked.

"Surely, Vi, uncle would not come as fast as possible if he had good news to bring," said Molly. "Perhaps it is that they are coming home. It is getting so late in the fall now that I'm expecting every day to here that."

"Let's go down to grandpa," cried Vi, rising, while a faint color stole into her cheek which had grown very pale at the thought that the little pet sister might be dead or dying. "No, no," as a step was heard on the stairs, "he is coming to us."

The door opened and Mr. Dinsmore entered. One look into his grief-stricken face and Violet threw herself into his arms and wept upon his chest.

He soothed her with silent caresses, his heart almost too full for speech. But, at length, "It is not the worst," he said in low, moved tones. "She is alive but has had a relapse. They are bringing her home."

"Home to die!" echoed Violet's heart, and she clung about her grandfather's neck, weeping almost convulsively.

Tears coursed down Molly's cheeks also; and Eddie, hardly less overcome than his sister, asked tremulously, "How soon may we expect them, grandpa?"

"In about two days, I think. And my dear children, we must school ourselves to meet Lily with calmness and composure lest we injure by exciting and agitating her. We must be prepared to find her more feeble than when she went away and much exhausted by the fatigue of the journey."

Worse than when she went away? And even then the doctors had no hope! It was almost as if they already saw her lying lifeless before them.

They wept themselves to sleep that night and in the morning it was as though death had already entered the house. A solemn stillness reigned in all its rooms, and the quiet tread, the sad, subdued tones, the oft falling tear, attested to the warmth of affection in which the dear, dying child was held.

A parlor car was speeding southward. It's occupants were a noble-looking man; a lovely matron; a blooming, beautiful girl of seventeen; a rosy babe in his nurse's arms; and a pale, fragile, golden-haired, blue-eyed child of seven. She was lying now on the couch with her head in her mother's lap, now resting in her father's arms for a little.

She seemed the central figure of the group. All eyes turned ever and again upon her in tenderest solicitude. Every ear was attentive to her slightest complaint, every hand ready to minister to her wants.

She was very quiet, very patient, answering their anxious, questioning words and looks with many a sweet, affectionate smile or whisper of grateful appreciation of their ministry of love.

Sometimes she would beg to be lifted up for a moment that she might see the rising or setting sun, or gaze upon the autumnal glories of the woods. And as they grew near their journey's end she would ask, "Are we almost there, papa? Shall I soon see my own sweet home and dear brothers and sisters?"

At last the answer was, "Yes, my darling, in a few moments we shall leave the car for our own easy carriage, and one short stage will take us home to Ion."

Mr. Dinsmore, his son, and Arthur Conley met them at the station and told how longingly their dear ones at home were looking for them.

The sun had set, and shadows began to creep over the landscape as the carriage stopped before the door and

Lily was lifted out, borne into the house and gently laid upon her own little bed.

She was nearly fainting with fatigue and weakness, and dearly as the others were loved, father and mother had no eyes for any but her. There was no word of greeting as the one bore her past. The others hastily followed with the doctor and grandfather to her room.

But Elsie and Vi quickly locked in each other's arms, mingling their tears together, while Rosie and the boys gathered round, waiting their turn.

"Oh!" sobbed Rosie, "mamma didn't speak to me; she didn't look at me. She doesn't love me anymore, nor my papa either."

"Yes they do, little pet," Elsie said, leaving Violet to embrace the little sister. "And sister Elsie loves you dearly; Harold and Herbert, too; as well as our big oldest brother," smiling up at Eddie through her tears, as he stood by her side.

He bent down to kiss her sweet lips.

"Lily?" he said in a choking voice.

With a great effort Elsie controlled her emotion, and answered low and tremulously, "She is almost done with pain. She is very happy — no doubt, no fear, only gladness that soon she will be 'Safe in the arms of Jesus, Safe on his gentle breast.' "

Eddie turned away with a broken sob. Vi uttered a low cry of anguish and Rosie and the boys broke into a wail of sorrow.

Till that moment they had not given up hope that the dear one might even yet be restored.

In the sickroom, the golden head lay on a snow-white pillow. The blue eyes were closed and the breath came in pants from the pale, parted lips.

"Cousin Arthur" had his finger on the slender wrist, counting its pulses while father and grandfather stood looking on in anxious solicitude. The mother bent low over her fading flower asking in tender whispered accents, "are you in pain, my darling?"

"No, mamma, only so tired, so tired!"

Only the mother's quick ear, placed close to the pale lips, could catch the low-breathed words.

The doctor administered a cordial, then a little nourishment was given, and the child fell asleep.

The mother sat watching her, lost to all else in the world. Arthur came to her side with a whispered word about her own need of rest and refreshment after her fatiguing journey.

"How long?" she asked in the same low tone, glancing first at the white face on the pillow, then at him.

"Some days, I hope. She is likely now to sleep for hours. Let me take your place."

Elsie bent over the child, listening for a moment to her breathing; then, accepting his offer, followed her husband and father from the room.

Rosie, waiting and watching in the hall without, sprang to her mother's embrace with a low, joyful cry. "Mamma, mamma! Oh, you've been gone so long! I thought you'd never come back."

"Mamma is very glad to be with you again," Elsie said, holding her close for a moment; then, giving her to her father, she sought the others — all near at hand, and waiting eagerly for a sight of her loved face, a word from her gentle lips.

They were all longing for one of the old confidential talks, Violet, perhaps, more than the others. But it could not be now. The mother could scarcely allow herself time for a little rest ere she must return to her station by the side of the sick bed.

But Molly was not forgotten or neglected. Elsie went to her with kind inquiries, loving cheering words and a message from Dick, whom she had seen a few days before.

"How kind and thoughtful for others she is! How sweet and gentle, how patient and resigned. I will try to be more like her. How truly she obeys the command 'be compassionate, be courteous.' But why should one so lovely, so devoted a Christian, be visited with so sore a trial? I can see why my trials were sent. I was so proud and worldly. They were necessary to show me my need of Jesus, but she has loved and leaned upon Him since she was a little child."

CHAPTER TWENTIETH

Let them die,
Let them die now, thy children! So thy heart
Shall wear their beautiful image all undimm'd
Within it to the last.

— MRS. HEMANS.

LILY SEEMED A LITTLE STRONGER in the morning and the brothers and sisters were allowed to go in by turns and speak to her.

Violet chose to be the last thinking that would, perhaps, secure a little longer interview.

Lily with mamma by her side lay propped up with pillows — her eyes bright, a lovely color on her almost transparent cheek, her luxurious hair lying about her like heaps of shining gold, her red lips smiling a joyous welcome, as Vi stooped over her.

Could it be that she was dying?

"Oh, darling, you may get well even yet!" cried Vi, in tones tremulous with joy and hope.

Lily smiled and stroked her sister's face lovingly with her little thin white hand.

Violet was startled by its scorching heat.

"You are burning up with fever!" she exclaimed, tears gushing from her eyes.

"Yes, but I shall soon be well," said the child clasping her sister close. "I'm going home to the happy land to be with Jesus, Vi. Oh, don't you wish you were going too? Mamma I'm tired; please tell Vi my text."

" 'And the inhabitant shall not say, I am sick; the people that dwell therein shall be forgiven their iniquity,' " the mother repeated in a low sweet voice.

"For Jesus' sake," softly added the dying one. "He has loved me and washed me from my sins in His own blood."

Vi fell on her knees by the bedside, and buried her face in the sheets, vainly trying to stifle her bursting sobs.

"Poor Vi," sighed Lily. "Mamma, comfort her."

Mamma drew the weeper to her bosom and spoke tenderly to her of the loving Savior and the home He has gone to prepare for His people.

"Our darling will be so safe and happy there," she said, "and she is glad to go, to rest in His bosom and wait there for us, as, in His own good time, he shall call one after another to Himself.

'Tis there we'll meet,
At Jesus' feet,
When we meet to part no more.'

Tears were coursing down the mother's cheeks as she spoke, but her manner was calm and quiet.

To her, as to her child standing upon the brink of Jordan, heaven seemed very near, very real. While mourning that soon that beloved face and form would be seen no more on earth, she rejoiced with joy unspeakable for the blessedness that should be hers forever and for evermore.

There were no tears in Lily's eyes. "Mamma, I'm so happy," she said smiling. "Dear Vi, you must be glad for me and not cry so. I have no pain today and I'll never have any more when I get home where the dear Savior is. Mamma, please read about the beautiful city."

Elsie took up the Bible that lay beside the pillow. And opening to the Revelation, read its last two chapters — the twenty-first and the twenty-second.

Lily lay intently listening; Violet's hand fast clasped in hers.

"Darling Vi," she whispered, "you love Jesus, don't you?"

Violet nodded assent; she could not speak.

"And you're willing to let Him have me, aren't you, dear?"

"Yes, yes," but the tears fell fast. "Oh, what shall I do without you?" she cried with a choking sob.

"It won't be long," said Lily. "Mamma says it will seem only a very little while when it is past."

Her voice sank with the last words, and she closed her eyes with a weary sigh.

"Go, dear daughter, go way for the present," the mother said to Violet, who instantly obeyed.

Lily lingered for several days, suffering little except for weakness. She was always patient and cheerful, talking so joyfully of "going home to Jesus," that death seemed robbed of all its gloom. For it was not of the grave they thought in connection with her, but of the glories of the upper sanctuary, the bliss of those who dwell forever with the Lord.

Father, brothers and sisters often gathered for a little while about her bed, for she dearly loved them all. But the mother scarcely left her day or night. The mother whose gentle teachings had guided her childish feet into the path that leads to God, whose ministry of love had made the short life bright and happy in spite of weakness and pain.

It was in the early morning that the end came.

She had been sleeping quietly for some hours, sleeping while darkness passed away till day had fully dawned and the east was flushing with crimson and gold.

Her mother sat by the bedside gazing with tender glistening eyes upon the little wan face, thinking how placid was its expression, what an almost unearthly beauty it wore, when suddenly the large azure eyes opened wide, gazing steadily into hers, while the sweetest smile played about the lips.

"Mamma, dear mamma, how good you've been to me! Jesus is here. He has come for me. I'm going now. Dear, darling mamma, kiss me goodbye."

"My darling! My darling!" Elsie cried, pressing a kiss of passionate love upon the sweet lips.

"Dear mamma," they faintly whispered — and were still.

Kneeling by the bedside, Elsie gathered the little wasted form in her arms, pillowing the beautiful golden head upon her bosom, while again and again she kissed the pale brow, the cheeks, the lips. Then, laying it down gently she stood gazing upon it with unutterable love and mingled joy and anguish.

"It was well with the child," and no rebellious thought arose in her heart; but, oh, what an aching void was there! How empty were her arms, though so many of her darlings were still spared for her.

A quiet step drew near, a strong arm was passed about her waist, and a kind hand drew her head to a resting-place on her husband's shoulder.

"Is it so?" he said in moved tones, gazing through a mist of tears upon the quiet face of the young sleeper. "Oh, darling, our precious lamb is safely folded at last. He has gathered her in His arms and is carrying her in His bosom."

They laid her body in the family burial ground and mamma and the children went very often to scatter flowers upon the graves, reserving the fairest and sweetest for the little mound that looked so fresh and new.

"But she is not here," Rosie would say, "She's gone to the dear home above where Jesus is. And she's so happy. She'll never be sick any more because it says, 'Neither shall there be any more pain.' "

Lily was never spoken of as lost or as dead. She had only gone before to the happy land where they all were journeying and where they should find her again, blooming and beautiful. They spoke of her often and with cheerfulness, though tears would sometimes fall at the thought that the separation must be so long.

Elsie was much worn out with the long nursing that she would not resign to other hands; and, as Mr. and Mrs. Daly were well pleased to have it so arranged, they still retained their posts in the household.

But the children again enjoyed the pleasant evening talks and the prized morning half-hour with mamma. They might go to her at other times also, and it was not long before Vi found an opportunity to unburden her mind by a full account of all the doubts and perplexities that had so troubled her. She also recounted the manner in which they had been removed, to her great comfort and peace.

It was in the afternoon of the second day after the funeral. The two older girls were alone with their mother in her boudoir.

Elsie was startled at the thought of the peril her child had been in.

"I blame myself," she said, "that I have not guarded you more carefully against these fearful errors. We will now take up the subject together, my children and I, and study it thoroughly. And we will invite Isa and Virgy to join with us in our search after truth."

"Molly also, mamma, if she is willing," suggested her namesake daughter.

"Certainly, but I count her among my children. Ah, I have not seen her for several days! I fear she has been feeling neglected. I will go to her now," she added, rising from the couch on which she had been reclining. "And you may both go with me, if you wish."

Isa had been with Molly for the last half-hour. "I came on that unpleasant business of making a call of condolence," she announced on her entrance. "But they told me Cousin Elsie was lying down to rest and her girls were with her — Elsie and Vi — so, not wishing to disturb them, I'll visit with you first, if you like."

"I'm glad to see you," Molly said. "Please be seated."

Isadore seemed strangely embarrassed and sat for some moments without speaking.

"What's the matter, Isa?" Molly asked at length.

"I think it was really unkind in mamma to send me on this errand. It was her place to come, but she said Cousin Elsie was so bound up in that child that she would be overwhelmed with grief. And she (mamma) would not know what to say. She always found it the most awkward thing in the world to try to console people under such afflictions."

"It will not be at all necessary," returned Molly dryly. "Cousin Elsie has all the consolation she needs. She came to me for a few minutes the very day Lily died, and though I could see plainly that she had been weeping, her face was perfectly calm and peaceful. And she told me that her heart sang for joy when she thought of her darling's blessedness."

Isa looked very thoughtful.

"I wish I were sure of it," she said half unconsciously. "She was such a dear little thing."

"Sure of what?" cried Molly indignantly. "Can you doubt for a moment that that child is in heaven?"

"If she had only been baptized into the true church. But there, don't look so angry! How can I help wishing it when I know it's the only way to be saved?"

"But you don't know it! You can't know it, because it isn't so. Oh, Isadore, how could you turn Roman Catholic and then try to turn Violet?"

"So you've heard about it? I supposed you had," said Isadore coloring. "I suppose too, that Cousin Elsie is very angry with me, and that is why I thought it so unkind in mamma to send me in her place, making an excuse of a headache. It was not a bad enough one to prevent her coming, I'm sure."

"I don't know how Cousin Elsie feels about it, or even whether she has heard it," said Molly. "Though I promise she has, as Vi never conceals anything from her."

"Well, I've only done my duty and can't feel that I'm deserving of blame," said Isadore. "But such a time as I've had of it since my conversion became known in the family!"

"Your perversion, you should say," interrupted Molly. "Was Aunt Louise angry?"

"Very, but principally, I could see, because she knew grandpa and Uncle Horace would reproach her for sending me to the convent."

"And did they?"

"Yes, grandpa was furious, and of course uncle said, 'I told you so.' He has only reasoned with me, though he let me know he was very much displeased about Vi. Cal and Art, too, have undertaken to convince me of my errors, while Virginia sneers and asks why I could not be content to remain a Protestant. Altogether, I've had a sweet time of it for the last two weeks."

"There's a tap at the door. Will you please open it?" asked Molly.

It was Mrs. Travilla, Elsie and Violet whom Isadore admitted. She recognized them with a deep blush and an embarrassed, deprecating air. For the thought instantly struck her that Vi had probably just been telling her mother what had occurred during her absence.

"Ah, Isa, I did not know you were here," her cousin said taking her hand. "I am pleased to see you."

The tone was gentle and kind and there was not a trace of displeasure in look or manner.

"Thank you cousin," Isa said, trying to recover her composure. "I came to — mamma has a headache, and sent me — ."

"Yes, never mind. I know all you would say," Elsie answered, tears trembling in her soft brown eyes, but a look of perfect peace and resignation on her sweet face. "You feel for my sorrow, and I thank you for your sympathy. But, Isa, the consolations of God are not small with me, and I know that my little one is safe with Him."

"Molly, my child, how are you today?"

"Very well, thank you," Molly answered, clinging to the hand that was offered her, and looking up with dewy eyes into the calm, beautiful face bending over her. "How kind you are to think of me at such a time as this. Ah cousin, it puzzles me to understand why afflictions should be sent to one who already seems almost an angel in goodness."

Elsie shook her head. "You cannot see my heart, Molly, and the Master knows just how many strokes of His chisel are needed to fashion the soul in His image. He will not make one too many! Beside should I grudge Him one of the many darlings He has given me, or her the bliss He has taken her to? Ah, no, no! His will be done with me and mine."

She sat down upon a sofa, and making room for Isa,

who had been exchanging greetings with her younger cousins, invited her to a seat by her side.

"I want to talk with you," she said gently. "Vi has been telling me everything. Ah, do not think I have any reproaches for you, though nothing could have grieved me more than your success in what you attempted."

She then went on to give, in her own gentle, kindly way, good and sufficient reasons for her dread and hatred of — not Catholics — but Popery. She concluded by inviting Isa to join with them in a thorough investigation of its arrogant claims.

Isa consented, won by her cousin's generous forbearance and affectionate interest in her welfare, and arrangements were made to begin the very next day.

Molly's writing desk stood open on the table by her side, and Violet's bright eyes catching sight of the address on a letter lying there exclaimed, "Oh, cousin, have you heard? And is it good news?"

"Yes," replied Molly, a flush of pride and pleasure mantling her cheek. "I should have told you at once, if — under ordinary circumstance — but —" and her eyes filled as she turned them upon Mrs. Travilla.

"Dear child, I am interested now and always in your plans and pleasures," responded the latter, "and shall heartily rejoice in any good that has come to you."

Then Molly, blushing and happy, explained that she had been using her spare time for months past in making a translation of a French story. She had offered it for publication, and, after weeks of anxious waiting, had that morning received a letter announcing its acceptance, and enclosing a check for a hundred dollars.

"My dear child, I am proud of you — of the energy, patience and perseverance you have shown," her cousin said warmly, and with a look of great gratification. "Success, so gained, must be very sweet, and I offer you my hearty congratulations."

The younger cousins added theirs, Elsie and Vi rejoicing as at a great good to themselves, and Isa expressing extreme surprise at the discovery that Molly had attained to so much knowledge, and possessed sufficient talent for such an undertaking.

CHAPTER TWENTY-FIRST

Vice is a monster of so frightful mien,
As to be hated needs but to be seen;
Yet seen too oft, familiar with her face,
We first endure, then pity, then embrace.

— POPE

THE WINTER AND SPRING PASSED very quietly at Ion. At Roselands there was more gaiety, the girls going out frequently and receiving a good deal of company at home.

Virginia was seldom at Ion, but Isadore spent an hour there almost every day pursuing the investigation proposed by her cousin Elsie.

She was an honest and earnest inquirer after truth, and at length acknowledged herself entirely convinced of the errors into which she had been led and was entirely restored to the evangelical faith. And more than that, she became a sincere and devout Christian — much to the disgust and chagrin of her worldly-minded mother and Aunt Delaford, who would have been far better pleased to see her a mere butterfly of fashion as were her younger sister and most of her younger friends.

But to her brother Arthur, and at both the Oaks and Ion, the change in Isa was a source of deep joy and thankfulness.

Also, it was a means of leading Calhoun, who had long been halting between two opinions, to come out decidedly upon the Lord's side.

Old Mr. Dinsmore had become quite infirm and Cal now took entire charge of the plantation. Arthur was busy in his profession, and Walter was at West Point preparing to enter the army.

Herbert and Meta Carrington were up north — the one attending college and the other at boarding school. Old Mrs. Carrington was still living, making her home at Ashlands. Through her the Rosses were frequently heard from.

They were still enjoying a large measure of worldly prosperity — Mr. Ross being a very successful merchant. He had taken his son Philip into partnership a year ago and Lucy's letter spoke much of the lad as delighting his father and herself by his business ability and shrewdness.

They had their city residence as well as their country place. Gertrude had made her debut into fashionable society in the fall and spent a very happy winter. The occasional letters she wrote to the younger Elsie were filled with descriptions of the balls, parties, operas and theatricals she attended, the splendors of her own attire, and the elegant dresses worn by others.

It may be that at another time Elsie, so unaccustomed to worldly pleasures, would have found these subjects interesting from their very novelty; but now, while the parting from Lily was so recent, when her happy death had brought the glories of heaven so near, how frivolous they seemed.

They had more attraction for excitable, excitement-loving Violet. Yet, even she, interested for the moment, presently forgot them again as something reminded her of the dear little sister who was not lost but gone before to the better land.

Vi had a warm, loving heart. No one could be fonder of home, parents, and brothers and sisters than she; but, as spring drew on, she began to have a restless longing for change of scene and employment. She had been growing fast and felt both weak and languid.

Both she and Elsie had attained their full height, Vi being a trifle the taller of the two. They grew daily in beauty and grace and were not lovelier in person than in character and mind.

They were as open as the day with their gentle, tender mother and their fond, proud father. He was proud of his lovely wife and his sons and daughters, whose equals he truly believed were not to be found anywhere throughout the whole length and breadth of the land. So Vi was not slow in telling her of desire for change.

It was on a lovely evening in May when all of the family were gathered on the veranda, serenely happy in each other's company. The babe was in his mother's arms, Rosie on her father's knee, the others grouped about them, doing nothing but enjoying the rest and quiet after a busy day with books and work.

Molly in her wheelchair was there in their midst, feeling quite like one of them, looking as contended and even blithesome as any of the rest. She was feeling very glad over her success in a second literary venture, thinking of Dick, too, and how delightful it would be if she could only talk it all over with him.

He had told her in his last letter that she was making him proud of her. What a thrill of delight the words had given her!

"Papa and mamma!" exclaimed Violet, breaking a pause in the conversation, "home is very dear and sweet, and yet — I'm afraid I ought to be ashamed to say it — I want to go away somewhere for awhile, to the seashore, I think; that is, if we can all go and be together."

"I see no objection if all would like it," her father said with an indulgent smile. "What do you say to the plan, little wife?"

"I echo my husband's sentiments as a good wife should," she answered with something of the sportiveness of other days.

"And we echo yours, mother," said Edward, "do we not?" as he appealed to the others.

"Oh, yes, yes!" they cried, "a summer at the seashore, by all means."

"In a cottage home of our own, shall it not be, papa?" added Elsie.

"Your mamma decides all such questions," was his smiling rejoinder.

"I approve the suggestion. It is far preferable to hotel

life," she said. "Molly, my child, you are the only one who has not spoken."

Molly's bright face had clouded a little. "I want you all to go and enjoy yourselves," she said, "though I shall miss you sadly."

"Miss us! Do you then intend to decline going along?"

Molly colored and hesitated. "I'm such a troublesome piece of furniture to move," she said half in jest, bravely trying to cover up the real pain that came with the thought.

"That is nothing," said Mr. Travilla, so gently and tenderly that happy, grateful tears sprang to her eyes. "You go, of course, with the rest of us — unless there is some more important objection — such as disinclination on your part. And even that should, perhaps, be overruled for the change would do you good."

"Oh, Molly, you will not think of staying behind?"

"We should miss you sadly," said Elsie and Vi.

"And if you go you'll see Dick," suggested Eddie.

Molly's heart bounded at the thought. "Oh," she said, her eyes sparkling, "how delightful that would be! And since you are all so kind, I'll be glad, very glad to go."

"Here comes grandpa's carriage. I'm so glad!" exclaimed Herbert, the first to spy it as it turned in at the avenue gate. "Now I hope they'll say they'll all go too."

He had his wish. The carriage contained Mr. and Mrs. Dinsmore, and their son and daughter. It soon appeared that they had come to propose the very thing Herbert desired — that adjacent cottages at the seashore should be engaged for the two families and that all spend the summer there together.

It was finally arranged that the Dinsmores should precede the others by two or three weeks, then Mr. Dinsmore would return for his daughter and her family. Then, Mr. Travilla would follow a little later in the season.

Also, it was decided that the second party should make their journey by water. It would be easier for Molly and newer to all than the land route that they had taken much more often in going north.

"Dear me, how I wish we were rich!" exclaimed

Virginia Conly when she heard of it the next morning at breakfast from Cal, who had spent the evening at Ion. "I'd like nothing better than to go north for the summer — not to the dull, prosaic life in a cottage though, but to some of the grand hotels where people dress splendidly and have dances and all sorts of gay times. If I had the means I'd go to the seashore for a few weeks and then off to Saratoga for the rest of the season. Mamma, couldn't we manage it somehow? You ought to give Isa and me every advantage possible, if you want us to make good matches."

"I shouldn't need persuasion to gratify you if I had the money, Virginia," she answered dryly, and with a significant glance at her father and sons.

There was no reason from them, for none of them felt able to supply the coveted funds.

"I think it very likely Cousin Elsie will invite you to visit them," remarked Arthur at length, breaking the silence that had followed his mother's remarks.

"I shall certainly accept if she does," said Isa, "for I should dearly like to spend the summer with her there."

"Making garments for the poor, reading good books and singing psalms and hymns," remarked Virginia with a contemptuous sniff.

"Very good employments, all of them," returned Arthur quietly, "though I feel safe in predicting that a good deal more time will be spent by the Travillas in swimming, riding, driving, boating and fishing. They are not ascetics, but the most cheerful, happy family I have ever come across."

"Yes, it's quite astonishing how easily they've taken the death of that child," said Mrs. Conly ill naturedly.

"Mother, how can you!" exclaimed Arthur, indignant at the insinuation.

"Oh, mamma, no one could think for a moment it was from want of affection!" cried Isadore.

"I have not said so. But you can't tell me, I suppose, how Molly assured you her cousin had no need of consolation?"

"Yes, mother, but it was that her grief was swallowed up in the realizing sense of the bliss of her dear departed child. Oh, they all talk of her to this day with glad tears in their eyes — sorrowing for themselves but rejoicing for her."

Elsie did give a cordial invitation to her aunt and the two girls to spend the summer with her. It was accepted at first, but declined afterward when a letter came from Mrs. Delaford inviting them to join her in some weeks' sojourn, at her expense, first at Cape May and afterward at Saratoga.

It would be the gay life of dressing, dancing and flirting at great hotels for which Virginia hungered, and so Virginia and her mother snatched at it with great eagerness.

Isadore would have preferred to be with the Travillas, but Mrs. Conly would not hear of it.

Aunt Delaford would be mortally offended. And the idea of throwing away such a chance! Was Isa crazy? It would be well enough to accept Elsie's offer to pay their traveling expenses and provide each with a handsome outfit, but her cottage would be no place to spend the summer when they could do so much better. There would be few gentlemen there. Elsie and Mr. Travilla were so absurdly particular as to whom they admitted to an acquaintance with their daughters. If there was the slightest suspicion against a man's moral character, he might as well wish for the moon as for entrance to their house — or so much as a bowing acquaintance with Elsie and Vi. It was really too absurd.

"But, mamma," expostulated Isadore, "surely you would not be willing that we should associate with anyone who was not of irreproachable character?"

Mrs. Conly colored and looked annoyed.

"There is no use in being too particular, Isadore," she said. "One can't expect perfection. Young men are very apt to be a little wild, and they often settle down afterward into very good husbands."

"Really, I don't think any the worse of a young fellow for sowing a few wild oats," remarked Virginia, with a toss of her head. "They're a great deal more interesting than your good young men."

"Such as Cal and Art," suggested Isa, smiling slightly. "Mamma, don't you wish they'd be a little wild?"

"Nonsense, Isadore! Your brothers are just what I would have them to be! I don't prefer wild young men, but I hope I have sense enough not to expect everybody's sons to be as good as mine and charity enough to overlook the imperfections of those who are not."

"Well, mamma," said Isadore with great seriousness, "I have talked this matter over with Cousin Elsie, and I think she takes the right view of it. The rule should be as strict for men as for women. The sin that makes a woman an outcast from decent society should receive the same condemnation when committed by a man. A woman should require the same absolute moral purity in the man she marries as men do in the women they choose for wives. So long as we are content with anything less, so long as we smile on men whom we know to be immoral, we are in a measure responsible for their vices."

"I endorse that sentiment," said Arthur, coming in from the adjoining room. "It would be a great restraint upon men's vicious inclinations, if they knew that indulgence in vice would shut them out of ladies' society."

"A truce on the subject — I'm tired of it," said Virginia. "Is it decided, mamma, that we take passage in the steamer with the Travillas?"

"Yes, and now let us turn our attention to the much more agreeable topic of dress. There are a good many questions to settle in regard to it — what we must have, what can be got here, and what after we reach Philadelphia."

"And how one dollar can be made to do the work of two," added Virginia, "for there are loads and loads of things I must have in order to make a respectable appearance at the watering places."

"And we have just two weeks in which to make our arrangements," added her mother.

Chapter Twenty-second

Such sheets of fire, such bursts of horrid thunder
Such groans of roaring wind and rain, I never
Remember to have heard.

— Shakespeare

Early in the morning of a perfect June day, the numerous parties arrived at the wharf where lay the steamer that was to carry them to Philadelphia.

The embarkation was made without incident. Molly had had a nervous dread of her share in it, but under her uncle's careful supervision was conveyed safely on board.

The weather was very warm, the sea perfectly calm, and as they steamed out of the harbor a pleasant breeze sprang up and the voyage began most prosperously.

There were a hundred lady passengers, and not more than a dozen were gentlemen. But to Virginia's delight one of the latter was a gay dashing young army officer with whom she had a slight acquaintance.

He caught sight of her directly, hastened to greet her and they were soon promenading the deck together, engaged in an evident flirtation.

Mr. Dinsmore, seated at some little distance with his daughter and her children about him, watched his niece's proceedings with a deepening frown. He was not pleased with either her conduct or her companion.

At length, rising and approaching his sister, he asked, "Do you know that young man, Louise?"

"Not intimately," she returned, bridling. "He is Captain Brice of the army."

"Do you know his character?"

"I have heard that he belongs to a good family and I can see that he is a gentleman. I hope you are satisfied."

"No, I am not, Louise. He is a wild, reckless fellow, fond of drink, gambles —."

"And what of it?" she interrupted. "I don't suppose he's going to teach Virginia to do either."

"He is no fit associate for her or for any lady. Will you interpose your authority?"

"No, I won't. I'm not going to insult a gentleman and I'm satisfied that Virginia has sense enough to take care of herself."

"Waiving the question whether a man of his character is a gentleman, let me remark that it is not necessary to insult him in order to put a stop to this. You can call your daughter to your side, keep her with you, take an early opportunity to inform her of the man's reputation and bid her discourage his attentions. If you do not interfere," he added in his determined way, "I shall take the matter into my own hands."

"Isadore," said Mrs. Conly, "go and tell your sister I wish to speak to her."

Virginia was extremely vexed at the summons, but obeyed it promptly.

"What can mamma want? I was having such a splendid time," she said peevishly to her sister when they were out of the captain's hearing.

"It is more Uncle Horace than mamma."

Virginia reddened. She knew her uncle's opinions and she was not entirely ignorant of the reputation of Captain Brice.

She feigned ignorance however, listened with apparent surprise to her uncle's account of him and promised sweetly to treat him with the most distant politeness in the future.

Mr. Dinsmore saw through her, but what more could he do, except keep a strict watch over both?

The captain, forsaken by Virginia, sauntered to the deck and presently approached an elderly lady who sat somewhat apart from the rest, lifted his cap with a smiling, "How do you do, Mrs. Noyes?" Taking an empty chair by her side, he entered into a desultory conversation.

"By the way," he said, "what an attractive family group is that over yonder," with a slight motion of his head in the direction of the Travillas. "The mother is my ideal of a lovely matron, in appearance at least. I have not the happiness of her acquaintance, and the daughters are models of beauty and grace. They are from your neighborhood, I believe?"

"Yes, I have a calling acquaintance with Mrs. Travilla. She was a great heiress. She has peculiar notions — rather puritanical — but is extremely agreeable for all that."

"Could you give me an introduction?"

She shook her head. "I must beg you to excuse me."

"But why?"

"Ah, captain, do you not know that you have the reputation of being a naughty man? Not very, but then, as I have told you, the mother is very strict and puritanical in her ideas. The father is the same. I should only offend them without doing you any good. The girls would not dare or even as much as wish to look at or speak to you."

Growing red and angry, the captain stammered out something about being no worse than nine-tenths of the rest of the world.

"Very true, no doubt," she said, "and please understand that you are not tabooed by me. I'm not so strict. But perhaps," she added laughing, "it may be because I've no daughters to be endangered by young fellows who are as handsome and fascinating as they are naughty." He bowed his acknowledgments; then, as a noble looking young man was seen to approach the group with the manner of one on a familiar footing, inquired, "Who is that fellow that seems so much at home with them?"

"His name is Leland, Lester Leland. He's the nephew of the Leland who bought Fairview from the Fosters some years ago. He's an artist and poor — the nephew — he had to work his own way in the world, has to yet for that matter. I should wonder at the notice the Travillas take of him, only that I've heard he's one of the good sort. Then, besides, you know he may make a good reputation some day."

"A pious fortune hunter, I presume," sneered Brice, rising to give his seat to a lady. Then, with a bow, he turned and walked away.

Mr. Dinsmore was taking his grandsons over the vessel, showing them the engine and explaining its complicated machinery.

Edward, who had quite a mechanical turn, seemed to understand it nearly as well as his grandfather. Harold and Herbert, bright, intelligent boys of ten and twelve, looked and examined with much interest, asking sensible questions and listening attentively to the replies.

They were active, manly little fellows, not foolhardy or inclined to mischief, nor was their mother the over-anxious kind. She could trust them. And when the tour of inspection with their grandpa was finished, they were allowed to roam about by themselves.

Captain Brice took advantage of this to make acquaintance with them and win their hearts by thrilling stories of buffalo hunts and encounters with wolves, grizzly bears and Indians, in which he invariably figured as the conquering hero.

He thought to make them stepping stones to an acquaintance with their sisters. He congratulated himself on his success when, on being summoned to return to their mother, they asked eagerly if he would not tell them more tomorrow.

"Just try me, my fine fellows," he answered, laughing.

"Mamma, what do you want with us?" they asked, running up to her. "A gentleman was telling us such nice stories."

"I think the call to supper will come very soon," she said. "I want you to smooth you hair and wash your hands. Dinah will take you to your stateroom and see that you have what you need."

"I'm afraid we're going to have a gust," remarked

Isadore as the lads hurried away to do their mother's bidding. "See how the clouds are gathering yonder in the northwest?"

"A thunder storm at sea, how romantic!" said Virginia. "'Twill be something to talk about all our lives."

"Silly child!" said her mother. "To hear you talk, one would think there was no such thing as danger."

"Pshaw, mamma! We're hardly out of sight of land — our own shores," she retorted.

"That would but increase our danger if the storm were coming from the opposite direction," said her uncle. "Fortunately, it is from a quarter to drive us out to sea."

"Do you think it will be a gust, grandpa?" asked Violet, a little anxiously.

"I fear so. The heat has become so oppressive, the breeze has entirely died down, and the clouds look threatening. But, my child, do not fear. Our Father, God, rules upon the sea as well as the land, the stormy wind fulfilling His word."

The storm came up rapidly, bursting on them in its fury before they had left the tea table. The lightning's flash and the crash and roll of the thunder followed in quick succession. The stentorian voices of the officers of the vessel, shouting their orders to the crew, the heavy hasty tramp of the men's feet, the whistling of the wind through the rigging, the creaking of the cordage, the booming of the sea mingling with the terrific thunder claps and the down pouring of the rain all combined in an uproar fit to cause the stoutest heart to quake.

Faces grew pale with fear. The women and children huddled together in frightened groups; the men looked anxiously at each other, and between the thunder peals, spoke in low tones of the danger of being driven out to sea. They asked each other of the captain's skill, on what part of the coast they were, and whether the vessel was strong enough to outride the tempest, should it continue very long.

"Oh, this is dreadful! I'm afraid we shall all go to the bottom if it keeps on much longer," Mrs. Conly was saying to her niece, when there came a crash as if the very sky were falling — as if it had come down upon them. There was a shock that threw some of them from their seats, while others caught at the furniture to save themselves. The vessel shivered from stem to stern, seemed to stand still for an instant, then rushed on again.

"It struck! We're lost!" cried a number of voices, while many women and children screamed, and some fainted.

"Courage, my friends!" called Mr. Dinsmore in loud clear tones that could be distinctly heard by all above the storm. "All is not lost that is in danger. And the 'Lord's hand is not shortened that it cannot save; neither his ear heavy that it cannot hear.' "

"Yes, it is time to pray," said an excited, answering voice. "The lightening has struck and shivered the mast. And look how it has run along over our heads and down yon mirror, as you may see by the melting of the glass. It has doubtless continued on to the hold and set fire to the cotton stored there." The speaker — a thin, nervous looking man who was pushing his way through the throng — added this in a whisper close to Mr. Dinsmore's ear.

"Be quiet, will you!" said the latter sternly. "These helpless women and children are sufficiently frightened already."

"Yes, yes, and I don't want to scare 'em unnecessarily, but we'd better be prepared for the worst."

Elsie had overheard the whispers and her cheek paled, a look of keen distress coming over her face as she glanced from one to another of her loved ones. They were dearer by far than was her own life.

But she showed no sign of agitation. Her heart sent up one swift cry to Him to whom "all power is given in heaven and in earth," and faith and love triumphed over her fear. His love to her was infinite and there was no limit to His power. She would trust Him that all would be well whether in life or death.

" 'Even the wind and the sea obey Him,' "she whispered to Violet who was asking with pale trembling lips, "Mamma, mamma, what will become of us?"

"But mamma, they say the vessel is loaded with cotton, and that the lightning has probably set it on fire."

"Still, my darling, He is able to take care of us. 'It is nothing with Him to help whether with many or with them that have no power.' He is the Lord our God."

Her father came to her side. "Daughter my dear, dear daughter!" he said with emotion, taking her in his arms as was his habit in her early years.

"Oh, grandpa, take care of mamma, whatever becomes of us!" exclaimed Elsie and Vi together.

"No, no!" she said, "Save my children and never mind me."

"Mamma, you must be our first care!" said Eddie hoarsely.

"Your sisters, my son, and your brothers. Leave me to the last," she answered firmly.

"We will hope to save you all," Mr. Dinsmore said, trying to speak cheerfully. "But, if you perish, I perish with you."

"Horace, is it true? Is it true that the vessel is on fire?" gasped Mrs. Conly, clutching his arm and staring him in the face with eyes wild with terror.

"Try to calm yourself, Louise," he said kindly. "We do not know certainly yet, though there is reason to fear it may be so."

"Horrible!" she cried, wringing her hands. "I can't die! I've never made any preparations for death. Oh, save me, Horace, if you can! No, no, save my girls, my poor dear girls, and never mind me."

"Louise, my poor sister," he said, deeply moved, "we will not despair yet of all being saved. But try to prepare for the worst. Turn now to Him who has said, 'Look unto Me and be ye saved all ye ends of the earth.' "

Virginia had thrown herself upon a sofa, in strong hysterics, and Isadore stood over her with smelling salts and a fan.

Mrs. Conly hurried back to them with tears rolling down her cheeks.

"Oh, what is to be done?" she sighed, taking the fan from Isadore's hand. "If only Cal and Art were here to look after us! Your uncle has his hands full with his daughter and her children."

"Mamma, let us ask God for help. He and He only can give it," whispered Isadore.

"Yes, yes, ask Him! You know how and He will hear you. Virgy, my child, try to calm yourself."

Isa knelt by her sister's side. There were many on their knees crying for succor in this hour of terrible danger.

The storm was abating. The rain had nearly ceased to fall and the wind to lash the waves into fury. The flashes of lightning were fewer and fainter and the heavy claps of thunder had given place to distant mutterings. They would not be wrecked by the fury of the tempest. Yet, alas, there still remained the more fearful danger of devouring fire.

It was a night of terror. No one thought of retiring, and few but young children closed an eye.

Every precaution was made for taking to the water at a moment's warning. Those that had life preservers — and all of this party were supplied with them — brought them out and secured them to their persons. Boats were made ready to launch, and those who retained sufficient presence of mind and forethought, selected and kept close at hand such valuables as it seemed possible they might be able to carry about them.

The Travillas kept together, Mr. Dinsmore with them. So was young Leland also.

He was to them only an ordinary friend, but one of them he would have died to save. And almost he would have done it for the others for her sake.

Poor Molly had never felt her helplessness more than now — fastened to her chair as with bands of steel, there was less hope of escape for her than for others.

Her thoughts fled to Dick in that first moment of terror, to Dick who loved her better than any other earthly thing. Alas, he was far away. But, there was One near, her Elder Brother, who would never leave her. With that thought, she grew calm and strong to wait and endure.

But her uncle did not forget her. With his own hands, he fastened a life preserver about her.

"My poor helpless child," he said low and tenderly,

"do not fear that you will be forgotten should there be any chance for rescue."

"Thank you, dear, kind uncle," she said with tears in her eyes, "but leave me to the last. My life is worth so much less than theirs," glancing toward her cousins. "There would be only Dick to mourn my loss — ."

"No, no, Molly, we all love you!" he interrupted.

She smiled a little sadly, but went on, "and it would be more difficult to save me than two others."

"Still, do not despair," he said. "I will not leave you to perish alone. And I have hope that in the good providence of God, we shall all be saved."

Gradually the screaming, sobbing and fainting gave place to a dull despairing waiting — waiting with a trembling, sickening dread, for the confirmation of their worst fears.

Rosie had fallen asleep upon a sofa with her head in her eldest sister's lap, Vi on an ottoman beside them, tightly clasping a hand of each.

Elsie had her babe in her arms. He was sleeping sweetly, and laying her head back, she closed her eyes. Her thoughts flew to Ion, to the husband and father who would perhaps learn tomorrow of the loss of all his treasures.

Her heart bled for him, as she seemed to see him bowed down with heart breaking sorrow.

Then arose the question, "What should the end bring to them — herself and her beloved children?"

For herself she could say, "Though I walk through the valley of the shadow of death, I will fear no evil; for Thou art with me." Elsie, Vi and Eddie she had good reason to hope were true Christians. But Harold and Herbert? A pang shot her heart. Good, obedient children though they were, she knew not that they had ever experienced that new birth without which none can enter heaven.

Jesus said, "Verily, verily, I say unto thee, except a man be born again, he cannot see the kingdom of God."

"Mamma, what is it?" Eddie asked, seeing her glance anxiously from side to side.

"Your brothers! I do not see them. Where are they?"

They went into their stateroom a moment ago. They were right here. Shall I call them?"

"Yes, yes, I must speak to them."

They came hand in hand in answer to Eddie's summons.

Herbert's eyes were full of tears, not of terror or grief; there seemed a new happy light in each boyish face.

"Mamma," whispered Harold, putting his arm around her neck, his lips to her ear, "we went away to be alone, Herbie and I. We knew what made you look so sorry at us — because you were afraid we didn't love Jesus. But we do, mamma, and we went away to give ourselves to Him. We mean to be His always, whether we live or die."

Glad tears rolled down her cheeks as she silently embraced first one and then the other.

And so slowly the night wore away. There was a reign of terror for hours while every moment they were watching with despairing hearts for the smell of fire or the bursting out of flames from the hold. Their fears gave way to a faint hope as time passed on and the catastrophe was still delayed. A hope grew gradually stronger and brighter, till at last it was lost in glad certainty.

The electricity, it appeared, had scattered over the iron of the machinery instead of running on down into the hold.

Some said, "What a lucky escape!" Others said "What a kind Providence."

CHAPTER TWENTY-THIRD

Sacred love is basely bought and sold;
Wives are grown traffic, marriage is a trade.

— RANDOLPH

THEY CAME SAFELY INTO PORT. A little crowd of eager, expectant friends stood waiting on the wharf. Among them was a tall, dark-eyed young man with a bright, intellectual face whom Molly, seated on the deck in the midst of the family group, recognized with almost a cry of delight.

The instant a plank was thrown out, he sprang on board, and in another moment she was in his arms sobbing, "Oh, Dick, Dick, I thought I'd never see you again!"

"Why?" he said with a joyous laugh. "We've not been so long or so far apart that you need have been in despair of that."

Then, as he turned to exchange greetings with the others, his ear caught the words, "We had an awful night, expecting every moment to see flames bursting out of the hold."

"What? — what does it mean?" he asked, grasping his uncle's hand, while his cheek paled and he glanced hastily from side to side.

"We have had a narrow escape," said Mr. Dinsmore.

The main facts were soon given, the details as they drove to the hotel. Dick rejoiced with trembling, as he learned how, almost, he had lost these dear ones.

A few days were spent in Philadelphia, and then Mr. Dinsmore and the Travillas sought their seaside homes. Dick went with them.

Mrs. Dinsmore and her daughter Rose, who had been

occupying their cottage for a week or more, hailed their coming with joy.

The Conlys would linger some time longer in the city, laying in a stock of finery for the summer campaign. The, joined by Mrs. Delaford, they too would seek the seashore.

The cottages were quite out of the town, built facing the ocean and as near it as consistent with safety and comfort.

The children hailed the first whiff of the salt sea breeze with eager delight. They were down upon the beach within a few minutes of their arrival. And until bedtime left it only long enough to take their tea, finishing their day with a long moonlit drive along the shore.

They were given perfect liberty to enjoy themselves to the full. The only restrictions were that they were not to go into danger, or out of sight of the house, or to the water's edge unless accompanied by some older member of the family or a trusted servant.

The next morning they were all out again for a ramble before breakfast. Immediately after prayers Vi, Rosie, Harold and Herbert, with a manservant in attendance, returned to the beach.

The girls were collecting shells and seaweed; the boys were skipping stones on the water. Ben, the servant, watched the sport with keen interest and occasionally joined in it.

Absorbed in their amusements, none of them noticed the approach of a young man in undress uniform.

He followed them for some moments in a careless way, as if he were but casually strolling in the same directions. Yet, he was watching with close attention every movement of Vi's graceful figure.

She and Rosie were unconsciously widening the distance between their brothers and themselves, not noticing that the boys had become stationary.

Perceiving this, and that they were now out of earshot, the stranger quickened his pace, and coming up behind the lads, hailed them with "So here you are, my fine fellows! I'm pleased to meet you again!"

"Oh," exclaimed Herbert, looking round, "It's the

gentleman that tells such nice stories! Good morning, sir. We're glad to see you, too."

"Yes, indeed," assented Harold, offering his hand, which the stranger grasped and shook heartily. "We're having a splendid time skipping stones. Did you ever do it?"

"I did, many a time when I was a little chap like you. I used to be a famous hand at it. Let's see if I can equal you now."

He was soon apparently as completely engrossed with the sport as any of them. Yet through it all, he was furtively watching Vi and Rosie as they strolled slowly onward — now stooping to pick up a shell, or pausing a moment to gaze out over the wide expanse of water, then sauntering on again in careless, aimless fashion. They were thoroughly enjoying the entire freedom from ordinary tasks and duties.

The boys knew nothing about their new companion except what they had seen of him on board the vessel. Their mother had not understood who was their story-telling friend, and in the excitement of the storm and the hasty visit to the city, he had been quite forgotten by all three. Nor were any of the family aware of his vicinity. Thus it happened that the lads had not been warned against him.

Vi, however, had seen him with Virginia and knew from what passed directly afterward between her grandfather and aunt (though she did not hear the conversation) that the stranger was not one whom Mr. Dinsmore approved.

Not many minutes had passed before she looked back, and seeing that she had left her brothers some distance behind, hastily began to retrace her steps — Rosie with her.

The instant they turned to do so, the captain, addressing Harold, artfully inquired, "Do you know that young lady?"

"I should think so! She's my own sister," said the boy proudly. "The little one is too."

"Pretty girls, both of them. Won't you introduce me?"

"Yes, I suppose so," returned the boy a little doubtfully. Taking a more critical survey of his new acquaintance than he had thought necessary before, "You — you're a gentleman and a good man, aren't you?"

"Don't I look like it?" laughed the captain. "Would you take me for a rogue?"

"I — I don't believe you'd be a burglar or a thief, but —."

"Well?"

"Please, don't think I mean to be rude, sir, but you broke the third commandment a minute ago."

"The third? Which is that? I really don't remember."

"I thought you'd forgotten it," said Herbert.

"It's the one that says, 'Thou shalt not take the name of the Lord thy God in vain,' " answered Harold in low reverent tones.

"I own to being completely puzzled," said the captain. "I certainly haven't been swearing."

"No, not exactly; but you said, 'by George,' and 'by heaven,' and mamma says such words are contrary to the spirit of the command. And no one who is a thorough gentleman and Christian will ever use them."

"That's a very strict rule," he said, lifting his cap and bowing low to Violet, who was now close at hand.

She did not seem to notice it, or to see him at all.

"Boys," she said with gentle gravity, "let us go home now."

"What for, Vi? I'm not tired of the beach yet," objected Herbert.

"I have something to tell you, something else to propose. Won't you come with me?"

"Yes," and with a hasty "goodbye" to the captain, they joined their sisters who were already moving slowly toward home.

"What have you to tell us, Vi?" asked Harold.

"That I know grandpa does not approve of that man, and I am quite sure mamma would not wish you to be with him. The sun is getting hot and there are Dick and Molly on the veranda. Let's go and talk with them for a while. It's nearly time now for our drive."

"Miss Wi'let," said Ben, coming up behind, "dat fellah's mighty pow'ful mad. He swored a big oath dat you's proud as Lucifer."

"Oh, then we won't have anything more to do with him!" exclaimed the boys. Herbert added, "But I do wish he was good for he does tell such famous stories."

They kept their word and were so shy of the captain that he soon gave up trying to cultivate their acquaintance, or to make that of their sisters.

Mrs. Noyes and he were boarding at the same hotel, and from her he learned that Mrs. Delaford and the Conlys were expected shortly, having engaged rooms on the same floor with her.

The information was agreeable, as, though he did not care particularly for Virginia, flirting with her would, he thought, be rather an enjoyable way of passing the time — all the more so because it would be in opposition to Mr. Dinsmore's wishes. The captain knew very well why, and at whose suggestion, Virginia had been summoned away from his society on board the vessel. And he had no love for the man who so highly disapproved of him.

The girl, too, resented her uncle's interference, and, on her arrival, with the perversity of human nature, went farther in her encouragement of the young man's attentions than she perhaps would otherwise have done.

Her mother and aunt looked on with indifference, if not absolute approval.

Isadore was the only one who offered a remonstrance, and she was cut short with a polite request to "mind her own business."

"I think I am, Virgy," she answered pleasantly. "I'm afraid you're getting yourself into trouble, and surely I ought to try to save you from that."

"I won't submit to surveillance," returned her sister. "I wouldn't live in the same house with Uncle Horace for anything. And if mamma and Aunt Delaford don't find fault, you needn't."

Isadore, seriously concerned for Virginia's welfare, was questioning in her own mind whether she ought to mention the matter to her uncle, when her mother set that doubt at rest by forbidding her to do so.

Isa, who was trying to be a consistent Christian, would neither flirt nor dance, and the foolish, worldly minded mother was more vexed at her behavior than at Virginia's.

Isa slipped away to the cottage homes of the Dinsmores and Travillas whenever she could. She enjoyed the quiet pleasures and the refined and intellectual society of her relatives and the privileged friends, both ladies and gentlemen, whom they gathered about them.

Lester Leland, who had taken up his abode temporarily in that vicinity, was a frequent visitor. He sometimes brought a brother artist with him. Dick's friends came, too, and old friends of the family from far and near.

Elsie sent an early invitation to Lucy Ross to bring her daughters and spend some weeks at the cottage.

The reply was a hasty note from Lucy saying that she deeply regretted her inability to accept, but they were extremely busy making preparations to spend the season at Saratoga and had already engaged their rooms and could not draw back. Besides that, Gertrude and Kate had set their hearts on going. "However," she added, "she would send Phil in her place. He must have a little vacation and he insisted that he would rather visit their old friends the Travillas than go anywhere else in the world. He would put up at a hotel (being a young man, he would of course prefer that) but hoped to spend a good deal of time at the cottage."

He did so and attached himself almost exclusively to the younger Elsie with an air of proprietorship, which she did not at all relish.

She tried to let him see it without being rude. But the blindness of egotism and vast self-appreciation was upon him and he thought her only charmingly coy, probably with the intent to thus conceal her love and admiration.

He was egregiously mistaken. She found him never

the most interesting of companions and at times, an intolerable bore. She was constantly contrasting his conversation which ran upon trade and money making to the exclusion of nearly everything else except fulsome flatteries of herself — with that of Lester Leland, who spoke with enthusiasm of his art. He was a lover of nature and nature's God and his thoughts dwelt among lofty themes, while at the same time he was entirely free from vanity. His manner was as simple and unaffected as that of a little child.

He was a favorite with all the family, his society enjoyed especially by the ladies.

He devoted himself more particularly to sculpture, but also sketched finely from nature, as did both Elsie and Violet. Violet was beginning to show herself a genius in both that and music. Elsie had recently, under Leland's instructions, done some very pretty wood carving and modeling in clay. This similarity of tastes made them very congenial.

Philip's stay was happily not lengthened, business calling him back to New York.

Letters came now and then from Mrs. Ross, Gertrude and Kate, telling of their gay life at Saratoga.

The girls seemed to have no lack of gentleman admirers, among whom was a Mr. Larrabee from St. Louis who was particularly attentive to Gertrude.

At length, it was announced that they were engaged.

It was now the last of August. The wedding was to take place about the middle of October and as the intervening six weeks would barely afford time for the preparation of the trousseau, the ladies hurried home to New York.

Then Kate came down to spend a week with the Travillas.

She looked tired and worn, complained of ennui, was already wearied of the life she had been leading, and had lost all taste for simple pleasures.

Her faded cheek and languid air presented a strange contrast to the fresh, bright beauty and animation of Elsie and Violet — a contrast that pained the kind motherly heart of Mrs. Travilla, who would have been glad to make all the world as happy as she and her children were.

Elsie and Vi felt a lively interest in Gertrude's prospects and had many questions to ask about her betrothed — "Was he young? Was he handsome? Was he a good man? But oh, that was of course."

"No, not of course at all," Kate answered, almost with impatience. "She supposed he was not a bad man; but he wasn't good in their sense of the word — not in the least religious — and he was neither young nor handsome."

A moment of disappointed silence followed this communication. Then Elsie said, a little doubtfully, "Well, I suppose Gerty loves him and is happy in the prospect of becoming his wife?"

"Happy?" returned Kate, with a contemptuous sniff. "Well, I suppose she ought to be; she is getting what she wanted — plenty of money and a splendid establishment. But as to loving Mr. Victor Larrabee — I could about as soon love a — snake, and so could she. He always makes me think of one."

"Oh, Kate! And will she marry him?" both exclaimed in horror.

"She's promised to and doesn't seem inclined to draw back," replied Kate with indifference. Then, bursting into a laugh, "Girls," she said, "I've had an offer too, and mamma would have had me accept it, but it didn't suit my ideas. The man himself is well enough. I don't really dislike him, but such a name! Hogg! Only think of it! I told mamma that I didn't want to live in a sty, if it was lined with gold."

"No, I don't believe I could feel willing to wear that name," said Violet laughing. "But if his name suited, would you marry him without loving him?"

"I suppose so. I like riches and mamma says wealthy men as Mr. Hogg and Mr. Larrabee are not to be picked up every day."

"But, oh, it wouldn't be right, Kate! You have to promise to love."

"Oh, that's a mere form!" returned Kate with a yawn.

"Gerty says she's marrying for love — not of the man but his money," and Kate laughed as if it were an excellent joke.

The other two girls looked grave and distressed. Their mother had taught them that to give the hand without the heart was folly and sin.

Chapter Twenty-fourth

There's many a slip
'Twixt the cup and the lip.

THE TRAVILLAS WERE ALL INVITED to Gertrude's wedding; but as it was to be a very grand affair, the invitation was declined because of their recent bereavement.

Mr. Ross had not seen his intended son-in-law, nor did he know how mercenary were Gertrude's motives. He took for granted that she would not, of her own free will, consent to marry a man who was not at least agreeable to her, though he certainly thought it odd that she should fancy one over forty years older than herself.

He made some inquiries relative to the man's character and circumstances, and learning that he was really very wealthy, and bore a respectable reputation as the world goes, gave his consent to the match.

The preparations went on — dresses and jewels were ordered from Paris, invitations issued to several hundred gucsts, and the reception rooms of their city residence refurnished for the occasion. Money was poured out without stint to provide the wedding feast and flowers, rich and rare, for the adornment of the house and the persons of the girls.

Gertrude did not seem unhappy, but was in a constant state of excitement. She would not allow herself a moment to think.

Ten days before that appointed for the ceremony, the bridegroom arrived in the city and called upon the family.

Mr. Ross did not like his countenance and wondered more than ever at his daughter's choice.

He waited till Mr. Larrabee was gone, then sent for her to come to him in the library.

She came, looking surprised and annoyed. "What is it, papa?" she said impatiently. "Please be as brief as you can, because I've a world of things to attend to."

"So many that you have not a moment to spare for the father you are going to leave so soon?" he said a little sadly.

"Oh, don't remind me of that!" she cried, a sudden change coming over her manner. "I can't bear to think of it!" and creeping up to him, she put her arms around his neck, while a tear trembled in her eye.

"Nor I," he said, caressing her, "not even if I knew you were going to be very happy so far away from me. But I fear you are not. Gertrude, do you love that man?"

"Why, what a question coming from my practical father!" she said, forcing a laugh. "I am choosing for myself, marrying of my own free will. Is that not sufficient?"

"I tell you candidly, Gertrude," he answered, "I do not like Mr. Larrabee's looks. I cannot think it possible that you can love him, and I beg of you if you do not, to draw back even now at this late hour."

"It is too late, papa," she returned, growing cold and hard. "And I do not wish it. Is this all you wanted to say to me?"

"Yes," he said, releasing her with a sigh.

She glided from the room and he spent the next half-hour in pacing slowly back and forth with his hands bowed upon his chest.

The doorbell rang and a servant came in with a card.

Mr. Ross glanced at it, read the name with a look of pleased surprise, and said, "Show the gentleman in here."

The next moment the two were shaking hands and greeting each other as old and valued friends.

"I'm very glad to see you, Gordon!" exclaimed Mr. Ross, "but what happy chance brought you here? Are you not residing somewhere in the West?"

"Yes, in St. Louis. And it is not a happy chance, but a painful duty that has brought me to you tonight."

He spoke hurriedly, as if to be done with an unpleasant task. Mr. Ross's pulses throbbed at the sudden recollection that Larrabee also was a resident of St. Louis.

He turned a quick, inquiring look upon his friend. "Out with it, man! I'm in no mood to wait, whether it be good news or ill."

Gordon glanced toward the door.

Mr. Ross stepped to it and turned the key. Then coming back, seated himself close to his friend with the air of one who is ready for anything.

"Phil, my old chum," said Gordon, clapping him affectionately on the shoulder, "I heard the other day in St. Louis that Larrabee was about to marry a daughter of yours. So I took the first eastern bound train and traveled night and day to get here in time to put a stop to the thing. I hope I am not too late."

"What do you know of the man?" asked Mr. Ross steadily, looking Gordon full in the eye, but with a paling cheek.

"Know of him? I know that he made all his money by gambling and that he is a murderer."

The last word was spoken low and close to the listener's ear.

Mr. Ross started back — horrified — deadly pale.

"Gordon, do you know whereof you affirm?" he asked low and huskily.

"I do. I had the account from one who was an eyewitness to the affair. He is dead now, and I do not suppose it would be possible to prove the thing in a court of justice; but, nevertheless, I assure you it is true."

"It was thirty years ago, on a Mississippi steamer, running between St. Louis and New Orleans, that the deed was done."

"Larrabee, then a professional gambler, was aboard plying his trade. My informant, a man whose veracity I could not doubt, was one of a group of bystanders who saw Larrabee fleece a young man out of several thousand dollars — all he had in the world. Then, enraged by some taunting words from his victim, pulled out a pistol and shot him through the heart, just as they sat there on opposite sides of the gambling table. Then, with his revolver still in his hand, he threatened with terrible oaths and curses to shoot down any man who should attempt to stop him. He rushed on deck, jumped into the river, swam ashore and disappeared into the woods."

"Horrible, horrible!" groaned Mr. Ross, hiding his face in his hands. "And this murderer, this fiend in human form, would have married my daughter!" he cried, starting up in strong excitement. "Why was he allowed to escape? Where is he now?"

"The whole thing passed so quickly, my informant said, that everyone seemed stunned, paralyzed with horror and fright till the scoundrel had made good his escape. Besides, there were several others of the same stamp on board — desperate fellows probably belonging to the same gang — who were evidently ready to make common cause with the ruffian.

"In those days that part of our country was, you know, infested with desperados and outlaws."

"Yes, yes, but what is to be done now? I shall of course send a note to Larrabee at his hotel telling him that all is at an end between him and Gertrude, forbidding him the house and intimating that the sooner he leaves the vicinity the better. But — Gordon, I can never thank you sufficiently for your kindness. Will you add to it by keeping this thing to yourself for the present? I wouldn't for the world have the story get into the papers."

"Certainly, Ross!" returned his friend, grasping his hand in adieu. "I understand how you feel. There is but one person beside ourselves who knows my errand here and I can answer for his silence."

"Who is it?"

"Mr. Hogg, a friend of your wife and daughters."

The news brought by Mr. Gordon sent both Gertrude and her mother into violent hysterics. Mr. Ross and an old nurse who had been in the family for years had their hands full for the rest of the night. It was a sore wound to the pride of both mother and daughter.

"The scoundrel! The wretch! The villain!" cried Gertrude. "I can never hold up my head again. Everybody will be talking about me. Those envious Miss Petitts and their mother will say, "It's just good enough for her. It serves her right for being so proud of the grand match she was going to make. Oh dear, oh dear! Why couldn't that Gordon have stayed away and held his tongue?"

"Gertrude!" exclaimed her father in anger and astonishment, "is this your gratitude to him for saving you from being the wife of a gambler and murderer? You might well be thankful to him and to a Higher Power for your happy escape."

"Yes, of course," said Lucy. "But what are we to do? The invitations are all out. Oh, dear dear, was there ever such a wretched piece of business? Phil, it's real good in you not to reproach me."

" 'Twould be useless now," he sighed, "and I think the reproaches of your own conscience must be sufficient. Not that I would put all the blame on you, though, a full share of it belongs to me."

By morning both ladies had recovered some degree of calmness, but Gertrude obstinately refused to leave her room or to see anyone who might call — even her most intimate friend.

"Tell them I'm sick," she said. "It'll be true enough, for I have an awful headache."

It was to her mother who had been urging her to come down to breakfast that she was speaking.

"Well, I shall send up a cup of tea," said Mrs. Ross. "But what is this?" as the maid entered with a note. "It's directed to you, Gertrude."

"From him, I presume," Gertrude said, as the girl went out and closed the door. "Throw it into the fire, mother, or I'll send it back unopened."

"It is not his hand," said Mrs. Ross, closely scrutinizing the address.

"Then give it to me, please," and almost snatching if

from her mother's hand, Gertrude tore it open and glanced hastily over its contents.

"Yes, I'll see him! He'll be here directly and I must look my best!" she exclaimed, jumping up and beginning to take down her hair.

"See him? Gertrude are you mad? Your father will not allow it."

"Mr. Hogg, mother."

"Oh!"

They exchanged glances and smiles. Mrs. Ross hurried down to breakfast, not to keep her husband waiting. Gertrude presently followed all dressed up and in apparently quite gay spirits — a trifle pale, but only enough to make her interesting, her mother said.

Mr. Ross and Philip, Jr., had already gone away to their place of business. Sophie and the younger boys were off to school and only Mrs. Ross and Kate were left. Kate had little to say but regarded her sister with a sort of contemptuous pity.

Gertrude had scarcely finished her meal when the doorbell rang and she was summoned to the drawing room to receive her visitor.

The wedding came off at the appointed time. There was a change of bridegrooms; that was all. And few could decide whether the invitations had been a ruse, so far as he was concerned — or if that was not so, how the change had been brought about.

In a long letter to Violet Travilla, Kate Ross gave the details of the whole affair.

A strange, sad story it seemed to Vi and her sister. They could not in the least understand how Gertrude could feel or act as she had, and fear she would find, as Kate expressed it, "even a gold-lined sty, but a hard bed to lie in, with no love to soften it."

"Still," they said to each other, "it was better, a thousand times better, than marrying that dreadful Mr. Larrabee."

For Kate had assured them Mr. Hogg was "an honest, honorable man, and not ill-tempered; only an intolerable bore — so stupid and uninteresting."

CHAPTER TWENTY-FIFTH

Whatsoever a man soweth, that shall he also reap.

— GALATIANS 6:7

ELSIE AND HER CHILDREN returned home healthful and happy with scarce any but pleasing recollections of the months that had just passed.

This was not so with Mrs. Conly and Virginia. They seemed soured and disappointed. Nothing had gone right for them. Their finery was all spoiled and they were worn out — with the journey they said, but in reality far more by late hours and dissipation of one sort and another.

The flirtation with Captain Brice had not ended in anything serious — except the establishment of a character for coquetry for Virginia — nor had several others that followed in quick succession.

The girl had much ado to conceal her chagrin. She had started out with bright hopes of securing a brilliant match, and now, though not yet twenty, began to be haunted with the terrible, boding fear of old maidenhood.

She confided her trouble to Isadore one day when a fit of depression had made her unusually communicative.

Isa could scarce forbear smiling, but checked the inclination.

"It is much too soon to despair, Virgy," she said. "But, indeed, I do not think the prospect of living single need make one wretched."

"Perhaps not you who are an heiress, but it's another thing for poor, penniless me."

Isadore acknowledged that that probably did make a difference.

"But," she added, "I hope neither of us will ever be so

silly as to marry for money. I think it must be dreadful to live in such close connection with a man you do not love, even if he is rolling in wealth. Suppose he loses his money directly? There you are tied to him for life without even riches to compensate you for your loss of liberty."

"Dear me, Isa, how tiresome! Where's the use supposing he's going to lose his money?"

"Because it's something not at all unlikely to happen. Riches do take wings and fly away. I do not feel certain that Aunt Delaford's money will ever come to me, or that if it does I may not lose it. So I intend to prepare to support myself if it should ever become necessary."

"How?"

"I intend to take up the study of English again, and also higher mathematics, and make myself thorough in them. I am far from being thorough now because they do not teach them thoroughly at the convent. I want be able to command a good position as a teacher. And let me advise you to do the same."

"Indeed, I've no fancy for such hard work," sneered Virginia. "I'd rather trust to luck. I'll be pretty sure to be taken care of somehow."

"I should think if anyone might feel justified in doing that it would be Cousin Elsie," said Isadore. "But Uncle Horace educated her in such a way to make her quite capable of earning her own living, and she is doing the same by every one of her children."

"Such nonsense!" muttered Virginia.

"Such prudence and forethought, I should say," laughed her sister.

A few days after this, Isadore was calling at Ion and in the course of conversation Mrs. Travilla remarked with concern, "Virginia looks really unhappy of late. Is her trouble anything it would be in my power to relieve?"

"No, unless she would listen to good counsel from you. It is really nothing serious, and yet, I suppose it seems so to her. I'm almost ashamed to tell you, cousin, but as far as I can learn it is nothing in the world but the fear of old maidenhood," Isa answered, half laughing.

Elsie smiled. "Tell her from me that there is plenty of time yet. She is two or three years younger that I was when I married, and" she added with a bright, happy look, "I never thought I lost anything by waiting."

"I'm sure you didn't, mamma," said Violet who was present. "But how very odd of Virgy to trouble about that! I'm glad people don't have to marry, because I shall never, never be willing to leave my dear home and my father and mother — especially not to live with some stranger."

"I hope it may be some years before you change your mind in regard to that," her mother responded with a loving look.

Elsie was not bringing up her daughters to consider marriage the chief end of woman. She had, indeed, said scarcely anything on the subject till her eldest was of an age to begin to mix a little in general society. Then, she talked quietly and seriously to them of the duties and responsibilities of the married state and the vast importance of making a wise choice in selecting a partner for life.

In their childhood she had never allowed them to be teased about beaux. She could not prevent their hearing, occasionally, something of the kind. But she did her best to counteract the evil influence. She had succeeded so well in that, and in making home a delight, that her children one and all shunned the thought of leaving it, and her girls were as easy and free from self-consciousness in the society of gentlemen as in that of ladies — never bold or forward. There was nothing in their manner that could give the slightest encouragement to undue familiarity.

And then, both she and their father had so entwined themselves about the hearts of their offspring that all shared the feeling expressed by Violet. They truly believed that nothing less than death could ever separate them from these beloved parents.

There was a good deal to bring the subject of marriage prominently before their minds at present. The event of the winter was the bringing home of a wife by their Uncle

Horace and "Aunt Rosie" was to be married in the ensuing spring.

The approaching Centennial was another topic of absorbing interest.

That they might reap the full benefit of the great Exhibition, they went north earlier than usual. The middle of May found them in quiet occupancy of a large, handsome, elegantly furnished mansion in the vicinity of Central Park.

Here they kept open house, entertaining a large circle of relatives and friends drawn thither by a desire to see the great World's Fair.

The Dalys were with them, husband and wife in the same capacities as at Ion, which left Mr. and Mrs. Travilla free to come and go as they wished — with or without the children.

They kept their own carriages and horses and when at home drove almost daily to the Exhibition.

Going there with parents and tutor and being able to devote so much time to it, the young people gathered a great store of general information.

Poor Molly's inability to walk shut her out of several of the buildings, but she gave the more time and careful study to those whose contents were brought within her reach by the rolling chairs.

Her cousins gave her glowing descriptions of the treasures of the Art Building, Horticultural Hall, and Women's Department and sincerely sympathized with her deprivation of the pleasure of examining them for herself.

But Molly was learning submission and contentment with her lot and would smilingly reply that she considered herself highly favored in being able to see so much, since there were millions of people even in this land who could not visit the Exhibition at all.

One morning, early in the season, when as yet the crowd was not very great, the whole family had gone in a body to Machinery Hall to see the Corliss engine.

They were standing near it, silently gazing, when a voice was heard in the rear.

"Ah, ha! Ah, ha! Um h'm, ah, ha! What think ye o' that now, my lads? Is it worth looking at?"

"That it is, sir!" responded a younger voice in manly tones, full of admiration, while at the same instant Elsie turned quickly round with the exclamation, "Cousin Ronald!"

"Cousin Elsie!" he responded as hand grasped hand in cordial greeting.

"I'm so glad to see you!" she said. "But why did you not let us know you were coming? Did you not receive my invitation?"

"No, I did not, cousin, and thought to give you a surprise. Ah, Travilla, the sight of your pleasant face does one good like a medicine. And these bonny lads and lasses, can they be the bairns of eight years ago? How they have grown and increased in number too?" he said glancing around the little circle.

He shook hands with each, then introduced his sons — two tall, well built, comely young men aged twenty and twenty-two respectively — whom he had brought with him over the sea.

Malcom was the name of the elder; the other he called Hugh.

They had arrived in Philadelphia only the day before and were putting up at the Continental.

"That will not do at all, Cousin Ronald," Elsie said when told this. "You must all come immediately to us and make our house your home as long as you stay."

Mr. Travilla seconded her invitation and, after some urging, it was accepted.

It proved an agreeable arrangement for all concerned. "Cousin Ronald" was the same genial companion that he had been eight years before. The two lads were worthy of their sire — intelligent and well-informed, frank, simple hearted and true.

The young people made acquaintance very rapidly. The Exposition was a theme of great and common interest, discussed at every meal and on the days when they stayed at home for rest. They all found it necessary to do so occasionally; some of the ladies and little ones could scarcely endure the fatigue of attending two days in succession.

Then through the months of July and August they made excursions to various points of interest, usually spending several days at each — sometimes a week or two.

In this way they visited Niagara Falls, Lakes Ontario, George and Champlain, the White Mountains and different seaside resorts.

At one of these last, they met Lester Leland again. The Travillas had not seen him for nearly a year but had heard of his welfare through the Lelands of Fairview.

All seemed pleased to renew the old familiar communication. This was an easy matter as they were staying at the same hotel.

Lester was introduced to the Scotch cousins as an old friend of the family.

Mr. Lilburn and he exchanged a hearty greeting and chatted together very amicably, but Malcom and Hugh were only distantly polite to the newcomer and eyed him askance, jealous of the favor shown him by their young lady cousins whose sweet society they would have been glad to monopolize.

But this they soon found was impossible even could they have banished Leland for Herbert Carrington, Philip Ross, Dick Percival and his friends, and several others soon appeared upon the scene.

Elsie was now an acknowledged young lady; Violet, in her own estimation and that of her parents, was still a mere child. But her height, her graceful carriage and unaffected ease of manner — which was the combined result of native refinement and constant association with the highly polished and educated, united to childlike simplicity of character and utter absence of self-consciousness — led strangers into the mistake of supposing her several years older than she really was.

Her beauty, too, and her genius for music and painting added to her attractiveness; so that altogether the gentlemen were quite as ready to pay court to her as to her sister. Had she been disposed to receive their attentions or to push herself forward in the least, her parents would have found it difficult to prevent her entering society earlier than was good for her.

But like her mother before her, Vi was in no haste to assume the duties and responsibilities of womanhood. Only fifteen she was

Standing with reluctant feet
Where the brook and river meet,
Womanhood and childhood fleet.

Hugh Lilburn and Herbert Carrington both regarded her with covetous eyes and both asked permission of her father to pay their addresses, but received the same answer — that she was too young yet to be approached on that subject.

"Well, Mr. Travilla, if you say that to everyone, as no doubt you do, I'm willing to wait," said Herbert going off tolerably contented.

But Hugh reddened with the sudden recollection that Violet was an heiress and his portion a very moderate one. Then he stammered out something about hoping he was not mistaken for a fortune hunter and that he would make no effort to win her until he was in circumstances to do so with propriety.

"My dear fellow," said Mr. Travilla, "do not for a moment imagine that has anything to do with my refusal. I do not care to find rich husbands for my daughters. If Violet were of proper age, I should have no objection to you as a suitor even though you would be likely to carry her far away from us."

"No, no, sir, I wouldn't" exclaimed the lad warmly. "I like America and I think I shall settle here. And sir, I thank you most heartily for your kind words. But, as I've said, I won't ask again till I can do so with propriety."

Leland, too, admired Violet extremely, but loved her with brotherly affection. It was Elsie who had won his heart.

But he had never whispered a word of this to her, or

to any human creature, for he was both poor and proud. He had firmly resolved not to seek her hand until his art should bring him fame and fortune to lay at her feet.

Similar considerations alone held Malcom Lilburn back. Each was tortured with the fear that the other would prove a successful rival.

Philip Ross, too, was waiting to grow rich, but he feared no rival in the meantime because he was so satisfied that no one could be so attractive to Elsie as himself.

"She's waiting for me," he said to his mother, "and she will wait. She's just friendly and kind to those other fellows, but it's plain she doesn't care a pin for any of them."

"I'm not so sure of that Phil," returned Mrs. Ross. "Someone may cut you out. Have you spoken to her yet? Is there a regular engagement between you?"

"Oh, no! But we understand each other — always have since we were mere babies."

Mrs. Ross and her daughters had accompanied Philip to the shore and it pleased Lucy greatly that they had been able to obtain rooms in the same house with their old friends, the Travillas.

Mr. Hogg was of the party also, and Elsie and Violet had now an opportunity to judge of the happiness of Gertrude's married life.

They were not greatly impressed with it. Husband and wife seemed to have few interests in common and to be rather bored with each other's company.

Mr. Hogg had a fine equipage and drove out a great deal — sometimes with his wife, sometimes without. Both dressed handsomely and spent money lavishly, but he did not look happy and Gertrude, when off her guard, wore a discontented, care-worn expression.

Mrs. Ross was full of cares and anxieties and one day she unburdened her heart to her childhood friend.

They were sitting alone together on the veranda upon which Mrs. Travilla's room opened, waiting for the call to the tea table.

"I have no peace with my life, Elsie," Lucy said fretfully. "One can't help sympathizing with one's children and my girls don't seem happy like yours. Kate's lively and pleasant enough in company, but at home she's dull and spiritless. And though Gertrude has made what is considered an excellent match, she doesn't seem to enjoy life. She's easily fretted and wants change and excitement all the time."

"Perhaps matters may improve for her," Elsie said, longing to comfort Lucy. "Some couples have to learn to accommodate themselves to each other."

"Well, I hope it may be so," Lucy responded, sighing as though the hope were faint indeed.

"And Kate may grow happier, too, dear. Lucy, if you could only lead her to Christ, I am sure she would," Elsie went on low and tenderly.

Mrs. Ross shook her head, tears trembling in her eyes. "How can I? I have not found him myself yet. Ah, Elsie, I wish I'd begun as you did. You have some comfort in your children. I've none in mine. That is," she added hastily, correcting herself, "not as much as I ought to have, except in Phil. He's doing well. Yet, even he's not half as thoughtful and affectionate toward his father and mother as your boys are. But then, of course, he's of a different disposition."

"Your younger boys seem fine lads," Elsie said, "and Sophie has a winning way."

Lucy looked pleased, then sighed, "they are nice children, but so willful; and the boys are so venturesome. I've no peace when they are out of my sight, lest they should be in some danger."

CHAPTER TWENTY-SIXTH

Oh, Lord! Methought what pain it was to drown!

— SHAKESPEARE

COUSIN RONALD was a great favorite with his young relatives. Harold and Herbert had long since voted him quite equal, if not superior, to Captain Brice as a storyteller. His narratives were fully interesting and, besides, always contained a moral or some useful information.

There were tales of the sea, wild tales of the Highlands and of the Scottish border, stories of William Wallace of the Bruce and the Black Douglass, in all of which the children greatly delighted. Mr. Lilburn's ventriloquial powers were used for their amusement also. Altogether, they found him a very entertaining companion.

Rosie, holding a shell to her ear one day, was sent into ecstasies of delight by hearing low, sweet strains of music, apparently coming from the inside of it.

At another time, as she stooped to pick up a dead crab while wandering alone the beach, she started back in dismay at hearing it scream out in a shrill, tiny voice, "Don't touch me! I'll pinch you if you do."

The merry laugh of the boys told her that it was "only Cousin Ronald," but she let the crab alone, keeping at a respectful distance from its claws. All of this was on the evening spoken of in the last chapter while mamma and Aunt Lucy were chatting together on the veranda waiting for the call to tea.

It sounded presently and Cousin Ronald and the children started on a run for the house, trying to see who would get there first. Harold showed himself the fleetest of foot, Herbert and Frank Daly were close at his heels, while Mr. Lilburn with Rosie in one hand and little Walter in the other came puffing and blowing not far behind.

"Won't you take us for another walk, cousin?" asked Rosie when they came out again after the meal.

"Yes," he said, "this is a very pleasant time to be down on the beach. Come lads," to Harold and Herbert, "will you go along?"

They were only too glad to accept the invitation and the four sauntered leisurely down to the water's edge where they strolled along watching the incoming tide.

"I love the sea," Rosie said. "I wish we could take it home with us."

"We have a lake and must be content with that," said Herbert, picking up a stone and sending it far out to fall with a splash in among the restless waves. "We can't have everything in one place."

"Did you ever see a mermaid, Rosie?" asked Mr. Lilburn.

"No, sir, what is it?"

"They're said to live in the sea and to be half fish and half woman."

"Ugh! That's dreadful! I wouldn't like to be half fish. But I wish I could see one. Are there any in our sea here, Cousin Ronald?"

"They're said to have very long hair," he went on, not noticing her query, "and to come out of the water and sit on the rocks sometimes while they comb it out with their fingers and sing."

"Sing! Oh, I'd like to hear 'em! I wish one would come and sit on that big rock way out there."

"Look sharp now and see if there is one there. Hark! Don't you hear her sing?"

Rosie and the boys stood still listening intently, and in another moment strains of music seemed to come to them from over the water from the direction of the rock.

"Oh, I do! I do!" screamed Rosie in delight. "Oh, boys, can you hear her too? Can you see her?"

"I hear singing," said Harold smiling, "but I think the rock is bare."

"I hear the music too," remarked Herbert, "but I suppose Cousin Ronald makes it. A mermaid's only a fabled creature."

"Fabled? What's that?"

"Only pretend."

"Ah, now, what a pity!"

At that instant a piercing scream seemed to come from the sea, out beyond the surf, some yards higher up the coast. "Help! Help! I'll drown! I'll drown!"

Instantly Harold was off like a shot, in the direction of the sound, tearing off his coat as he went; while Herbert, screaming "somebody's drowning! The life boat! The life boat!" rushed off toward the hotel.

"Lads! Lads!" cried Mr. Lilburn, putting himself to his utmost speed to overtake Harold in time to prevent him from plunging into the sea. "Are ye mad? Are ye daft? There's nobody there, lads. 'Twas only Cousin Ronald at his old tricks again."

As he caught up to Harold, the boy's coat and vest lay on the ground and he was down beside them, tugging at his boots and shouting, "Hold on! I'm coming," while a great wave came rolling in and dashed over him, wetting him from head to foot.

"No, ye're not!" cried Mr. Lilburn, laying a tight grasp upon his arm. "There's nobody there; and if there was, what could a bit, frail laddie like you do to rescue him? You'd only be dragged under yourself."

"Nobody there? Oh, I'm so glad," cried Harold with a hearty laugh as he jumped up, snatched his clothes from the ground and sprang hastily back just in time to escape the next wave. "But you gave us a real scare this time, Cousin Ronald."

"You gave me one," said Mr. Lilburn, joining in the laugh. "I thought you'd be in the sea and maybe out of reach of help before I could catch up to you. You took no time to deliberate."

"Deliberate when somebody was drowning? There wouldn't have been a second to lose."

"You'd just have thrown your own life away, lad, if

there had been anybody there. Don't you know it's an extremely hazardous thing for a man to attempt to rescue a drowning person? They're so apt to catch and grip you in a way to deprive you of the power to help yourself and to drag you under with them."

"I honor you for your courage, but I wish, my boy, you'd promise me never to do the like again; at least, not till you've grown up and have some strength."

"And have a fellow creature to perish!" cried the boy almost indignantly. "O cousin, could you ask me to be so selfish?"

"Not selfish, lad, only prudent. If you want to rescue a drowning man, throw him a rope or reach him the end of a pole or do anything else you can without putting yourself within reach of his hands."

Rosie, left behind by all her companions, looked this way and that in fright and perplexity, then ran after Herbert. That was the direction to take her to her father and mother.

Mr. Travilla and Eddie had started toward the beach to join the others. They were the first to hear Herbert's cry.

"Oh, it was Cousin Ronald," said Eddie. "Nobody goes bathing at this hour."

"Probably," said his father, "yet — ah, there's the life boat out now and moving toward the spot."

With that, they ran in the same direction and came up to Mr. Lilburn and Harold just as the boy had put on his coat and the gentleman had concluded his exhortation.

They all saw at once that Eddie had been correct in his conjecture.

"Hello! Where's the drowning man?" he called. "Or was it a woman?"

"Ask Cousin Ronald," said Harold laughing, "he's better acquainted with the person."

"A hoax was it?" asked Mr. Travilla. "Well, I'm glad things are no worse. Run home my son, and change your clothes. You're quite wet."

"I fear I owe you an apology, sir," said Mr. Lilburn, "but the fact is I'd a great desire to try the mettle of the lads. I believe they're brave fellows, both, and not lacking in the very useful and commendable quality called presence of mind."

"Thank you, sir," Mr. Travilla said, turning upon his boys a glance of fatherly pride that sent a thrill of joy to their young hearts.

Chapter Twenty-seventh

Nursed by the virtues she hath been
From childhood's hour.

— Halleck

Count all th' advantage prosperous vice attains,
'Tis but what virtue flies from and disdains;
And grant the bad what happiness they would,
One they must want — which is to pass for good.

— Pope

Mrs. Travilla was sitting on the veranda of the hotel, reading a letter her husband had handed her at the tea table, when Violet came rushing toward her in wild affright.

"Mamma, mamma! Something's wrong! Something's happened! Herbie just came running up from the beach calling for the lifeboats. Papa and Eddie have gone back with him, running as fast as they can. Oh, I'm afraid Harold or Rosie has fallen into the water!" she added, bursting into hysterical weeping.

Her mother rose hastily, thrusting the letter into her pocket, pale but calm.

"Daughter, dear, we will not meet trouble half way. I do not think it could be they for they are not disobedient or venturesome. But come." And together they hurried toward the beach.

In a moment they perceived that their fears were groundless, for they could see their dear ones coming to meet them.

Violet's tears were changed to laughter as Harold gave a humorous account of "Cousin Ronald's sell," as he called it. And the latter's praise of the boy's bravery and readiness to respond to the cry for help brought proud, happy smiles to the lips and eyes of both mother and sisters.

Elsie had joined them as had Mrs. Ross and a handsome, richly dressed, middle-aged lady, whom she introduced as her friend, Mrs. Faude, from Kentucky.

They, as Lucy afterward told Elsie, had made acquaintance the year before at Saratoga, and were glad to meet again.

Mrs. Faude was much taken with Elsie and her daughters, pleased, indeed, with the whole family; and from that time forward sought their company very frequently.

Elsie found her an entertaining companion, polished in manners, refined, intelligent, highly educated and witty, but very worldly, caring for the pleasures and rewards of this life only.

She was a wealthy widow with but one child, a grown son of whom she talked a great deal. "Clarence Augustus" was evidently, in his mother's eyes, the perfection of manly beauty and grace — a great genius, and indeed everything that could be desired.

"He is still single," she one day said significantly to the younger Elsie, "though I know plenty of girls, desirable matches in every way, who would have been delighted with the offer of his hand. Yes, my dear, I am quite sure of it," she added, seeing a slight smile of incredulity on the young girl's face. "Only wait till you have seen him. He will be here tomorrow."

Elsie was quite willing to wait, and no dreams of Mrs. Faude's idol disturbed either her sleeping or waking hours.

Clarence Augustus made his appearance duly the next day at the dinner table. He was a really handsome man, if regular features and fine coloring be all that is necessary to constitute good looks. But his face wore an expression of self-satisfaction and contempt for others, which was not attractive to the Ion clan.

It soon became evident to them that to most of the other ladies in the house, he was an object of admiration.

His mother seized an early opportunity to introduce him to the Misses Travilla, coming upon them as they stood talking together on the veranda.

But they merely bowed and withdrew, having, fortunately, an engagement to drive at that hour with their parents and cousins along the beach.

"What do you think of him?" asked Violet when they had reached their room.

"He has good features and a polished manner."

"Yes, but do you like his looks?"

"No, I do not desire his acquaintance."

"Nor I. He's not the sort that papa and grandpa would wish us to know."

"No, so let us keep out of his way."

"But without seeming to do so?"

"Oh, yes, as far as we can. We don't wish to hurt his feelings or his mother's."

They carried out their plan of avoidance so skillfully that neither mother nor son was quite sure it was intended. In fact, it was difficult for them to believe that any girl could wish to shun the attentions of a young man so attractive in every way as was Clarence Augustus Faude.

"I should like you to marry one of those girls," the mother said to her son, chatting alone with him in her own room. "You could not do better. They are beautiful, highly educated and accomplished, and will have large fortunes."

"Which?" he added sententiously, with a smile that seemed to say he was conscious that he had only to take his choice.

"I don't care. There's hardly a pin to choose between them."

"Just my opinion. Well, I think I shall go for the brown eyes. You tell me the other is not out yet, and I hear the father refuses, on that plea, to allow any one to court her — though, between you and me, Mrs. F., I fancy he might make an exception in my favor."

"It would not surprise me, Clarence Augustus," she

responded, regarding him with a proud, fond smile. "I fancy he must be aware that there's no better match in the Union. But you have no time to lose. They may leave here any day."

"True, but what's to hinder us from following? However, I will take your advice and lose no time. Let me borrow your writing desk for a moment. I'll ask her to drive with me this morning, and while we're out secure her company for the boating party that's to come off tomorrow."

A few moments later the younger Elsie came into her mother's room with a note written in a manly hand, on delicately perfumed and tinted French paper.

"What shall I do about it, mamma?" she asked. "Will you answer it for me. Of course, you know I do not wish to accept."

"I will, daughter," Mrs. Travilla said, "though if he were such a man as I could receive into my family on friendly terms, I should prefer to have you answer it yourself."

Mr. Faude's very handsome carriage and horses were at the door, a liveried servant holding the reins. The gentleman himself waited in the parlor for the coming of the young lady, who, he doubted not, would be well pleased to accept his invitation. He was not kept waiting long. He had, indeed, scarcely seated himself and taken up the morning paper, when Mr. Travilla's Ben appeared with a note, presented it in a grave silence, and with a respectful bow, withdrew.

"Hold on! It may require an answer," Mr. Faude called after him.

"No, sah, Mrs. Travilla say dere's no answer," returned Ben, looking back for an instant from the doorway, then vanishing through it.

"All right!" muttered Clarence Augustus, opening the missive and glancing over the contents, an angry flush suffusing his face as he read.

"What is it? She hasn't decline, surely?" Mrs. Faude asked in an undertone, close at his side.

"Just that. It's from the mother. She thanks me for the

invitation, but respectfully declines, not even condescending to a shadow of an excuse. What can it mean?"

"I don't know, I'm sure. But if they knew you had serious intentions — it might make a difference."

"Possibly. I'll soon bring it to the proof."

He rose and went out in search of Mr. Travilla. He found him alone and at once asked his permission to pay court to Elsie.

The request was courteously but decidedly and firmly refused.

"May I ask why?" queried the young man in anger and astonishment.

"Because, sir, it would not be agreeable to either my daughter herself, to her mother or to me."

"Then I must say, sir, that you are all three hard to please. But pray, sir, what is the objection?"

"Do you insist upon knowing?"

"I do, sir."

"Then let me answer your query with another. Would you pay court to a young woman — however wealthy, beautiful, or high-born — whose moral character was not better, whose life had been no purer than your own?"

"Of course not!" exclaimed Faude, coloring violently, "but who expects — ."

"I do, sir. I expect the husbands of my daughters to be as pure and stainless as my sons' wives."

"I'm as good as the rest, sir. You'll not find one young fellow in five hundred who has sowed fewer wild oats than I."

"I fear that may be true enough, but it does not alter my decision," returned Mr. Travilla, intimating by a bow and a slight wave of the hand that he considered the interview at an end.

Faude withdrew in anger, but with an intensified desire to secure the coveted prize. The more difficult the acquisition, the more desirable it seemed.

He persuaded his mother to become his advocate with Mrs. Travilla.

She at first fully refused, but at length yielded to his

entreaties, and undertook the difficult, and to her haughty spirit, humiliating mission.

Requesting a private interview with Elsie, she told her of the wishes of Clarence Augustus, and pleaded his cause with all the eloquence of which she was mistress.

"My boy would make your daughter a good husband," she said. "Indeed, I think any woman might feel highly honored by the offer of his hand. I do not understand how it is, Mrs. Travilla, that a lady of your sense fails to see that."

"I appreciate your feelings, my dear Mrs. Faude," said Elsie gently. "I am a mother, too, you know. And I have sons of my own."

"Yes, and what possible objection can you have to mine? Excuse my saying it, but the one your husband advanced seems to me simply absurd."

"Nevertheless, it is the only one — except that our child's heart is not enlisted. But either alone would be insuperable."

"She hardly knows him yet, and could not fail to learn to love him if she did. Be persuaded my dear Mrs. Travilla, to give him a chance to try. It is never well to be hasty, especially in declining a good offer. And this, let me tell you, is such an one as you will not meet with every day — lovely and attractive in every way as your daughters are.

"Ours is an old, aristocratic family. There is none better to be found in our state or in the Union. We have wealth, too, and I flatter myself that Clarence Augustus is as handsome a man as you would find anywhere. He is amiable in disposition, also, and would, as I said before, make an excellent husband. Will you not undertake his cause?"

"Believe me, it is painful to me to refuse, but I could not, in good conscience."

"But why not?"

"Simply for the reason my husband gave. We both consider moral purity more essential than anything else in those we admit to even friendly acquaintance with our children, especially our daughters."

"My son is not a bad man, Mrs. Travilla. Very far from it!" Mrs. Faude exclaimed in the tone of one who considers herself grossly insulted.

"Not, I am sure, as the world looks upon those things," said Elsie. "But the Bible is our standard, and guided by its teachings we desire above all things else, purity of heart and life in those who seek friendship of our children. We especially desire it in those who are to become their partners for life and the future fathers or mothers of their offspring, should it please God to give them any."

"That is certainly looking ahead," returned Mrs. Faude, with a polite sneer.

"Not farther than is our duty, since after marriage it is too late to consider, to any profit, what kind of parent our already irrevocably chosen partner for life will probably make."

"Well, well, everyone to her taste!" said Mrs. Faude, rising to go. "But, had I a daughter, I should infinitely prefer for her husband such a young man as my Clarence Augustus to such as that poor artist who is so attentive to Miss Travilla.

"Good morning. I am sure I may trust you not to blazon this matter abroad?"

"You certainly may, Mrs. Faude," Elsie returned with sweet and gentle courtesy, "and, believe me, it has been very painful to me to speak words that have given pain to you."

"What is it, little wife?" Mr. Travilla asked, coming in a moment after Mrs. Faude's departure and finding Elsie alone and seemingly sunk in a painful reverie.

She repeated what had just passed, adding, "I am very glad now that we decided to return to Philadelphia tomorrow. I could see Mrs. Faude was deeply offended, and it would be unpleasant to both of us to remain longer in the same house. As she and her son go with the boating party today and we leave early in the morning, we are not likely to encounter each other again."

"Yes, it is all for the best," he said, "but I wish I could have shielded you from this trial."

CHAPTER TWENTY-EIGHTH

The brave man is not he who feels no fear,
For that were stupid and irrational;
But he whose soul its fear subdues,
And bravely dares the danger nature shrinks from.

— BAILLIE

THE TRAVILLAS RETURNED HOME to Ion in November and took up with new zest the old and loved routine of study, work and play.

Elsie was no longer a schoolgirl, but still devoted some hours of each day to the cultivation of her mind and the keeping up of her accomplishments. She also pursued her art studies with renewed ardor under the tutelage of Lester Leland. Leland's health required a warmer climate than that of his northern home so he had come at the urgent request of his relatives to spend the season at Fairview.

Elsie had a number of gentlemen friends, some of whom she highly esteemed, but Lester's company was preferred to that of any other.

Malcom Lilburn had grown very jealous of Lester and found it difficult indeed to refrain from telling his love, but he had gone away without breathing a word of it to anyone.

He'd not gone to Scotland, however; he and his father were traveling through the West, visiting the principal points of interest. They had partly promised to take Ion in their way, as they returned which would probably not be before spring.

Mr. and Mrs. Travilla were not exempt from the cares and trials incident to our fallen state, but no happier parents could be found. They were already reaping as they had sowed. Indeed, it seemed to them that they had been reaping all the way along, so sweet was the return of affection from the clinging, helpless ones — the care of whom had been no less a pleasure than a sacred, God-given duty. With each passing year, the harvest grew richer and more abundant. The eldest three had become companionable and the exchanges between the two Elsies were more like that of sisters than of mother and daughter. The young girl loved her mother's company above that of any other of her sex. "Mamma" was still, as she had ever been, her most intimate friend and confidante.

And was it not wise? Who could be a more tender, faithful and prudent guide and counselor than the mother to whom she was dearer than life?

It was the same with the others also — both sons and daughters. And they were scarcely less open with their wisely indulgent father.

Life was not all sunshine. The children had their faults that would occasionally show themselves; but the parents, conscious of their own imperfections, were patient and forbearing. They were sometimes tried with sickness, too, but it was borne with cheerful resignation. No one could say what the future held in store for any of them; but God reigned — the God whom they had chosen as their portion and their inheritance forever. And they left all with Him, striving to obey the command to be without carefulness.

The winter passed quickly, almost without incident — save one.

Eddie had been spending the afternoon with his cousins at Pinegrove — some of them were lads near his own age — fine, intelligent, good boys. He had stayed to tea and was riding home alone, except that he had an attendant in the person of a young Negro boy, who rode some yards in the rear.

It was already dark when they started, but the stars

shone down from a clear sky and a keen, cold wind blew from the north.

Part of the way lay through woods, in the midst of which stood a hut occupied by a family by the name of Smith, belonging to the class known as "poor whites." They were shiftless, lazy and consequently very poor indeed. Many efforts had been put forth on their behalf by the families of the Oaks and Ion and by others also; but thus far with small results, for it is no easy matter to effectually help those who will not try to help themselves.

As Eddie entered the woods, he thought he smelled smoke, and presently a sudden turn in the road brought into view the dwelling of the Smiths all wrapped in flames.

Putting spurs to his horse at the sight, Eddie flew along the road shouting at the top of his lungs, "Fire! Fire! Fire!" Jim, his attendant, followed his example.

But there was no one within hearing save the Smiths themselves.

The head of the family, half stupefied with rum, stood leaning against the fence, his hands in the pockets of his ragged coat, a pipe in his mouth, gazing in a dazed sort of way upon the work of destruction. All the while the wife and children ran hither and thither, screaming and wringing their hands with never a though of an attempt to extinguish the flames or save any of their few poor possessions.

"Sam Smith," shouted Eddie, reining in his horse close to the individual addressed, "why don't you drop that old pipe, take your hands out of your pockets, and go to work to put out the fire?"

"Eh!" cried Sam, turning slowly round so as to face his interlocutor, "why — I — I — I couldn't do nothin'; it's bound to go — that house is. Don't you see how the wind's a blowin'? Well, 'tain't much 'count nohow, and I wouldn't care, on'y she says she's left the baby in there — so she does."

"The baby?" and almost before the words had left his

lips, Eddie had cleared the rough rail fence at a bound and was rushing toward the burning house.

How the flames crackled and roared, seeming like demons greedily devouring all that came in their way.

"That horse blanket, Jim! Bring it here quick, quick!" he shouted back to his servant. Then to the half-crazed woman, "Where is your baby? Where did you leave it?"

"In there, in there on the bed. Oh, oh, it's burnin' all up! I forgot it an' I couldn't get back."

Eddie made one step backward and ran his eye rapidly over the burning pile, calmly taking in the situation, considering whether the chances of success were sufficient to warrant the awful risk.

It was the work of an instant to do that. He snatched the blanket from Jim, wrapped it around his person, and plunged in among the flames, smoke, and falling firebrands, regardless of the boy's frightened protest. "Oh, Mr. Eddie, don't; you'll be killed! You'll burn all up!"

He had looked into the cabin but a day or two before and remembered in which corner stood the rude bed of the family, their only one. He groped his way to it, half suffocated by the heat and smoke, and in momentary dread of the falling in of the roof, reached it at last. Feeling about among the scanty covering laid hold of the child which was either insensible or sound asleep.

Taking it in his young, strong arms, holding it underneath the blanket which he drew closer about his person, he rushed back again, stepping from the door just as the roof fell in with a crash.

The woman snatched her babe and its gallant rescuer fell fainting to the ground. A falling beam had grazed his head and struck him a heavy blow upon his shoulder.

With a cry Jim sprang forward, dragged his young master out of reach of the flying sparks, the overpowering heat and suffocating smoke; and dropping, blubbering down by his side, tried to loosen his cravat.

"Fetch some wattah!" he called. "Quick dar! You gwine let young Marse Eddie die, when he done gone saved yo' baby from burnin' up?"

"Take the gourd and run to the spring Celestia Ann. Quick, quick as you kin go," said the mother hugging her rescued child and wiping a tear from her eye with the corner of a very dirty apron.

"There ain't none," answered the child. "We uns ain't got nothin' left; it's all burnt up."

But a keen, fresh air was already reviving the hero.

"Take me home, Jim." He faintly said, "Stop that wagon," as one was heard rumbling down the road still at some distance away.

"Hello dar! Jes stop an' take a passenger aboard!" shouted Jim, springing to his feet and rushing into the road, waving his cap above his head.

"Hello!" shouted back the other, "dat you Jim Yates? Burnin' down Smith's house. Dat's a powerful crime, dat is, sah!"

"Oh, go 'long, you fool, Pete White!" retorted Jim as the other drew rein close at his side. "You bet you don't catch dis niggah a burnin' no houses. 'Spect ole Smith set de fire goin' hisself wid dat ole pipe o' his'n!"

"An' its clar burnt down to de ground," observed Pete, gazing with eager interest at the smoldering ruins. "What you s'pose dey's gwine to do for sheltah for dem po' chillen?"

"Dat ain't no concern ob mine," returned Jim indifferently. "Ise consarned 'bout getting young Marse Ed'ard safe home, an' don't care nuffin' for all de others in de country. Jes hitch yo' hoss an' help me lift him into de wagon."

"What's de mattah?" queried Pete, leisurely dismounting and slowly hitching his horse to a tree.

"Oh, you hurry up, you ole darkey!" returned Jim impatiently. "Mr. Ed'ard's lyin' dar in de cold. He catch his diff if you's gwine to be all night 'bout gittin to him."

"Ise got de rheumatiz, chile. Ole folks can't turn roun' like young uns," returned Pete quickening his movements somewhat as he clambered over the fence and followed Jim to the spot where Eddie lay.

"Hurt, sah?" he asked.

"A little, I fear I can hardly sit my horse — for this faintness," Eddie answered low and feebly. "Can you put me into your wagon and drive me to Ion?"

"Yes, sah, wid de greatest pleasah in life, sah. Mr. Travilla and de Ion ladies ben berry kind to me an' my ole woman an' de chillen."

Mrs. Smith and her dirty ragged little troop had gathered round, still crying over their fright and their losses, curious about the young gentleman who had saved the baby and was lying there on the ground so helpless.

"Are ye much hurt, Mr. Edward?" asked the woman. "Oh yer mother'll never forgive me fur lettin' ye risk yer life that away!"

"I don't think the injury is serious, Mrs. Smith, at least I hope not. And you were not to blame," he answered, "so make yourself easy. Now, Pete and Jim, give me an arm, each of you."

They helped him into the wagon and laid him down, putting the scorched horse blanket under his head for a pillow.

"Now drive a little carefully, Pete," he said, suppressing a groan. "And look out for the ruts. I'd rather not be jolted."

"And you, Jim, ride on ahead and lead Prince. I want you to get in before us. Ask for father and tell him I've had an accident. Tell him that I'm not seriously hurt but want my mother prepared. She must not be alarmed by seeing me brought in unexpectedly in this state."

His orders were obeyed. Jim reached Ion some ten minutes ahead of the wagon and gave due warning of its approach. He met his master in the avenue and told his story in a tolerably straightforward manner.

"Where is Mr. Edward now?" asked Mr. Travilla.

"De wagon's jes down de road dar a piece, sah, be here in 'bout five minutes, sah."

"Then off for the doctor, Jim, as fast as you can go. Here, give me Prince's bridle. Now don't let the grass grow under your horse's feet. Either Dr. Barton or Dr. Arthur — it doesn't matter which — only get him here speedily." And vaulting into the saddle, Mr. Travilla rode back to the house, dismounted, throwing the bridle to Solon, and went in.

Opening the door of the drawing room where the family was gathered, "Wife," he said cheerfully, "will you please step here for a moment?"

She came at once and followed him down the hall, asking, "What is it, Edward?" for her heart warned her that something was wrong.

"Not much, I hope, dearest," he said, turning and taking her in his arms. "Our boy, Eddie, has done a brave deed and suffered some injury by it, but nothing serious, I trust. He will be here in a moment."

He felt her cling to him with a convulsive grasp. He heard her quick coming breath, the whispered words, "Oh, my son! Dear Lord, help!" Then, as the rumble of the wagon wheels was heard nearing the door, she put her hand in his, calm and quiet, and went forth with him to meet their wounded child.

His father helped him to alight and supported him up the veranda steps.

"Don't be alarmed, mother, I'm not badly hurt," he said, but staggered as he spoke, and would have fallen but for his father's sustaining arm. By the light from the open door she saw his eyes close and a deadly pallor overspread his face.

"He's fainting!" she exclaimed, springing to his other side. "Oh, my boy, this is no trifle!"

Servants were crowding about them and Eddie was quickly borne to his room, laid upon the bed, and restoratives administered.

"Fire!" his mother said with a start and shudder, pointing to his singed locks. "Oh, where has the child been?"

Her husband told her in a few words.

"And he has saved a life!" she cried with tears of mingled joy and grief, proud of her brave son, though her tender mother's heart ached for his suffering. "Thank God for that, if — if he has not sacrificed his own."

The door opened and Arthur Conly came in.

Consciousness was returning to the lad and looking up at his cousin as he bent over him, he murmured, "Tell mother that I'm not much hurt."

"I have to find that out first," said Arthur. "Do you feel any burns, bruises? Whereabouts are you injured, do you think?"

"Something — a falling beam, I suppose — grazed my head and struck me on the shoulder. I think, too, that my hands and face are scorched."

"Yes, your face is and your hands — scorched? Why, they are badly burned! And your collarbone's broken. That's all, I believe enough to satisfy you, I hope?"

"Quite," Eddie returned with a faint smile. "Don't cry, mother dear. You see it's nothing but what can be made right in a few days or weeks."

"Yes," she said, kissing him and smiling through her tears. "Oh, let us thank God that it is no worse!"

Eddie's adventure created quite a stir in the family and among outside relatives and friends he was dubbed the hero of the hour. Attention was lavished upon him without stint.

He bore his honors meekly. "Mother," he said privately to her, "I don't deserve all this praise and it makes me ashamed. I am not really brave. In fact, I'm afraid I'm an errant coward. Do you know I was afraid to rush in among those flames, but I could not bear the thought of leaving that poor baby to burn up. You taught me that it was right and noble to risk my own life to save another's."

"That was not cowardice, my dear boy," she said, her eyes shining, "but the truest courage. I think you deserve far more credit for bravery than you would if you had rushed in impulsively without a thought of the real danger you were encountering."

"Praise is very sweet from the lips of those I love, especially my mother's," he responded with a glad smile. "And what a nurse you are, mother mine! It pays to be ill when one can be so tended."

"That is when one is not seriously ill, I suppose?" she

said playfully, stroking his hair. “By the way, it will take longer to restore these damaged locks than to repair any of the other injuries caused by your escapade.”

“Never mind,” he said, “they'll grow again in time. What has become of the Smiths?”

“Your father has found temporary shelter for them at the quarter and is rebuilding their hut.”

“I knew he would; it is just like him — always so kind, so generous.”

Chapter Twenty-ninth

Oh, gentle Romeo,
If thou dost love, pronounce it faithfully.
Or if thou think'st I'm too quickly won,
I'll frown and be perverse, and say thee nay,
So thou wilt woo; but else nor for the world.

— Shakespeare

One lovely morning in the ensuing spring, the younger Elsie wandered out alone into the grounds and sauntering aimlessly along with a book in her hand, at length found herself standing on the shore of the lakelet.

It was a lovely spot, for the limpid waters reflected grassy banks sprinkled here and there with wild violets and shaded by beautiful trees.

A gentle breeze just ruffled the glassy surface of the pond and rustic seat invited rest. It seemed just the place and time for a reverie, and Elsie, with scarce a glance about her, sat down to that enjoyment. It was only of late that she had formed this habit, but it was growing upon her.

She sat for some time buried in thought, her cheek upon her hand, her eyes upon the ground, and smiles and blushes chasing each other over the fair sweet face.

The dip of an oar followed instantly by a discordant laugh and a shrill voice saying, "What are you sittin' there for so still and quiet? Wouldn't you like to get in here with me?" caused her to start and spring to her feet with a cry of dismay.

About an hour before, a little, oddly dressed woman, with gray hair hanging over her shoulders, a large doll in one arm and a sun umbrella in the other hand, might have been seen stealing along the road that led from Roselands to Ion. She kept close to the hedge that separated it from the fields and now and then glanced over her shoulder as if fearing or expecting pursuit.

She kept up a constant gabble — now talking to herself, now to the doll, hugging and kissing it with a great show of affection.

"Got away safe this time, didn't we, Grissy? And we're not going back in a hurry, are we, dear? We've had enough of being penned up in that old house ever so long. Now we'll have a day in the woods, a picnic all to ourselves. Hark! What was that? Did I hear wheels?" Pausing a moment to listen, she said, "No, they haven't found us out yet, Grissy, so we'll walk on."

Reaching the gate leading into the avenue at Ion, she stood a moment peering in between the bars.

"Seems to me I've been here before, must have been a good while ago. Guess I won't go up to the house; they might catch me and send me back. But let us go in, Griselda, and look about. Yonder's a garden full of flowers. We'll pick what we want and nobody'll know it."

Putting down her umbrella and pushing the gate open just far enough to enable her to slip through, she stole cautiously in, crossed the avenue and lawn, and entered the garden unobserved.

She wandered here and there, plucking remorselessly whatever seized her fancy, till she had an immense bouquet of the choicest blossoms.

At length, leaving the garden, she made a circuit through the shrubbery and finally came out upon the shore of the little lake.

"Oh, this is nice!" she said. "Did I ever see this before? It's cool and shady here. We'll sit down and rest ourselves under one of those trees, Grissy." Then catching sight of a pretty rowboat moored to the shore, "No, we'll jump into this boat and take a ride!" And springing nimbly in, she laid the doll down on one of the seats, the bouquet beside it, saying, "I'm tired carrying you, Griselda, so just lie there and rest." Then quickly loosing the little craft from the moorings and taking up the oars, she pushed off into the deep water.

She laid down the oars presently and amused herself with the flowers, picking them to pieces and scattering the petals in the water. She leaned over the side of the boat, talking to the fishes, and bidding them eat what she gave them, "For it was good, much better and daintier than bread crumbs."

The breeze came from the direction to take her farther from the shore and soon wafted her out to the middle of the lake. But she went on with her new diversion, taking no note of her whereabouts.

It was just about this time that Elsie reached the spot and sat down to her daydreams.

Enna, for it was she who occupied the boat, did not see her niece at first. After a little while, growing weary of her sport with the flowers, she threw them from her, took up an oar again. Glancing toward the land as she dipped the oar into the water, her eye fell upon the graceful white-robed figure seated there underneath the trees and she instantly called out to her.

Elsie was much alarmed — concerned for the safety of the poor lunatic. There was no knowing what madness might seize her at any moment. No one was within call and, that being the only boat there, there was no way of reaching her until she should return to the shore of her own accord. All this was if, indeed, she was capable of managing the boat so as to reach land and if she desired to do so.

Elsie did not lose her presence of mind. She thought very rapidly. The breeze was wafting the boat farther from her, but nearer to the opposite shore. If let alone, it would arrive there in the course of time and Enna, she perceived, did not know how to propel it with the oars.

"Will you come?" she was asking again. "Will you take a ride in this pretty boat with me?"

"I'll run round to the other side," Elsie called in reply. "I wouldn't bother with those heavy oars if I were you.

Just let them lie in the bottom of the boat while you sit still and rest. The wind will carry it to the land."

"All right!" Enna answered, laying them down. "Now you hurry up."

"I will," Elsie said, starting upon a run for the spot where she thought that the boat would be most likely to reach the shore.

She reached it first. The boat being several yards away floating upon very deep water, she watched it a moment anxiously.

Enna was sitting still in the bottom, hugging the doll to her bosom and singing a lullaby to it. Suddenly, as Elsie stood waiting and watching in trembling suspense, she sprang up, tossed the doll from her, leaped over the side of the boat, and disappeared beneath the water.

Elsie tore off her sash, tied a pebble to one end, and as Enna rose to the surface, spluttering and struggling, threw it to her crying, "Catch hold and I will try to pull you out."

"Oh, don't! You will but sacrifice your own life!" cried a manly voice in tones of almost agonized entreaty. Lester Leland came dashing down the bank.

It was too late. Enna seized the ribbon with a jerk that pulled Elsie also into the water. They were struggling together, both in imminent danger of drowning.

It was but an instant before Lester was there also. Death with Elsie would be far preferable to life without her and so he would save her or perish with her.

It was near being the latter. It would have been had not Bruno come to his aid. With the help of the faithful dog, he at length succeeded in rescuing both ladies, dragging them up the bank and laying them on the grass, both in a state of insensibility.

"Go to the house, Bruno. Go and bring help," he said panting, for he was well nigh overcome by his exertions. The dog bounded away in the direction of the house.

"Lord, grant it may come speedily," entreated the young man, kneeling beside the apparently lifeless form of her whom he loved so well. "Oh, my darling, have those sweet eyes closed forever?" he cried in anguish, wiping the water from her face and chafing her cool hands in his. "Elsie, my love, my life, my all! Oh! I would have died to save you!"

Enna had been missed almost immediately and Calhoun, Arthur and several servants at once set out in different directions in search of her.

Arthur and Pomp got upon the right scent, followed her to Ion, and joined by Mr. Travilla, soon traced her through the garden and shrubbery down to the lake. They came upon the scene of the catastrophe, or rather the rescue, but a moment after Bruno left.

"Why, what is this?" exclaimed Mr. Travilla in alarm. "Is it Elsie? Can she have been in the water? Oh, my child, my darling!"

Instantly he was down upon the grass by her side, assisting Lester's efforts to restore her to consciousness.

For a moment she engrossed the attention of all to the utter exclusion from their thoughts of poor Enna, for whom none of them entertained any great amount of affection.

"She lives! Her heart beats! She will soon recover!" Arthur said presently. "See, a faint color is coming into her cheek. Run, Pomp, bring blankets and more help. They must be carried at once to the house."

He turned to his aunt, leaving Mr. Travilla and Lester to attend to Elsie.

Enna seemed gone. He could not be sure that life was not extinct. Perhaps it were better so, but he would not give up till every possible effort had been made to restore her.

Both ladies were speedily conveyed to the house. Elsie, already conscious, was committed to the care of her mother and Aunt Chloe. Arthur, Dr. Barton, and others used every exertion for Enna's resuscitation. They were at length successful in fanning to a flame the feeble spark of life that yet remained; but fever intervened, and for weeks afterward she was very ill.

Elsie kept her bed for a day, then took her place in the family again, looking quite herself except for a slight paleness. And yet, a close observer might have detected another change — a sweet glad light in the beautiful brown eyes that was not there before.

Lester's words of passionate love had reached the ear that seemed closed to all earthly sound. They were heard as in a dream, but afterward recalled with a full apprehension of their reality and of all they meant to her and to him.

Months ago she had read the same sweet story in his eyes, but how much sweeter by far it was to have heard it from his lips.

She had sometimes wondered that he held his peace so long, and again had doubted the language of his looks. Now those doubts were set at rest and their next meeting was anticipated with a strange flutter of the heart, a longing for, yet half shrinking from the words he might have to speak.

But the day passed and he did not come — another and another — and no word from him. How strange! He was still her tutor in her art studies. Did he not know that she was well enough to resume them? If not, was it not his place to inquire?

Perhaps he was ill. Oh, had he risked his health, perhaps his life in saving hers? She did not ask. Her lips refused to speak his name. Would nobody tell her?

At last she overheard her father saying to Eddie, "What has become of Lester Leland? It strikes me as a little ungallant that he has not been in to inquire after the health of your aunt and sister."

"He has gone away," Eddie answered. "He left the morning after the accident."

"Gone away," echoed Elsie's sinking heart. "Gone away, and so suddenly! What could it mean?" She stole away to her room to indulge, for a brief space, in the luxury of tears; then, with a woman's instinctive pride, carefully removed their traces and rejoined the family with a face all wreathed in smiles.

CHAPTER THIRTIETH

Love is not to be reasoned down or lost,
In high ambition, or a thirst for greatness;
'Tis second life, it grows into the soul,
Warms ev'ry vein, and beats in ev'ry pulse;
I feel it here; my resolution melts.

— ADDISON

ENNA LAY AT THE POINT OF DEATH for weeks. Mrs. Travilla was her devoted nurse, scarcely leaving her day or night, and only snatching a few hours of rest occasionally on a couch in an adjoining room whence she could be summoned at a moment's notice.

Mr. Travilla at length remonstrated, "My darling, this is too much. You are risking your own life and health, which are far more valuable than hers."

"Oh, Edward," she answered, the tears shining in her eyes, "I must save her if I can. I am praying, praying that reason may come back and her life be spared till she has learned to know Him, whom to know aright is life eternal."

"My precious, unselfish little wife!" he said embracing her with emotion. "I believe your petition will be granted, that the Master will give you this soul for your hire, saying to you as to one of old, 'according to your faith be it unto you.' But, dearest," he added, "you must allow others to share your labor. There are others upon whom she certainly has a nearer claim. Where is Mrs. Conly?"

"Aunt Louise says she has no talent for nursing," Elsie answered with a half smile, "and that Prilla, mammy and Dinah are quite capable. And I am foolish to take the work off their hands."

"I am partly of her opinion," he responded playfully;

then, more seriously, "Will you not, for my sake and for your children's spare yourself a little?"

"And for your father's," added Mr. Dinsmore, whose quiet step as he entered the room they had not heard.

Elsie turned to him with both hands extended, a smile on her lips, a tear in her eye, "My dear father, how are you?"

"Quite well, daughter," he said, taking the hands and kissing the rich, red lips, as beautiful and sweet now, as in her childhood and youth, "but troubled and anxious about you. Are you determined to be quite obstinate in this thing?"

"No," she said, "I hope not; but what is it you and my husband would have me do?"

"Take your regular rest at night," answered the one, the other adding, "and go out for a little air and exercise every day."

Arthur, coming in at that moment from his morning visit to his patient, who lay in the next room, joined his entreaties to theirs, and upon his assurance that Enna was improving, Elsie consented to do as they desired.

Still, the greater part of her time was spent at Enna's bedside and her family saw but little of her.

This was a trial to them all, but especially to the eldest who was longing for "mamma's" dear company. She fully appreciated Molly's and Eddie's companionship, dearly loved that of her father, and esteemed Vi's as very sweet, but no one could fill her mother's place.

Probably not even to her would she have unburdened her heart. She could scarce bear to look into it herself. But the dear mother's very presence, though she might only sit in silence by her side, would be as a balm to her troubled spirit.

She forced herself to be cheerful when with the others and to take an interest in what interested them, but when left alone she would drop her book or work and fall into a reverie. Or she would wander out into the grounds, choosing the most quiet and secluded parts — often the shady banks of the lakelet where she and Lester had passed many an hour together in days gone by.

She had gone there one morning, leaving the others at home busied with their lessons. She was seated on a rustic bench, her hands folded in her lap, her eyes on the ground and a book lying unheeded in the grass at her feet. She was startled by a sound as of some heavy body falling from a height and crashing through the branches of a thick clump of trees on the other side of the lake.

She sprang up and stood looking and listening with a palpitating heart. She could see that a large branch had broken from a tall tree and that it lay upon the ground and — yes, something else lay beside or on it, half concealed from her view by the green leaves and twigs, and — did she hear a groan?

Perhaps it was only fancy, but it might be that someone was lying there in pain and needing assistance.

Instantly she flew toward the spot, her heart beating wildly. She drew near, started back and caught at a young sapling for support. Yes, there lay a motionless form among the fallen branches. It was a man, a gentleman as she discerned by what she could see of his clothing; her heart told her the rest.

Another moment and she was kneeling at his side, gazing with unutterable anguish into the still white face.

"He is dead; the fall has killed him." She had no hope of anything else at the moment. There seemed no possibility of life in that rigid form and death-like face, and she made no effort to give assistance or to call for it. She was like one turned to stone by the sudden crushing blow. She loved him and she had lost him — that was all she knew.

But, at length, this stony grief gave place to a sharper anguish. A low cry burst from her lips and hot scalding tears felling upon his face.

They brought him back to consciousness and he heard her bitter sighs and moans. He knew she thought him dead and mourned as for one who was very dear.

He was in terrible pain, for he had fallen with his leg

bent under him and it was badly broken. But a thrill of joy shot through his whole frame. For a moment more he was able to control himself and remained perfectly still, then his eyelids quivered and a groan burst from him.

At the sound Elsie started to her feet, then bending over him she said, "You're hurt, Lester," unconsciously addressing him for the first time by his Christian name. "What can I do for you?"

"Have me carried to Fairview," he said faintly. "My leg is broken and I cannot rise or help myself."

"Oh, what can I do?" she cried. "How can I leave you alone in such pain? Ah!" as steps were heard approaching, "here is grandpa coming up in search of me."

She ran to meet him and told him what had happened.

He seemed much concerned. "Solon is here with the carriage," he said. "I was going to ask your company for a drive, but we will have him take Leland to Fairview first. Strange what could have taken him into that tree!"

That broken limb kept Lester Leland on his back for six weeks.

His aunt nursed him with the utmost kindness, but could not refrain from teasing him about his accident, asking what took him into the tree, and how he came to fall. At last, in sheer desperation, he told her the whole story of his love. He told of his hopelessness on account of his poverty, his determination not to go back to Ion to be thanked by Elsie and her parents for saving her life, his inability to go or stay far away from her. And finally he owned that he had climbed the tree simply that he might be able to watch her, himself unseen.

"Well, I must say you are a sensible young man!" laughed Mrs. Leland. "But it is very unromantic to be so heavy as to break the limb and fall."

"True enough!" he said, half laughing, half sighing, while a deep flush suffused his face. "Well, what are you going to do next?"

"Go off to — Italy, I suppose."

"What for?"

"To try to make fame and money to lay at her feet."

"That is all very well, but I think —."

"Well?"

"It just struck me that I was about to give unasked advice, which is seldom relished by the recipient."

"Please, go on. I should like to have it whether I make use of it or not."

"Well, I think the honest, straightforward, and therefore best course, would be to seek an interview with the parents of the young lady. Tell them frankly your feelings toward her, your hopes and purposes, and leave it with them to say whether you shall go without speaking to her."

"They will take me for a fortune hunter, I fear," he said, the color mounting to his very hair.

"I think not, but at all events, I should risk it. I do not pretend to know Elsie's feelings, but if she cares for you at all, it would be treating her very badly indeed to go away without letting her know yours — unless her parents forbid it."

"There, I've said my say, and will not mention the subject again till you do. But I will leave you to consider my advice at your leisure."

Lester did so during the next week, which was the last week of enforce quietude. And the more he pondered it, the more convinced was he of the soundness of his aunt's advice. At length, he fully resolved to follow it.

Mr. Travilla had called frequently at Fairview since his accident, always inquiring for him — sometimes coming up to his room, at others merely leaving kind messages from himself, wife and family, or some dainty to tempt the appetite of the invalid. Eddie had been there, too, on similar errands; but there was never a word from her whose lovely image was ever present to his imagination.

. . . .

ENNA WAS RECOVERING. She was now able to sit up and to walk about the room. There was partial restoration of reason, also. Elsie's prayers had been granted, and though still feeble in intellect, Enna had sense enough to comprehend the plan of salvation and seemed to have entered into the kingdom as a little child. She was gentle, patient and submissive — very different, indeed, from the Enna of old. Elsie rejoiced over her with joy akin to that of the angels "over one sinner that repenteth."

. . . .

ELSIE'S CHILDREN WERE FULL of content and happiness in having mamma again at leisure to bestow upon them her accustomed care and attention. Her husband was contented, also, in that he was no longer deprived of the large share of her sweet company, which for weeks past had been bestowed upon Enna.

"Let us have a quiet walk together, little wife," he said to her one lovely summer evening as she joined him on the veranda after coming down from seeing her little ones safe in their nests. "Suppose we call on the Lelands. Lester, I hear, is talking of going north soon, and I believe contemplates a trip to Europe."

"I have never seen him yet to thank him for saving our darling daughter's life, and Enna's too. Yes, let us go."

Lester and his aunt were alone in the drawing room at Fairview when their visitors were announced.

There seemed a slight air of embarrassment about the young man at the moment of their entrance, but it was quickly dispelled by the kindly warmth of their greeting.

The four chatted together for some time on indifferent topics, then Mrs. Leland found some excuse for leaving the room and Mrs. Travilla seized the opportunity to pour out her thanks to Elsie's rescuer from a watery grave.

This made a favorable opening for Lester, and modestly disclaiming any right to credit for what he had done, he frankly told the parents all that was in his heart toward their daughter. He told why he had refrained from speaking before, and his purpose not to seek to win her until he could bring fame and fortune to lay at her feet.

He began in almost painful confusion, but something in the faces of his listeners reassured him. They expressed neither surprise nor displeasure, though tears were trembling in the soft brown eyes of the mother.

Lester had concluded, and for a moment there was silence, then Mr. Travilla said with a slight huskiness in his voice, "Young man, I like your straightforward dealing; but do you know the worth of the prize you covet?"

"I know, sir, that her price is above rubies, and that I am not worthy of her."

"Well, Mr. Leland, we will let her be the judge of that," the father answered. "Shall we not, little wife?" turning to Elsie with a look that had in it all the admiring homage of the lover, as well as the tender devotion of the husband.

"Yes," she sighed, seeming already to feel the pang of parting with her child.

"Do you mean that I may speak now?" Lester asked, half-incredulous of his happiness.

"Yes," Mr. Travilla said. "Though not willing to spare our child yet, we would not have you part in doubt of each other's feelings. And," he added with a kindly smile, "if you have won her heart, the want of wealth is not much against you. 'Worth makes the man.' "

They walked home together — Elsie and her husband — sauntering along arm in arm by the silvery moonlight, like a pair of lovers.

There was something very lover-like in the gaze he bent upon the sweet, fair face at his side. She was almost sad in her quietness.

"What is it, little wife?" he asked.

"Ah, Edward, how can we spare her — our darling, our first-born?"

"Perhaps we shall not be called upon to do so; he may not have won her heart."

She shook her head with a faint smile.

"She has tried to hide it — dear innocent child! But I know the symptoms. I have not forgotten." And she looked up into his face, blushing and happy as in the days when he had wooed and won his bride.

"Yes, dearest, what a little while ago it seems! Ah, those were gladsome days to us, were they not?"

"Gladsome? Ah, yes! Their memory is sweet to this hour. Yet I do not sigh for their return; I would not bring them back. A deeper, calmer blessedness is mine now. My dear husband,

I bless thee for the noble heart,
The tender and the true,
Where mine hath found the happiest rest
That e'er fond woman's knew;

I bless thee, faithful friend and guide,
For my own, my treasur'd share,
In the mournful secrets of thy soul,
In thy sorrow and thy care."

"Thank you, my darling," he said, lifting her hand to his lips, his eyes shining. "Yes,

We have lived and loved together,
Through many changing years,
We have shared each other's sorrows,
And we've wept each other's tear.

Let us hope the future
As the past has been, may be,
I'll share with thee thy sorrows,
And thou my joys with me.

The End